I0574576

NEWB

NEWB

CHRONICLES OF KIERAFREYA™ BOOK 01

MICHAEL ANDERLE

This book is a work of fiction. All of the characters, organizations, and events portrayed in this novel are either products of the author's imagination or are used fictitiously. Sometimes both.

Copyright © 2019-20 LMBPN Publishing
Cover by Mihaela Voicu http://www.mihaelavoicu.com/
Cover copyright © LMBPN Publishing
A Michael Anderle Production

LMBPN Publishing supports the right to free expression and the value of copyright. The purpose of copyright is to encourage writers and artists to produce the creative works that enrich our culture.

The distribution of this book without permission is a theft of the author's intellectual property. If you would like permission to use material from the book (other than for review purposes), please contact support@lmbpn.com. Thank you for your support of the author's rights.

LMBPN Publishing
PMB 196, 2540 South Maryland Pkwy
Las Vegas, NV 89109

First US edition, June 2020
eBook ISBN: 978-1-64971-001-7
Print ISBN: 978-1-64971-047-5

THE NEWB TEAM

Thanks to our Beta Team

Daniel Weigert, Erika Everest, John Ashmore, Kelly O'Donnell, Sarah Weir, and Mary Morris

Thanks to our JIT Readers

Jeff Eaton
Dave Hicks
Dorothy Lloyd
Misty Roa
Peter Manis
Joshua Ahles
Daniel Weigert

If We've missed anyone, please let us know!

Editor
The Skyhunter Editing Team

To Family, Friends and
Those Who Love
To Read.
May We All Enjoy Grace
To Live The Life We Are
Called.

PROLOGUE

Demetri stepped aside to allow an elderly woman to walk through the space he'd occupied but a second before. Taking the last few steps, he opened the door to the small mom-and-pop restaurant.

The cafe was bustling. It was a cute little diner with plastic gingham tablecloths and a handful of overweight matron-types serving food to tables and holding coffee jugs.

Demetri scanned across the tops of heads, over a sea of families, the elderly, and the unemployed before he spotted the person he was looking for. She was sitting in a corner, raising a stained cup of something to her lips. Looking as beautiful as ever.

He took a breath and waited for his heart to finish skipping its beat, and waded through the patrons to her table.

"We've got to stop meeting like this," Demetri called, displaying his widest grin and holding his arms wide as if to say, "Here I am."

Mia Denton, his old college flame, smiled back, then stood and wrapped her arms around his shoulders in the way she had when they were high school sweethearts.

Already it felt so familiar. Although they hadn't seen each other in —how many decades must it have been?—it felt completely right, like jigsaw pieces locking into place. He began to wonder why they'd ever parted in the first place.

"You've gotten fat," Mia mock-struggled, pretending to not be able to touch her hands together behind his back.

"I'd say you've gotten taller, but we both knew that would never happen." He winked.

They took their seats across the table from each other and the waitress took their order. Coffee, black, and a scrambled egg on toast for Demetri, and another tea for Mia.

It seemed she had already eaten. She had arrived way ahead of their meeting time and found herself too hungry to hold back.

He eyed her plate, one eyebrow raised. "You never could wait, could you?"

Mia looked abashed, her cheeks flushing. "You know me. If I see something I want, I do everything in my power to get it. Turned out my stomach wanted food." She smirked. "Who am I to deny such a thing?"

They laughed then, going down memory lane and collecting the fun times along the way. Their friends at school, their families, how life had treated them, and how it was treating them now.

It was so easy to talk to each other, as though not a second had passed since they had stalked the lakes and countryside together and held hands. Demetri studied her face as she talked, noticing the cute age lines that now decorated the corners of her eyes and mouth.

She was certainly older, *Damn, she has aged well,* he thought.

"So tell me," Demetri said after a pause in which they found themselves staring into each other's eyes. His mind raced as he wondered what was going on in her head. "What are you doing these days? Still flower-arranging for old Ted down Viking Street?"

Demetri remembered the last time he had seen Mia, a flying visit as he'd hurried on his way to yet another exam for his Professional Practice in Psychology license.

He had already been cutting it close, having three minutes to make the five-minute journey when he had seen her. He'd paused for a quick hello, sweat dripping from his forehead, before hurrying off and making the exam by the skin of his teeth.

She rolled her eyes, "Oh, that old job. Hell, no. As much fun as it is slicing your fingers open with thorns on a day-to-day basis, I packed that in."

Demetri smirked. "You sound a bit bitter about it?"

She eyed her plate, perhaps hoping a bit of her breakfast was still available. "Well, once I realized that old Ted was a perv who used to make me bend down to pick up the bundles and collect debris off the floor for his own enjoyment, the job lost some of its charm. Well, that, and…"

Mia leaned in conspiratorially, holding her hand by her mouth and waiting for Demetri to lean in too. "You know roses cost nothing to grow, right? Like, literally *zero* dollars, yet guys buy them for over thirty dollars a dozen."

He winked as he whispered back, "Wow, you did them cheap."

Mia playfully slapped Demetri's face.

Demetri feigned shock and they hovered near each other for a moment, electricity passing between them.

"Well, that's over now, anyway," Mia said, leaning back. Demetri wondered if there had been a double meaning to those words. Probably not, judging by the foot sliding up his trouser leg. "Change of careers for me."

"Yeah?" He waved down the waitress and asked her for more coffee. "What's the switch?"

"Game development," she said simply and took a dramatic sip of her tea.

"Game development?" Demetri asked, eyebrows raised skeptically. "*You*? Miss 'Can-you-please-spend-time-with-me-in-the-real-world' is now creating the very games that led to some of the biggest arguments I've ever had with anyone in my life?" He added after a moment, "*Ever.*"

His accusation of hypocrisy was set aside with a shrug. "Yeah. I mean, the stuff I'm working on right now is a *bit* different than when I used to find you sitting day after day in the same pair of sweatpants playing *Relic Hunter: 2*. We're more into the VR space now, creating full-immersion multiplayer experiences. Something you can really get your teeth into." She lifted an eyebrow. "Not rubbing your crotch while you watch elves screwing elves by your lonesome."

"Keep your voice down." Demetri looked at the other tables, checking that no one had overheard Mia's words. "Please! I have a reputation to maintain."

"Oh, that's right," Mia said, playfully. Her voice grew louder as she turned her head toward the cafe, but her eyes never moved from his face. "Mr. Bigshot Psychologist doesn't want people to know he used to live down on the ground with us mere mortals. That he used to drop Cheetos down the side of the couch and use the fallen items as nourishment when he couldn't be bothered to wash plates or get his lazy ass off the couch."

Demetri blushed, crouching and hiding his face with his hand.

He glanced over his fingers, finding that literally no one was paying attention. The diner's customers were all too involved in their own gossip and conversation to give a crap about two high school sweethearts playing catch-up.

"Are you done?" Demetri hissed.

"For now." Mia smirked. "*But,* since we're on the subject of our careers, it seems like as good a time as any to get to the bottom of why I asked you to meet with me today."

"Aw, man, can't a pretty girl ask a handsome guy to breakfast without wanting *something* in return?" Demetri feigned exasperation. "A man can feel used, you know."

"Hey, if a girl *really* wanted something, she'd ask the man to dinner at a decent restaurant." She pointed around the café. "Not a crummy diner in the early morning light," Mia said, biting her tongue coyly.

She reached down to the seat beside her and pulled out a magazine. A devilishly groomed man beamed on the cover, a hand pinching the knot of his tie. "You know who this is, right?"

Demetri scoffed. "You know I do, but I'm not exactly sure what you're getting at here."

Mia grinned and fanned through the pages, finding the center spread with the same man, who stood at the forefront of a V of sophisticated-looking men and women with similar features. They were all dressed in power suits. Some had their arms folded, others had their hands in their pockets. Eight of them in total. A headline at the top of the page read Hector's Heights Soar Ever Higher.

Mia slapped the magazine down as if her point had been made. "The Lagardes are one of the wealthiest families in America. Like, we're talking *stupid* ridiculous money. More zeroes than anyone can count. More zeroes than I can scribble onto this page before running out of space."

She paused, meeting Demetri's eyes.

"And what does their wealth have to do with me?" Demetri said, already feeling like he knew where this conversation was headed.

She tapped one of the guys in the image. "Hector has just invested 3.5 *billion* into the Tesla program to support Elon Musk, acting as a primary contributing benefactor to his programs of development. Stocks have skyrocketed—excuse the pun—and he's tripled his investment."

She moved her finger across the page to a man and woman, around their early-thirties who looked near enough identical had it not been for the clear difference in gender.

"Henry and Henrietta Lagarde, just last month invested half a million dollars into Occulus and the development of advanced AI embedment into AR and VR. Already the reports are coming back in, and they've *doubled* their investment."

Another move of her finger.

"Mum and Dad. Hugo and Helena, one of the richest couples in the world. A couple whose own investments into the development of advanced technologies for the human race brought about 5g, 6g, and created power sources so efficient that they make the old Duracell bunnies look like dehydrated tortoises."

Demetri leaned back and sighed, grabbing his cup of cold coffee.

"And, here..." Mia turned the page, finding where a small square thumbnail showcased an image of Demetri in his office, a plush purple-leather couch behind his beaming smile and a wall of books.

She continued, "The live-in psychologist of the family, who Hector boasts is the *hidden gem*. The good luck charm. The advisor who has helped the Lagardes see through the fog and put the stamp on their investments for the last twenty years."

Demetri removed his glasses and polished them on his shirt. "Let me guess: you've got a recommendation for software you'd like me to bend Hector's ear on. Make him your next investor?"

Mia's smile grew, and her eyes twinkled.

She shook her head and turned the page back to the V of Lagardes, pointing to the very back of the line where a young woman stood. Stood in the shadows of her brothers and sisters, a false smile strapped on her face. Whereas the other family members had small boxes near their heads detailing their financial worth, this girl didn't, just a title and her name.

"I want *her*. I want Chloe."

Demetri took a sip of his coffee, wincing as his lips met the cold liquid. "What's the project? I won't suggest a project unless I believe it will have a good return for the family. You are fantastic, but not *that* fantastic."

Mia smiled. "Please. I *am* that fantastic, but I wouldn't do anything like that to you."

Then she told Demetri everything.

CHAPTER ONE

Something was screeching at the top of its lungs, a grating sound that rattled the very bones of Chloe's hollow skull. She rolled over, the light from her alarm clock causing her to squint as she slapped a hand on top. Once...twice...third time's the charm.

"Eurgh."

She sat up slowly, the pounding hangover taking her. Her mouth tasted like someone had opened it and taken a dump straight inside. Her hair stood out at all angles. She closed her eyes, rested her head against the wall and tried to recall what the hell had happened.

Cosmos at some hipster joint on the square. Chloe and her girlfriends gossiping and living the high-life. Weekend binges and shopping sprees. Her girlfriends pulling the guys while she sat and held their bags. Round after round on Chloe, the youngest daughter of the Lagarde legacy. It was all she had ever known.

Then why didn't it feel right anymore?

"Good morning, Miss Lagarde," Tabitha, Chloe's personal assistant, said. Chloe jumped. How long had she been standing there?

"Already? Can't I have a few more hours?"

"Actually, I was being polite. It's almost noon, and you have appointments to keep. Your father won't be pleased if you miss them."

Tabitha studied her tablet, tapping the screen and casting the information to a projector built into the end of Chloe's bed. A holographic image appeared several feet from Chloe's face.

"Wow. Much excitement," Chloe said, scanning the list of board meetings and project reviews with bleary eyes. Things she had learned to abhor after she realized she offered no real value to them. Her brothers and sisters? They came prepared. They knew the ins and outs. Chloe just sat quietly in the corner, nodding at the right moments and casting votes whenever necessary.

"Can't you just tell my father to shove it? And Mother too, for that matter."

Tabitha rolled her eyes. "For the millionth time, Miss Lagarde, your mother and father are my employers, not you. My job is to serve the family and ensure that *you* are where you need to be at the right times." She checked her watch. "Speaking of which, in ten minutes, you will be exactly one minute late for your weekly appointment with Mr. Smythe."

Chloe sat up, cleared her throat, and said in her best version of a pompous British woman, "Well, we wouldn't want that, would we, Tabitha? If you would be so kind as to get me some ibuprofen, a sick bag, and something to comb the chunks of last night's meal out of my hair, I'll gladly chop-chop toward Master Smythe's quarters." She paused, putting her finger on her chin before pointing it into the air. "Lickety-split!"

Tabitha rolled her eyes once more and left the room.

Chloe made it to the office exactly three minutes late. The ibuprofen had kicked away some of the headache, but she still felt the overwhelming sense of shame that was customary after an evening of late-night drinking. She rapped on the door three times, heard the cursory, "Come in," and took her place on the couch.

"Heavy night?" Demetri said without even turning to look at Chloe. He was prepared, one leg crossed over the other and a notepad in hand with which he scribbled notes feverishly. Chloe always hated that. Before she'd even opened her mouth, she was being judged. If it hadn't been a condition of her receiving her full inheritance, she'd likely have blown off every last one of these sessions. It wasn't like they'd helped her at all over the years.

"Something like that," Chloe said, tapping her fingers on her chest. "You know, I've always thought it'd be fun to bring my own notepad and write my notes about you during our sessions. See how you'd like it."

Demetri looked over the rim of his glasses. "And how would that make you feel?"

Despite herself, Chloe chuckled. As useless as these sessions had been, he'd always had a knack of making her laugh.

"So what is it today, Doc? Going to probe my subconscious? Take another trip down memory lane? Going to dive down farther into my deep-seated family issues and tell me why every one of my siblings is a success and I'm just a layabout who pisses away her money on the weekends with a bunch of girls who only use me for it?"

Chloe's face straightened. She definitely hadn't meant to say that much.

Demetri straightened in his chair. "Something like that." He smirked. "Chloe, I've known you and your family for a great number of years now, and if there's one thing I've always been astounded by, it's the question of how can such a rich, talented, successful, charismatic family raise six children, yet only five of them inherited the characteristics of the mother and father?"

Chloe rolled her eyes and crossed her arms as if to say, "Oh, here we go again."

"I mean, it doesn't make sense. If we break this down into theory and look at the nature versus nurture debate, there's no reason that this should be so." Demetri stood up and moved to the bookshelf, eyeing the tomes as if studying them. "If we look at Freud or Frankl or Skinner or Pavlov, there's nothing there that correlates or makes sense."

"Bring it on, Doc. Tell me I'm a failure. Tell me I bring shame to my ridiculously talented family. Tell me I'm the mortal among the gods. I can take it. It's not like I haven't tried to keep up with the Kardashians."

"Kardashians?"

"You don't… You've never watched… Never mind."

Demetri turned his attention back to the shelf, humming a little as he did so. He thumbed through a stack of books and extracted a thin, colorful item. "You know what you are?" He spun the book, displaying a cover that showcased a fluffy gray duck swimming amid its bright yellow siblings.

Chloe squinted at the cover. "A rat?"

"No." Demetri chuckled. "An ugly duckling."

"Gee, thanks."

"A duckling who just needs some encouragement and persuasion to reach the heights of her brothers and sisters." He flicked through the pages, showing the duckling as it left its family, only to return as a beautiful swan. "Sometimes, it simply takes the removal of a person from their natural environment to discover who they are inside. To discover where their strengths lie, and what can help them excel in the world." He replaced the book on the shelf. "A flower cannot grow in the shade."

"So what are you suggesting? That I run off to Ibiza and spend some time discovering myself? Because I could really get on board with that." Chloe's wrist vibrated. She looked at her watch, noting the reminder that her next meeting was due to start in 20 minutes.

"Not exactly," Demetri said, returning to his seat. He picked up a tablet, unlocked the screen, and passed it to Chloe.

"*Finally*! You're ditching the pen and paper for something digital. I told you, Doc! Welcome to the twenty-first century. You don't need paper anymore." Chloe looked at the screen in her hand. There was an image of a blackened piece of glass in the shape of a rough-cut diamond. "What's '*Obsidian*?'"

Demetri leaned forward, encouraging Chloe to swipe the screen as he went through the information Mia had given him, describing the fully immersive experience of the online virtual reality game and paying particular attention in relaying the potential well-being and health benefits the game offered its players. There were in-game images that looked as if a photo had been taken at a Renaissance fair, only with advanced CGI graphics for the trolls, dragons, and goblins.

"You see? With this, you can dive into a world in which you're no longer a Lagarde. You can build colonies and alliances and guilds and towns and hash out any issues you have in the real world. You'll start as a nobody from scratch. I can monitor you as you go, and we can track your progress as you develop. A clean slate."

"This looks amazing," she said, flicking through the screens. Her shoulders slumped as a realization struck her. "But you know my mother and father will never allow this, not with all the meetings and events I'm scheduled to attend. When will I ever get a chance to play?"

"That's the best part," Demetri said, handing over a crisp white sheet of paper with her father and mother's scrawling signature at the bottom. "I've already spoken to your parents. You're officially off-duty for the next two years. Doctor's orders." He winked.

"Two... Wait. I can do whatever I want for the next two years without a single interruption from my family?"

"You sure can," Demetri said, pointing to the tablet. "As long as it's in *that* world. You heard me say that it's a *fully immersive* experience, right?"

Chloe didn't know what to say. The idea that she could literally leave her life behind and see what her world would be like out from under the shadow of her family was an absolute dream. Would she miss them? Sure. But two years wasn't forever, and the promises and benefits *Obsidian* offered seemed unbelievable. Almost too good to be true.

Which made her pause.

"Hold on a minute. What's the catch?"

Demetri held out a second piece of paper. The black *Obsidian* logo on the top right, and there was a monetary figure in bold on the middle of the page. "This game is in early development. You will be among the first players to jump in and test out the environment. This could be your legacy, Chloe." He held out a pen, clicking the top. "Are you ready to make your first real investment?"

CHAPTER TWO

"All ready to go?" Mia's voice said, appearing in Chloe's ear as if the woman were standing right next to her.

Chloe took a deep breath and looked around the pod, a huge egg-shaped thing that had been painted a sleek black. When she had first seen it, she couldn't quite believe it was real, particularly among the detritus, loose cabling, and mess of an office Demetri had taken her to.

They had walked halfway across the city to get here, finally going through a rusted back door in the seedy part of town. Chloe had to admit she had been surprised to find the attractive woman waiting to usher them both inside. She wasn't sure what she had expected—maybe a crazed scientist with hair askew and coke-bottle glasses. Not this pretty young thing whom Demetri seemed to have known from childhood—

Oh. Now she got it.

Chloe shifted to make herself comfortable, the nodes strapped to her head and the electrodes all over her body creating an unusual feeling. "I think so." She looked at the IV drips dangling out of her arm. They would be her lifeblood and sustenance for the next two years. "I'll be honest, I feel like a friggin' pincushion right now. It doesn't help that I can see through this small window here, too. Don't you think it might ruin the effect somewhat if I can see outside while trying to play the game?"

Mia's blurry face appeared, a broad smile on her face. "Don't worry, that'll go dark when we get started. That's just so we can see inside and check that you're okay. It'll also help you slowly readjust to the real world when you come out of the experience. We predict some...disorientation upon your return to the surface."

Chloe swallowed hard, sweat peppering her brow. "At least you're confident that I'll be coming back out."

"Everything should be fine," Mia assured her as she pressed a few buttons on a computer and a timer appeared in front of Chloe's eyes. "And you're sure I'll be okay when I resurface? Won't I, like, wither away and get bedsores and stuff?"

Mia smiled. "It's covered. These patches here are electrical stimulation devices designed to trigger muscle movement and keep them primed for re-entry. We'll also work with your body a couple of times a week for...preventive maintenance."

Chloe was about to ask what "preventive maintenance" involved when a voice started speaking, accompanied by text in an old-fashioned font.

WELCOME TO OBSIDIAN, ADVENTURER.

"Shit," Mia exclaimed.

Chloe leaned forward, trying to see what was going on through her tiny window. "What? What is it?"

It was almost impossible to see. What with the letters literally floating in her vision and the blur of the glass, she could just make out a wide-eyed Mia running a hand through her hair. Demetri stood watching over her shoulder, eyes wide with alarm.

PLEASE ENSURE THAT ALL JEWELRY AND LOOSE OBJECTS HAVE BEEN REMOVED FROM YOUR PERSON AND THAT YOU ARE LYING IN A COMFORTABLE POSITION.

"No. It was supposed to take 5 minutes..." Mia flapped, elbowing Demetri away from her screen. "We haven't done the official safety check—"

PLEASE CONFIRM THAT YOU HAVE READ THE SAFETY

INSTRUCTIONS BEFORE ADVENTURING.

Y / N

"Aha!"

Chloe leaned forward, trying to blink the messages away. Even with her eyes closed, she could see the images as clear as day. "What's going on?"

"Er...nothing. Just a minor hiccup. Teething problems. Just think 'no' and we can reset and get this started again."

Chloe tried to move her hands to select the option for no but remembered that she was strapped in tight. She looked at both options, but her eyes must have hovered over 'yes' for just a moment too long because the text faded and another message appeared.

GREAT. PLEASE NOTE THAT PRAXIS GAMES LTD. TAKES NO RESPONSIBILITY FOR ANY OF THE FOLLOWING CONDITIONS:

Chloe could hardly blink before a long list of conditions swam before her eyes. She managed to pick out words such as cancer, epilepsy, chronic bleeding, and body dysmorphia before her vision went black.

CONGRATULATIONS, ADVENTURER. YOU HAVE LANDED. GOOD LUCK.

Chloe felt herself fall, and she landed with an *oof* on something soft and bristly. A moment of silence followed as the voice echoed inside her head. Chloe kept her eyes screwed shut, a horrible feeling of displacement washing over her.

"Hello? Guys? Ha. That was all really funny, but can we stop all the pretend and get this going properly, please? Guys?"

Chloe shivered, her skin prickling. A chill wind gushing past her. Instinctively she folded her arms, brushing hands up her sleeves... Wait. Not sleeves. Where had her sleeves gone? Hold on... Where had the IV drips gone?

Opening her eyes, Chloe's breath caught. She was in a forest clearing surrounded by monumental pines. They towered over her, casting dark shadows across the needle-strewn floor. Somewhere to her left, the sun was setting behind the trees, its golden glow casting fractal rays of warmth on her skin that were fast torn away by the wind.

"Holy…" Chloe said, rising to her feet. It all felt so *real*. She took a deep breath in and smelled the earthen scent of the forest. She tasted the wind on her tongue, and the images in front of her were in such high definition that she had a hard time believing all of this wasn't real.

"Great work, guys!" Chloe shouted to the sky, impressed. "Seriously! These graphics are the bomb!"

She expected to hear a response come down from the sky. Half-expected Demetri's and Mia's faces to appear as images in the clouds, ready to respond and guide her. Until she remembered Demetri's caution that he'd only be able to communicate with her at certain times, once certain conditions were met.

"Damn. Should've asked what those conditions were." She turned to the sky. "Don't worry, I got this!"

The smile was ripped off Chloe's face as she heard the roar of some great beast somewhere back in the trees. "Shit. Right. You're in the wild, *genius*. Keep your voice down. Now, how the hell do I make any of this work…"

Chloe scanned her avatar. She was wearing a rough-spun tunic, shorts, and a pair of leather sandals. Her hair cascaded down her back. She noted, taking a handful of locks, that her hair was not her usual brunette, but instead was a dark emerald, black in the shadows and green in the sun's rays. "Strange. Apparently, they don't give anyone customization options in this game. Maybe that's a feature that'll be built in later?"

Looking down at her chest, she smirked as she cupped her breasts in her hands. In reality, she had been a rather modest and fair size (as described by blockhead ex-boyfriends). Now, though, they were at least double what they had been. Her waist had definitely lost a few inches, too. She had heard about guy gamers, and how they lived out their dirty fetishes through the objectification of women in their games but found she actually didn't mind all that much now that the change applied to her.

"Well, maybe I'll keep *these* as they are." She glanced skyward. "I see how it is, you *pervs!*"

Another roar—closer this time—and Chloe shut her mouth, fleeing from the clearing into the woods.

She wandered aimlessly through the forest until the sun had set and night had fallen. The entire time she wracked her mind, wondering what to do and where to go. Although she hadn't been a big gamer, her last boyfriend, Blake, had been *obsessed* with the *Relic Hunter* series, an open-world single-player RPG in which players had free reign to accept quests and explore the land. Surely this had to be something similar? Hadn't Mia said Chloe would come across quests and meet other players in this game? So far, she'd circled around the woods and had no interaction from anyone or anything other than a couple of squirrels hopping through the branches above, and the occasional hooting owl. Only once more had she heard the roar, and that time, it had been far enough away that she had felt a lot safer going in the direction she had been headed.

"Come on, Chloe, think. What happens in these games? Think. Think… Well, there's usually a menu, of some kind. No?" She looked around in every direction, finally noticing a blinking pixel in the lower right of her vision. She tried to capture it in her direct sight, but every time she tried, it moved farther away. She felt like a friggin' dog chasing its tail.

"Okay, fine. That's not working. What was it that Mia had said when those messages popped up? 'Just think 'no.'" Think… Think? Think!"

Chloe thought about the menu appearing and was surprised to find that it literally popped into view. A message box swamped her vision.

Congratulations, you've discovered the menu! You've just taken the first step to becoming a functional being in Obsidian.

There were a series of icons and buttons available for selection. The background was see-through, allowing Chloe to see the world beyond.

She focused on the Character icon and a character sheet appeared before her, interrupted by a message box.

Congratulations! You've discovered your character sheet. Monitor your progress and keep on top of your attributes and skills by accessing this screen.

Chloe turned her attention to a small question mark beside the notification.

Attributes: Your attributes are the lifeblood of your character in Obsidian. For the first 5 levels, your attributes will be locked. Based on your playing style for the first 5 levels, Obsidian's system will distribute 30 starter points across 5 primary attributes. You will also gain bonuses for unlocking new skills. Basic skills will earn you 1-2 skill points, intermediate skills will earn 3-5 skill points, while advanced skills will earn 6-10 points. With every new level you gain, you will acquire—

"Boring!" Chloe said, waving the text away and moving to the next message.

You've unlocked a new skill: Creature Identification (Lv 1)

You are now able to access useful information about creatures in the overworld. Gain the advantage over both enemies and friends by stripping them naked and studying them with greedy eyes. (Note: Creature Identification is not to be confused with x-ray vision and does not allow you to see through clothes. Perv.)

Requirements: Search the menu

Bonuses: +1 intelligence

Nice! Somehow Chloe felt like she was already bossing this game. Three congratulatory notes in quick succession *and* a new skill available, just by accessing the menu. If the game was going to be *this* easy, she clearly had nothing to worry about.

The message disappeared, shattering into a mini-firework display before the character sheet reappeared.

<u>**Bio**</u>

Character name: Untitled (*click to select a new character name*)

Level: 1

Class: Null

Race: Human

Stats
HP: 13/15
MP: 15/15
Stamina: 20/30
Active effects: Null
Attributes (Unavailable until level 5)
Skills
Languages: Human
Available Points: 0

"Okay, so that's somewhat useful," she mused, looking at the numbers. "Hey, when did I lose health?"

She focused on the button Activity Log and scanned a small list of actions that had occurred since landing.

Ouch! Talk about a crash landing. Maybe spread some butter on your feet and you'll land the right way next time?

-2 HP

It didn't seem fair to lose 2 hit points just by entering the game? Chloe made a note to bring that up with Mia when she was next able to check in.

She looked around the menu, searching for an area where she could keep a list of potential bugs, but she found nothing.

What she did find, however, was an inventory. She focused, and two boxes appeared in her vision.

Congratulations! You've found the inventory. From this menu, you'll be able to see all the treasured possessions you have on your person in one place. Currently, your item number matches the number of friends you've made here in Obsidian. That is to say, 0.

Well, that was unnecessary.

Chloe blinked away the message screen and sighed. She had been hoping to find some kind of weapon in her inventory. Even a rusty dagger or a hatchet would have worked. She tried to think back to when Blake had played his games. She was sure every character had started with some kind of weapon to get the action going.

"At this point, I'd take something as simple as a stick for a weapon." She picked up the most pathetic stick she could find. About the length of her hand, it flopped flaccidly, as if begging to be returned to the ground. She slashed it through the air. "Take that, dragon. Feel the mighty wrath of my unbelievable blade!"

You have a new weapon: Tiny stick

Hey! Good work. You've found the very thing all enemies cower and bow down to—a small stick! Let all enemies fear and turn from your might.

Damage: 0-1 (slashing)

Durability: 2/5

You've unlocked a new skill: Armed combat (Lv 1)

Good job. You can now fight stuff. Y'know, so long as they're low level, like bunnies and stuff. Let the battles begin!

Requirements: Acquisition of first weapon

Bonuses: +1 strength

Chloe wasn't sure whether to laugh or cry. It seemed like interaction with *anything* in this game could be beneficial, even just picking up a stick. She gripped her weapon tightly in her hand and held it in front of her like a sword. Advancing on the trunk of the closest tree, she said, "I shall have at thee, maiden oak. Bow down and fear the destroyer of things," before slashing and attacking the tree until her arms grew tired. She wasn't sure what she was expecting from this, perhaps some more level-up gains in the skills she'd acquired. Unfortunately, that was not what happened. Instead, the stick broke in two.

"Aw, man," she said, taking half in each hand.

You've unlocked a new skill: Dual wielding (Lv 1)

Excellent display of swordsmanship (stickmanship?), young lady. Now you can confidently wield low-level weapons with both hands. Give yourself a pat on the back...with both hands!

Requirements: Hold a small weapon in each hand

Bonuses: +1 dexterity

"Sweet!" She chuckled quietly, somehow feeling that, although the gains were small, she'd started making progress. Now, if only she could find somewhere warm and safe to sleep. The night had begun to envelop her, and upon inspection of her character sheet, she noted that she had already lost another 3HP.

Flicking up her Activity Log, she soon discovered why.

Ouch! It's freezing out, and you're wearing that? Best find somewhere warm before hypothermia sets in.

-1 HP

Ouch! It's freezing out, and you're wearing that? Best find somewhere warm before hypothermia sets in.

-1 HP

Ouch! It's freezing out, and you're wearing that? Best find somewhere warm before hypothermia sets in.

-1 HP

As she read through the messages, another appeared.

Ouch! It's freezing out, and you're wearing that? Best find somewhere warm before hypothermia sets in.

-1 HP

"All right! I get it. I'll find somewhere warm."

Then she felt a drop of water hit her shoulder. Another. A third. Within seconds, the storm came, unleashing bucketsful of rain. Chloe's clothes soaked through as she sprinted in any direction she could, doing her best to avoid hitting trees.

She bumped and scratched her shoulder on trunks and noted that the Activity Log notification blinked in the corner of her vision. She wasn't sure how long she'd have before her count went to zero. She hadn't even contemplated what that might mean for her.

The cuts and grazes begun to burn with a real pain that she couldn't quite explain, given that she was in a goddamn video game! If they were hurting now, what would death be like?

"Come on, Chloe." She was panting, her strength beginning to flag, and she slowed down. Her legs felt like they were made of lead. She gasped, drawing in as much breath as possible, noticing as she went light-headed that a small flicker of something orange had appeared through the trees ahead.

With heavy steps, she crashed toward the fire—for a fire it was. Flickering flames lit the inside of the cave entrance. Chloe approached as cautiously as possible, wondering what kind of creature could be dwelling inside.

CHAPTER THREE

The heat rolled over Chloe as she tiptoed into the cave. The walls were rough-hewn stone, and it already appeared much larger on the inside than it had from outside.

The cave bent around a tunnel, the glowing orange of the fire flickering gently. She could hear gruff voices but couldn't understand their speech.

She clung to the wall, her hair dripping wet. She did her best to stay quiet, but every step echoed as if she were deliberately stomping —the same noise she used to make when she was trying to piss off her stupidly successful brother in the bedroom below hers by jumping and stamping her feet on the floorboards.

Taking another step, she raised her leg as delicately as possible and tried her best to lower her foot without making a sound. In her head, the process went smoothly and not an iota of dust stirred. In reality…

Her foot *clapped* on the floor and the sound traveled down the tunnel, echoing along its length as it raced toward the voices. For a heart-wrenching moment, the voices were silent. Chloe could feel them listening for her, until they apparently decided it was nothing, resuming their raucous talk.

What the hell, I can't tiptoe? What's that about?

Then Chloe remembered. Blake had always been fond of being a thief assassin in his run-throughs of *Relic Hunter*. A necessary component of that role had been spending hours and hours grinding to gain the Sneak ability.

Chloe took another thunder-clapping step before slapping her face. *How am I supposed to learn Sneak if I'm going to be caught just by walking in a cave!*

And then it struck her—the way that she had seen animals sneaking on TV documentaries. She sighed, lowered herself to her hands and knees, and began crawling along the floor.

The shuffling sound still carried down the chamber, but it didn't make half as much noise as when she was walking. She gritted her teeth, doing her best not to cry out or moan as small shards of rock wore away the bare skin of her knees.

Ouch! Just in case you've forgotten, babies crawl. Consider getting your wittle tooshy up to avoid taking any more damage.

-1HP

Oh, come on!

She knew she had to stick to crawling as her curiosity got the better of her. As she slowly made her way deeper into the cave, she flicked open her character sheet.

<u>Bio</u>

Character name: Untitled (*click to select a new character name*)

Level: 1

Class: Null

Race: Human

<u>Stats</u>

HP: 8/15

MP: 15/15

Stamina: 20/30

Active effects: Null

<u>Attributes</u> (Unavailable until level 5)

<u>Skills</u>

Languages: Human

Creature Identification: Lv 1

Armed Combat: Lv 1
Dual Wielding: Lv 1
<u>**Available Points:**</u> 0

Damn. She'd only been in the game a couple of hours, and she'd already lost almost half of her health without even meeting a monster! If things kept on as they were, she'd be dead by the time she found a place to lie by the fire.

She glanced at the stats one more time, making a mental note to think of a kickass name for her character when she wasn't crawling along the floor on her way toward unknown voices. Maybe now wouldn't be the best time to accidentally call herself something stupid.

She didn't even know if by selecting a name, that name would stick forever in the game. If she couldn't customize her buxom character, what were the chances she'd be able to rename her?

Eventually, Chloe peeked around a sharp corner and found the source of the fire. The bend led to an open chamber about the size of a small house with a bonfire in the middle. Sitting around the bonfire, silhouetted by the flames, were two creatures she recognized instantly.

Goblins.

She had seen them before. They were Blake's favorite blade fodder, a great way to gain experience at the lower levels due to their stupidity and low HP. Chloe studied them for a moment, almost recoiling at the smell that accompanied each wave of heat pushed toward her. They had long, wide ears that protruded from the sides of their heads. Their skin was a darkish green, with patches of black fur here and there. They wore stained and torn loincloths that barely covered their private bits.

Chloe pulled in a deep breath of disgust. The sound was much louder than she'd liked.

She ducked behind the wall as the goblins turned to face her.

"You 'ear that?" one of the goblins croaked.

Chloe heard a slap. "Jus' the wind, idiot. You ain't scared o' the wind, are ya?"

The first goblin sniffled. *"Heeeey,* don' hit me."

A chuckle. "Quit your whining, Skud, or I'll give ya somethin' to whine about."

Chloe waited a moment before poking her head back around the corner.

You've unlocked a new skill: Sneak (Lv 1)

Who goes there? Oh, it must have been nothing...

With every level of the sneak skill, you will dissolve more into shadow. Monsters and enemies will have a harder time detecting your presence with each level gained. Don't get cocky though, kid. Remember, you've only just made Lv. 1.

Requirements: Avoid detection from a low-level monster

Bonuses: +1 dexterity

Nice! Another skill gained. Chloe glanced at her HP. *Damn, but another 2HP down... And another 10 stamina?* At this rate, she was going to be too exhausted to move before she could find a place to safely rest.

Chloe blinked away her notifications, wondering if she'd be able to find a setting later that might make the pop-ups a little less intrusive. This one had surprised her, and it would probably make the difference between life and death if she was unable to see because she'd gained a skill at the moment when she should've been stabbing a goblin's face.

Not only that, she wasn't sure she liked the tone of these notifications. She thought she remembered that Blake's messages had been a lot more friendly and straight-talking. With every message and notification received, Chloe was feeling more and more like she was being teased by her siblings.

Shaking away the thought, Chloe scoured her character sheet and spotted the Creature Identification skill.

Right! That could be useful. Let's test this baby out.

Chloe focused her attention on the first goblin, and somehow she *knew* how to use the skill. A small pop-up box appeared above the goblin's head.

Goblin.

That was all that it said. Nothing more. Nothing less.

Are you friggin' kidding me? I know it's a goblin.

She moved her focus to the second goblin.

Skud (Goblin).

Great. At least I know this one's name. I'm sure that'll come in useful.

Chloe backed away and weighed her options. The way that she saw it, she could do one of three things. She could find a way to sneak around the goblins and get closer to the fire, testing her new sneak ability, she could charge in there and take her chances using her pieces of floppy stick as a weapon, or she could head back out into the rain and try to find somewhere safer.

Well, the whole point of this game was to learn to be more confident and take control, right? No point hiding and whining like a baby.

Chloe unconsciously rubbed the scratches on her arms, hoping that if the goblins did attack, the pain wouldn't be anything like she had already felt. Surely it wouldn't in a game like this, right?

Chloe stepped around the corner into the firelight. "Good evening, gentlemen."

The goblins turned and jumped to their feet, mouths agape.

Skud took a step back. "Intruder!"

"No, no." Chloe waved her hands in front of her. "No, I'm not an intruder, I'm just looking for somewhere to dry off."

The second goblin reached into his pocket and withdrew a crooked dagger. "Intruder! Get her, Skud!"

Skud looked from Chloe to the other goblin, his lip quivering with fear. He nodded, reached into his own pocket, and pulled out a stick.

"Hey!" Chloe said brightly. "We've got the same weapon—"

"Aaaargh!" Skud roared as he ran at Chloe, her mind only now registering that *his* stick had been tapered to a sharp point.

Before Chloe could register what was happening, the stick found its mark in her stomach. She clutched at the wound, looking down in disbelief. White-hot pain bolted through her insides. With wide eyes, she raised her head and saw a flash of rusted silver as the second goblin slashed at her neck.

There was a final electric pulse of immense pain before her vision faded to black. The pain immediately subsided.

Wup-wup. You're dead.

Perhaps you should look before you leap. Walk before you run. Swim before you sink. What we're trying to say is, maybe don't approach hostile goblins while holding nothing but a stick.

-50n experience (where n equals your character's level)

-1/2 your equipment

Time to respawn: 2 hours

"Hey! I had *two* sticks!" Chloe blinked as she opened her eyes in the whitest room she had ever seen.

The room was empty apart from the chair she found herself sitting in, a desk with a 90s-style computer on top, and an old rotary telephone. On the far wall was a large countdown timer, now reading 01:59:24.

Chloe instinctively reached for the computer's mouse before she suddenly remembered what had brought her here. She pulled up her pristine white t-shirt and checked her stomach, then ran a hand across her neck. There was no sign of the goblin attack. A quick examination of her knees and arms revealed that they were as clean as whistles.

What a strange system this is, Chloe mused, trying not to think too much about the pain she had felt as the goblin's stick pierced her flesh. It had felt so *real*. She had experienced every single prod and poke, and when the second goblin had sliced her throat...

She shuddered, looking around for something—anything—to distract her from her thoughts.

She turned on the old computer, grimacing as a dial-up modem screeched and beeped. When the computer loaded, she found only an icon for exploring the internet.

With curious fingers, she typed the words "Obsidian game help," wondering if anyone else was online and had started adding information on the game to potential players. Mia had said that they would be piloting the game with more than just Chloe; they just needed her to get the bankroll going.

Maybe she'd find that some of these players had already died before her and uploaded useful tips.

The searches came back empty, just a rudimentary splash page on the Praxis Games website announcing the up-and-coming title.

"I wonder if I get a new skill or ability by being the first ever in the game to die." She pouted, then jumped when the phone began to ring.

Chloe picked up the phone. "Good morning, Haversham Dogs' Home. If you're looking to re-house your canine, please press 1."

Demetri spoke on the other side. "Chloe? Is that you?"

Chloe smirked. "I'm sorry, I don't understand that command. Would you like to re-listen to the options?"

Demetri exhaled loudly. "Ha-ha. Very funny. I'm glad to hear the game hasn't wiped out your sense of humor. Goblins, huh? That looked like a painful way to go."

Chloe's eyebrow raised. "Wait, you *saw* that? And, hold on…is this what you were talking about with 'conditions'? I have to *die* to be able to talk to you?"

"Yeah." Demetri sighed. "Not ideal, we know, but it's the only way to maintain the illusion of the game while you're in play. Nice work, by the way. We've been watching every step of your journey. Mia's wired the game so we can watch a livestream of your play-through. Way to go attacking that tree with a stick. That oak was definitely asking for it."

Chloe found herself blushing. "I was getting to grips with the game, okay? If Mia *is* still there, perhaps you might suggest that new players shouldn't be thrown into the ass-end of nowhere with literally nothing on them to help them survive. Oh, and for that matter, she might want to think about smoothing out the onboarding process. Forget about the fact that I was thrown into this world after she panicked and forgot to pass on the safety instructions, but that *fall*! I don't think I'll ever get rid of the bruise on my ass from the landing."

Chloe rubbed her behind, noticing once again that all the pain and marks had gone. "Huh. What do you know?"

"See?" Mia's voice came on as if she had just seen her. "The pain isn't real. It's all simulated by the full-emersion VR. State-of-the-art. It's fantastic, right?" A pause. "Sorry the onboarding wasn't as smooth as we wanted, but every new game has its bugs, right?"

"Speaking of bugs, perhaps it might be worth putting in an option to customize your character from the start." Chloe cupped her breasts. "You got lucky with me since I don't mind lugging around these fun bags, but some ladies might find the 'standard' size for tits in this world a bit offensive."

Chloe thought she could detect a hint of a smile in Mia's words. "Noted."

Chloe reclined in her chair, holding the phone between her shoulder and chin. She kicked her legs up onto the desk and twirled the coil between her fingers. "So what can I do now? Just sit and wait for the timer to count down?"

"Pretty much," Mia replied. "Feel free to browse the computer there for anything you need. The internet is hooked up to the real-world internet, although you don't have access to any live messaging systems."

"What the hell? So I'm alone in here?"

Mia's voice dropped. "It's a security measure. Something the board required we fit in to keep the game under wraps as much as possible. If you need anything, you're going to have to go through us, I'm afraid."

Chloe thought about that. Stuck in a video game with no one but her family's psychologist and an overenthusiastic game developer to relay her messages and keep in contact with the real world. Not the best situation to be in, but definitely not the worst she'd ever had.

After all, the whole point of her taking this..."vacation.." was to get a break from the real world. Maybe a detox from social media and a deep dive into this new life would yield some sort of benefits. Not that she wanted to tell Mia that. She quite liked picking up on these bugs and winding her up. Even deep into this VR experience, she felt that she had some power and sway over them both.

"Can you put Demetri back on the phone, please? I'd like to speak to someone that I trust knows what they're doing."

Mia's mouth flapped before the shuffling indicated Demetri coming back onto the line. "So what's the next step, Chloe?"

"Isn't it obvious?" Chloe sat forward, a confident grin on her face.

"I resurrect with full health, I charge the cave, and I take the goblins by surprise."

Demetri breathed in sharply. "Are you sure that's a good idea?"

"Look, I need weapons to move forward in this game. Those goblins have weapons. I will steal them before they even have a second to think. I know where they are. They won't know I'm coming."

Chloe let out a quiet chuckle. "What can possibly go wrong?"

CHAPTER FOUR

"Oh, you guys are just friggin' sick!" Chloe shouted to the air as she reappeared in the white room. Once again, she checked her body for cuts and wounds from where the goblins had slaughtered her a second time, but she found none.

The phone rang.

Chloe's nostrils flared as she picked up the receiver. "Are you friggin' kidding me?" On the other end, Demetri and Mia were clearly trying their hardest not to laugh.

"I'm so sorry." Mia snorted. "I had no idea how this would impact the lower levels. The punishments for death are meant to be balanced to make character's think more intelligently about their future actions."

Chloe threw her arms in the air. "I was nearly *naked!* How the hell am I supposed to defeat goblins when I'm stripped of my clothes!"

"Hey, it's not our fault that you've collected so few items of equipment that the system chose to take your clothes, too," Mia argued. "Maybe try stuffing your pockets with pinecones or something. Nice breasts, by the way."

Chloe scoffed. The whole experience had lasted less than two minutes. Luckily for her, the system had respawned Chloe back near the entrance of the cave. The night had been darker, with stars glowing overhead and the moon higher in the sky. It seemed that in-game time didn't pause while Chloe waited to return.

She had found herself topless with one sandal and a single broken stick in her hand. Hurrying out of the rain as the familiar notification blinked to tell her that she was losing health due to the cold, she snuck back into the cave and found her tunic and the other half of her stick floating in the spot where she had been slain. There was a sparkling aura around them as they hovered in the air. The goblins seemed to be oblivious to them.

"At least the NPCs can't steal your items after you've died," Demetri offered.

Mia added, "Or other gamers. They remain so that only *you* can collect them. For a limited time, at least."

"Fat load of good that is to me." Chloe folded her arms, sulking in her chair. "How am I supposed to get the items back now?" She sat up suddenly. "*Wait.* I'm going to be wearing *less* when I go into the game next time, aren't I?"

Mia mused on the other end of the phone, "Definitely something to consider when we take the live broadcasts to the public. I'll have to patch through to Development and see if they've added censor filters for genitalia. The game is to be rated 15 at least, so I'm sure boobs won't matter too much."

Chloe growled and slammed the receiver down. Two hours of pacing and waiting, and she was back in the game.

Once more, she made her way to the cave. This time she put aside the idea of sneaking and sprinted toward her gear. The cold wind blew past her bare lower parts, stones pinching her feet. She dashed into the cave, spotting her clothing hovering in a bundle, just waiting for her to collect.

"Aha—*ooof!*"

Chloe cried out as the goblins, who had been made aware of her approach by the footsteps echoing down the tunnel, appeared once more. Chloe reached for her clothing as she fell, desperately trying to grab them before appearing once more in the white room.

"*Son-of-a-mother—*" Chloe's words were lost as a strange beeping sound filtered the nasties from the rest of the words. "What the—" *beep*.

The phone rang.

Chloe threw the receiver to her ear. "*What?* Did you get a good view of my ass as I fell to the floor?"

To her surprise, Demetri sounded relatively calm, though that didn't muffle the sniggers from Mia behind him. "Take a breath, Chloe. Think about what you're doing. What have we gone over a hundred times in our sessions before? Look for another way. Don't let your anger cloud your mind."

Chloe pulled the receiver away and stared incredulously at the phone. "Are you trying to *therapize* me? Over the—" *beeeeep* "phone? *Argh!* What is that beeping noise?"

Mia took the line. "It's our in-built censoring mechanism. Pretty cool, huh? It uses the latest voice technology to remove any unnecessary cursing in-game. It keeps the modest words like 'bastard' and 'twat' but disables any mention of the harder ones. Makes it a bit more friendly for families during the livestreams. We have to be socially conscious and all that jazz if this is going to get mainstream approval."

Chloe's lip curled. "So cussing is bad, but a full display of my lady parts is fine?"

"A minor oversight. You'll be happy to hear Development is reviewing your footage to map the sensitive areas and ensure that a correct filtration method is implemented for future players."

"Hooray. I'm ecstatic," Chloe said blankly. "Put Demetri back on the line."

"Hey, Chloe!"

"You mentioned finding another way before? What did you mean?"

"Isn't it obvious?" Demetri replied. "You're in a game of infinite possibilities. You don't *have* to tackle that cave. By the time you've been killed enough times, the sun will be up and the daylight will return if that's the method you choose to take."

Chloe remembered the feeling of being stabbed over and over again. How many times had it been now? Three. She had been stabbed and sliced three times. How many times would she be willing to take those hits before she went insane from the pain?

Chloe twiddled her fingers. "I'd rather not. I want my clothes, Doc."

"Then look for an alternative route." Demetri chuckled. "Use your head. Take it slowly. No matter what happens in life, there's always another way."

"Why do I feel like you're trying to work in a secondary meaning here?"

"Seriously. Just keep your head up and take a look around. You've got this. You're smarter than you know."

This time it was Demetri who hung up. Chloe placed the receiver back down and turned her attention to the computer. Once more she looked online to see if there was any record of anyone else playing the game, but it still looked like maybe she was the only person to have died.

Not once.

Not twice.

Three times.

"Okay, you son of a bitch." Chloe paused, surprised. "Oh, so 'bitch' is fine. That's good to know." She turned skyward. "I'll save that one for you, Mia!" She turned back to the clock, watching as it counted down the final 10 seconds. She steeled herself, ready for the cold. "Let's do this."

Dropping back into the game, Chloe readied herself for her landing, twisting her body mid-air so her feet were the first to hit the ground. She blinked in surprise as notifications met her vision.

You've unlocked a new skill: Acrobatics (Lv 1)

You've learned from your mistakes and managed to survive a 3-foot fall without hurting yourself. What a champion! Now you'll have minor sensory awareness of your center of gravity when you're in the air or jumping. Try launching off a 20-foot wall and

see what you can accomplish with your new skill. Go on, we dare you.

Requirements: Survive a fall by landing on your feet.

Bonuses: +1 dexterity

You've unlocked a new (unique) skill: Reckless (Lv 1)

Damn, girl. You are stubborn. You have no qualms in rushing into a situation and taking charge, strategy be damned! You're grabbing this minotaur by the horns and swinging it around the pen.

Requirements: Throw caution aside and charge at an enemy

Bonuses: +5 strength, +2 endurance

(NOTE: Reckless is a unique skill unlocked by meeting hidden requirements. Hidden skills yield hidden benefits to your character. Find more throughout the game by walking the road less traveled.)

Damn! Not too shabby, Chloe grinned, feeling a slight boost in her own strength as she stood up. It was nice to know that there had been *some* benefits to her stupidity in rushing back in to grab her clothes.

Speaking of which...

Chloe sprinted once more out of the rain, struggling to run elegantly as her hands cupped her naked parts. The only item left on her person now was the mud-soaked sandal that splashed in a puddle. She found the cave entrance and kicked off her sandal, wondering if being barefoot would make her approach quieter.

Instinctively she moved toward the fire. She peeked around the corner and saw her clothes floating once more, more items now added to the bundle. She wondered how long they'd remain there, and how much time she had to come up with another plan.

Could she charge them once more? Her strength had gone up a lot since the last encounter, she presumed, realizing then that she had no idea what her base stats were and how the skill increases worked in comparison.

"Okay, Chloe, think," she mouthed, looking up and down the tunnel once more. Something caught her eye—a crack she hadn't noticed on her way into the cave. It was hidden around a shallow bend that made it impossible to see from the other direction. Inside was a dull green light.

Chloe ducked back down the tunnel, her footsteps as quiet as possible.

Skill increased: Sneak (Lv 2)

You've heard of crouching tiger, hidden dragon, right? Well, consider yourself crouching pussy, squashed lizard.

Bonuses: +2 dexterity

(NOTE: Increases in skill override any previous bonuses gained from the skill).

Sweet! Hold on,"pussy" is allowed, too?

Chloe shook the thought aside and continued tiptoeing, detecting a notable decrease in the sound her feet were making. Perfect timing too, since she noticed the goblins had fallen silent once more. A moment later, they were chattering again.

Chloe breathed a sigh of relief and soon found herself at the crack in the wall. She tried to glance inside, but couldn't see because of the limited angle. What she did notice, however, was a thin line that trailed around from the crack, creating an outline of what appeared to be a door.

Sparing a glance over her shoulder, Chloe tugged at the rock, feeling it give a little. She tugged a bit harder, and the rock began to move on hinges she couldn't see. A great grinding screech filled the cave as rock grated on rock.

"What's that?" Skud's voice called from farther inside the cave.

"Intruder?" the second goblin called.

"Intruder!"

Chloe's heart leapt to her mouth. She pulled and pulled until her veins bulged out, adrenaline shooting through her as she tried not to consider what the possibility of dying a fourth time would mean. She'd already lost her clothes, and she was sure she would have lost *any* experience she might have gained along the way, but she most definitely didn't want to feel the pain of being cut open again.

"Bug report," Chloe said through gritted teeth, hoping Mia would hear her through the livestream. The door swung wide open. "Maybe turn down the pain receptors when characters die!"

The goblins approached through the tunnel, charging toward where the noise had come from. By the time they'd reached the wall, there was nothing to be seen—just a small puff of dirt floating in the air.

CHAPTER FIVE

Chloe breathed a sigh of relief as she heard the goblins' voices retreating back down the corridor on the other side of the door. She took a quick peek through the crack, then turned her attention back to the narrow tunnel that now presented itself.

This tunnel seemed different from the one she had walked (and run) through to find the goblins. There was a musty smell, and while the main entrance's rock walls were smoothed by years of use from travelers and creatures alike, this tunnel's walls were rough, and the floor was bumpy and uneven. It was as if no one had been this way in a thousand years.

Not a thousand years. Remember that this is a game, Chloe.

The strangest thing about the tunnel was the faintly pulsing green light that emanated from somewhere ahead. It was almost hypnotic. The rhythmic pulses were making Chloe's belly heave.

She took one more baleful look back through the crack and shrugged. "Well, whatever's down there is probably going to be better than meeting the pointy end of a goblin's blade again," she mused, taking a single step forward.

There was a small flash of white light and Chloe leaped back, doing her best to stifle her scream.

In the space where she had been just a second ago, there hovered a ball of white light. The light was dazzling in the tunnel, illuminating the walls. A moment later, the orb morphed into the shape of a question mark. A notification popped up.

HINT: You'll find handy tips and tricks like this littered around Obsidian. Touch the Help icon to find out more information.

Chloe laughed, reaching forward to touch the question mark. Despite its incorporeal appearance, her hand met a solid mass.

HELP: Great job, adventurer! You've found a hidden cave. The land of Obsidian is home to a thousand secrets, and thanks to you, there are now only 999 left to find! (Just kidding. There are more than a thousand. Don't count them all. Even we can't).

Quest unlocked: Walk the Deathwalk of the Gods

Before you lies the Deathwalk of the Gods, a herculean trial to test your might and valor. Survive the Deathwalk of the Gods and you shall be named victorious!

Difficulty: 8/10

Rewards: 10,000 exp + bonus items (locked).

Accept quest: Y/N

Chloe punched the air. "Yes! At last, a quest!"

She read through the notification again.

"The Deathwalk of the Gods, eh?" She craned her head over the question mark and looked down the tunnel. The way ahead seemed relatively quiet and empty. She thought back to the goblins on the other side of the wall, remembering the searing pain at each death she had encountered from their weapons.

Surely whatever lay down this tunnel couldn't bring much more pain than death by stabbing with a rusty blade. Chloe pondered her chances of just running through the Deathwalk and seeing what would happen. Surely the worst that could occur would be a swift death by some OP monster with big teeth, or the melting of her skin in fire and flames.

Actually, Chloe didn't like the sound of that last one.

Chloe spared one more glance back at where she had come from before focusing on selecting Y. Treading around the help icon, she started down the tunnel.

Ten steps in, another blinding light appeared. Chloe tapped the question mark.

HELP: A Lv 1 tackling this quest? Seriously? We advise you to turn back. Higher-level players, please. Exclusive club. Er...paid members only.

Paid members onl— Now this I've got to see.

Chloe stepped around the second question mark with a sly grin on her face. Her curiosity now flared, reminding her of the times her brothers and sisters had told her to stay out of their rooms. She'd found that the more she was told not to do something, the more she wanted to do the opposite.

Words from her mother: "Don't waste your life partying every weekend."

Words from her father: "Don't piss your money away on magazines and friends."

Words from her eldest sister, Hilary: "Stay *out* of my makeup drawer and leave my clothes alone. Just because we're the same size, doesn't mean you automatically get to share."

Chloe had ignored all those suggestions and would admit she'd had a great time doing the opposite. On a couple of occasions, she had done all three at once, the exhilaration of getting caught an additional buzz on top of the alcohol.

Chloe kept walking, ignoring the third question mark that appeared, this time deep red in color. Side-stepping, she strode down the tunnel.

She felt like she had been walking for *ages* before the tunnel finally started to draw to an end. She could hear strange noises up ahead. The hammering of steel on steel. The roaring of fire. A few steps more and the tunnel opened into a gigantic cavern. Chloe stepped out onto a platform, her mouth open in awe.

"Holy..."

The floor dropped away before her, a fall that looked to be several hundred yards down a bumpy shaft. A few feet ahead and across the gap were a series of platforms held up by pillars of dark rock. All around the cavern walls were large outcrops of the rock that held strange green fires which emanated no heat but made the whole cave appear to rock and sway. At the farthest reaches of the cave were two giant rock statues of what appeared to be dark trolls.

Chloe leaned forward, trying to judge the distance between where she stood and the first platform. The whole setup certainly looked higher-level than the primitive cave in which she had met the goblins. Each platform was around ten feet away from the next, so a person would have to take a running jump and leap from platform to platform to make their way to the end.

Chloe closed her eyes and took a steadying breath before turning her face skyward. "You know, you guys really need to sort out your entrance exams for this game. How the hell is a beginner supposed to level up when there's no way to ease into them?"

Her voice echoed around the cave, working its way from wall to wall before heading straight back to her. She was surprised to hear how nervous she sounded. A second later, she heard something that took her breath away.

An impossible roaring, then the grunt of some monumental beast. Chloe searched for the noise, her heart dropping when the objects she had thought were statues began to move. The trolls' dark skin reflected the green light of the fires as they turned to search for the source of the noise that had just reverberated around the cavern.

Chloe sighed. "Mum always told me my mouth would get me in trouble someday. I just thought it would be with boys." She tilted her head as the trolls took a step toward her. Something large and bulky swayed out from under their loincloths for a fleeting moment. "Hmm. I guess I was right."

With every step they took, the ground shook, and the huge trolls roared. Without even thinking about what she was doing, Chloe tested her new acrobatics skill, taking a few steps back and running toward the first platform.

She jumped, feeling as though the run-up should have given her wings but finding that her legs hardly gave her any spring.

"No, no, no!" she cried, the platform falling away before her vision. She stretched her arms out and managed to grab the edge. The rock felt loose and she scrambled for purchase, trying to haul herself back up.

One of the trolls turned and punched the wall, managing to break out a chunk of rock the size of a small house. With a grunt, it hurled the rock toward Chloe, missing by a good measure. The rock bounced off the wall, scattering pebbles and debris before rolling toward the abyss below.

"Erm, guys? A little help here? Maybe a hard respawn, or an option to self-detonate?"

Chloe closed her eyes, hoping that when she opened them, she'd find herself back in the white room. Instead, she opened them to find a chunk of rock coming toward her, perfectly aimed but slightly underthrown.

The platform ahead of her crumbled and began to topple. It tilted and knocked into the one she was clinging to, tilting it enough to angle it into a position where she could scramble up. She placed her feet on top, the pillar of her own platform now crumbling beneath her, and tried to remember what she had learned the day she had gone skateboarding as a kid with her brothers.

"Keep your knees bent, Chloe. It's all in the knees, and about supporting your center of gravity."

Chloe steeled herself, knees bent, hoping that the flat of the platform would provide some kind of protection as the pillar fell away, the trolls faded from view, and the darkness came up to swallow her whole.

The only respite came in the form of a blinking notification informing Chloe that 1HP of her health had been restored.

Great.

CHAPTER SIX

"What the hell is she thinking?" Demetri shouted at the screen, adjusting the camera angles to get a better look at the image of a scrambling Chloe trying to hold onto the platform. "Every time she respawns, it's like she's *trying* to get herself killed.

"Oh, *relax*," Mia said, settling into her chair with a steaming mug of something. She kicked her feet up next to the TV, grinning slightly as Demetri's eyes slid to her smooth legs.

Demetri shook his head, trying to focus on the girl flailing on the screen before him. Although he had to admit that part of the reason he had wanted to convince Chloe to work on this project was the idea that he'd be seeing a lot more of Mia, the fact was that he had been trusted with the safety and welfare of the Lagardes' little girl—the *Lagardes'* little girl—and here she was finding every opportunity in-game to kill herself.

"How can I relax?" Demetri asked, throwing his hands in the air and standing up. "There's no beginner level. There's no starter pack. We've thrown the child of one of the wealthiest families in America into a game of self-destruction. You promised me that this would help her grow as a person. That it would be the key to unlocking her confidence and helping her become a full-fledged Lagarde. All I've seen is goblins reveal the inside of her stomach, rain sap her health, and a cavern of legendary proportions in which giant trolls are hurling rocks at her!"

Mia rolled her eyes and placed her drink down. She stood up, meeting Demetri's eyes. She was wearing a pair of shorts and an old college hoody. He could smell her perfume, and it was intoxicating.

Mia rubbed his arm. "Teething problems, Doc. That's exactly why we needed a test dummy in there. Someone who *isn't* a gamer to test the system. What she's doing is *perfect* for development. It means the system's AI is having to deal with situations we couldn't even dream possible."

"That, and the fact she's bankrolling your entire operation." Demetri frowned, staring at the screen again, where the *very* naked Chloe now appeared to be surfing on a giant chunk of rock that had begun to fall.

"Well, that too," Mia teased, grabbing his other arm.

They stood only a foot away from each other now. He could feel her breath. They stared into each other's eyes for an endless moment before Mia rose on her tiptoes and kissed him on the cheek.

"That, and because I've missed you."

Mia winked and returned to her seat, her steaming mug in her hand once more.

Demetri fell back into his own chair, his heart beating double-speed as the ghost of Mia's lips caressed his skin. He turned his attention back to the screen, which was now totally black.

With a confused expression, he leaned forward and hit the side of the screen. When nothing happened, he turned to Mia.

Mia shrugged, reclining into her chair.

A low ringing whine echoed around Chloe's head. She took a large gulp of oxygen and found that it was mixed with dust.

She coughed, a great racking paroxysm that sent spasms of pain through her body.

"Well, I guess we're not in Kansas anymore, Toto."

She tried to laugh, but it hurt too much. She then tried to sit up but found she physically couldn't. Only one of her arms was able to move.

Panic set in.

Oh, shit. What happens if I reach 1HP and find myself trapped somewhere I can never get out of? Will I stay at 1HP forever? Is it possible that, wherever I am, I could be down here for the rest of my life? Trapped? Paralyzed? A lonely creature with just 1 friggin' hit point available for the rest of my life?

No. Impossible. After 2 years, Demetri and Mia will pull me out, right?

Chloe pondered the possibilities, wondering where the hell she was. Wondering what her situation was. Wondering just how the hell she was going to get out of this one.

Remembering that the option was there, Chloe brought up her menu and selected her character sheet:

<u>Bio</u>

Character name: *Untitled (click to select a new character name)*

Level: 1

Class: Null

Race: Human

<u>Stats</u>

HP: 1/15

MP: 15/15

Stamina: 0/30

Active effects: Null

<u>Attributes</u> (Unavailable until level 5)

<u>Skills</u>

Languages: Human

Acrobatics: Lv 1

Armed Combat: Lv 1

Creature Identification: Lv 1

Dual Wielding: Lv 1

Sneak: Lv 2

Reckless: Lv 2

<u>Available Points:</u> 0

She scoured the information, finding it hard to process what was in her view.

Okay, so I am somehow down to 1HP. That's not good. I wonder what saved me.

"Hey! At least I have all my mana. *That's* friggin' useful!" Chloe called, coughing again as the words hacked out of her throat.

Maybe try not shouting, genius. That was what got you into this situation in the first place.

Chloe studied her sheet, noting that her stamina was 0. She knew that much was true. She felt like if she closed her eyes, she could sleep forever.

Felt like if she…

She…

Chloe wasn't sure how long she slept, but when she woke up, it was to the sound of tinkling bells.

Rolling over as slowly as she dared, Chloe opened her eyes and saw how far she had fallen. The fires were nothing more than twinkling green lights overhead. She moved her head left and right, feeling the ache in her neck. The high-pitched whine was gone, and she felt as though she could move more parts of her than before.

Pulling up the activity log, Chloe saw a plethora of messages outlining her last few interactions of play, from escaping the goblins to her tumble through the cave:

Hooray! You've managed to make it for enough time without getting hurt that you regain 1HP. Keep it up, and perhaps you can function as a regular being in society.

+1HP

Ouch! It's raining stones! Consider taking cover before the rocks bash your skull into pulp. So much for being a functional being, huh?

-2HP

Skill increased: Acrobatics (Lv 2)

Congratulations on performing a full rotating front flip while falling. You've proven you have the coordination of a child gymnast. Have a sticker.

Bonuses: +3 dexterity

(NOTE: Increases in skill override any previous bonuses gained from the skill).

Skill increased: Acrobatics (Lv 3)

Congratulations on performing a full triple rotating front flip while falling. Front flips can be quite the crowd pleaser. There are some who make an honest buck performing tricks. Like jesters and acrobatic hobos. Welcome to their ranks.

Bonuses: +5 dexterity

(NOTE: Increases in skill override any previous bonuses gained from the skill).

Skill increased: Reckless (Lv 3)

Do I even need to say it? I mean, you launched yourself over a chasm in an attempt to run toward two trolls. That takes guts, kid.

Bonuses: +10 strength, +5 endurance

(NOTE: Increases in skill override any previous bonuses gained from the skill).

Ouch! You fell 213 feet down a solid rock face. Congrats on surfing most of the way. At least you did it with skill. Unfortunately, skill can only take you so—

#ERROR404

CMD_SCRIPT_ID_595.28

BOOT.BIOS

#ERROR404

INITIATE_LAUNCH_SEQ_RESPAWN_LV1_DEATH-WALK_ID_38

LAUNCH=(DIV_INTERVENTION)_2.2

Divine Intervention activated

Congratulations! For some unknown reason, the gods have taken pity on you. Not too hard to believe, really. You are rather pitiable. You have been given a second chance.

+1HP

WARNING: CRITICAL. You have 1HP remaining. Drink potions or find a place to rest.

Divine Intervention? What did that even mean? Chloe raised an arm and scratched her head, feeling the stickiness of something matted in her hair. None of this made sense to her. She couldn't believe the game had taken pity on her. *Obsidian* had been ruthless since she had first logged on. Killed three times by pathetic goblins, yet somehow saved dying in a nearly 300-foot fall by some deity?

"Man, this game really has it all," Chloe muttered, closing her eyes and letting her body rest once more. A small smile reaching her face as she wondered what the impact of those skill increases would be. Reckless Lv 3, +10 strength. Surely that would *have* to mean something if she came across those trolls again.

Guess it's always worth taking risks in this place...

Chloe had no idea how long she was down there or how long she let herself rest, but soon enough, she was able to sit up. She pulled herself to her feet, noticing for the first time that her stomach was rumbling and her mouth was as a dry as troll balls...

Or so she imagined.

Again she marveled at how detailed this game was. Although her body was being fed and watered in the real world (or she presumed it was), this hunger and thirst felt real, as if her body needed the nourishment to continue going. She checked once more on her character sheet, looking at the great big 0 next to her stamina. Maybe food and drink would affect her stamina. Maybe in order to properly recover, she'd need to find some halloumi and a cosmopolitan.

Chloe gasped, her hand finding her mouth. *What if halloumi and cosmos don't exist in this world?* Another gasp, eyes wide, now. *Or avocados, or piña coladas?*

Before Chloe could continue pondering the lack of twenty-first-century metropolitan delicacies in an online fantasy RPG, something caught her attention. Her ears pricked as she heard the bells tinkling nearby, quiet enough to have been missable as she had endured her migraine from falling, loud enough now to draw her infamous curiosity.

Chloe took a careful step, wobbling as she did so. Each step felt as though her feet weighed fifty pounds each. She squinted into the darkness toward the direction of the noise, hands in front of her so she wouldn't walk into a wall in the pitch-darkness—or fall through another hole, for that matter.

She felt a rock beneath her foot and nearly fell. The tinkling was getting louder. Somewhere up ahead, she could make out a very dull yellow glow. Chloe focused hard on trying to make out what she was seeing.

You've unlocked a new skill: Dark Vision (Lv 1)

By staring feebly into the dark for so long that your corneas cracked, you've managed to improve your perception of what lies in the darkness. Now you'll be able to make out minor silhouettes in the—*watch out for that hole*!

Chloe stopped suddenly, only realizing then that she had been walking while reading the notifications. She looked down and felt the floor with her hand, but there was no hole there.

Huh?

She opened her notifications again.

GOTCHA!

I guess you'd like to read your bonuses now, huh?

Requirements: Try with all your might to see through the darkness.

Bonuses: +1 intelligence, +2 etheric potential

Great. Talk about kicking me while I'm down.

Putting aside the ever more obnoxious notifications, Chloe kept walking, impressed that, true to its word, the AI had been right. She could now see vaguely where she was walking. She continued, finding a bend in the tunnel and discovering a small alcove in which she was able to stand up straight and stretch her arms.

There was no exit tunnel, only a small shrine built into the back wall. There were candles that looked to have not been lit in eons, dead flowers, and bells.

Hovering in a glowing orb of sparkles and stars, in front of them all was the item that was tinkling.

Chloe cautiously reached forward, feeling a strange power emanating from the bracers, for that was what they were. She could hear something or someone whispering behind the tinkle of bells, but she couldn't make out the words. Her fingertips touched the item and—

Snap!

The item was gone. The light went out. The tinkling quieted to nothing.

Chloe waited with bated breath for something to happen.

Suddenly, a blinding light swallowed her whole, accompanied by music.

CHAPTER SEVEN

Chloe called out in surprise, unable to see through the blinding lights. She felt a great rush of exhilaration as she was lifted off her feet, and her hair blew in all directions as a mini-tornado built around her body.

Her feet hit solid ground. She half-saw grass around her feet before the light reappeared and pulsed around her. She was lifted once more as if cupped by the hand of a giant.

Her feet hit the ground for the briefest of moments before the whole process repeated.

Once.

Twice.

Three times.

After the fifth time, Chloe started to wonder if the game was glitching. She supposed it was possible, although it would be incredibly annoying. Had Mia built in some kind of contingency or hard reset for if anything like this occurred? She felt helpless. Hopeless.

And yet, somehow Chloe felt stronger than she ever had before.

After one final lift, Chloe's feet touched the cool softness of grass. She cautiously opened her eyes and was surprised to find herself at the mouth of the goblin's cave.

The sun was bright in a cloudless blue sky. All around her, she could hear the calls and voices of the forest.

"What in the name of all that is good and holy happened?" she murmured, patting her person and noting that all of her cuts, scrapes, and bruises were gone. A large gash that must have been the result of falling from the slab was visibly still knitting shut on her thigh. She glanced at her bare breasts, suddenly remembering that she was bare-ass naked, and crossed her legs, folding her arms around her chest.

"Mmmphhmmhampphm…" a muffled voice said.

Chloe whirled, sure that someone was watching her from the tree line. Getting a good eyeful of her avatar.

"Hmmmphghhpppmgh!" Louder this time.

Chloe looked down at where the voice was coming from, which was her chest. She unfolded her arms and darted back, examining the shimmering gold and green bracers that now adorned her wrists. They gleamed in the sunlight, looking as though they had been made from the finest precious metals, yet they were feather-light on her arms.

"Thank fuck for that," the voice said. Chloe's eyes widened as she realized the voice was coming *from* the bracers. "Do you have any idea how sweaty you are? Shit!"

Chloe's eyebrow raised. "You…you can talk?"

"I know, pretty freaky, right? Who'd have thought it, eh? Kiera-Freya, trapped in a piece of enchanted armor. It's a bit humiliating, really, but there we are. I'm actually quite glad you found me. There I was at the end of that Godforsaken quest, and who knew how long I'd be down there for?"

Despite herself, Chloe let out a laugh. She hadn't realized how much she had been missing company since arriving in Obsidian. Even if her first friend turned out to be a piece of enchanted armor, at least she had *someone* to talk to who didn't try to stab her on first sight.

"*You're* the reward for the Deathwalk?" Chloe asked.

"Well, *that* and a crapload of experience, apparently. Not that it'll make much difference to you, eh? 10,000 experience must be nothing at your character's level. Barely even made a notch on your progress bar, I'll bet."

Chloe lowered her arms and pulled up her character sheet.

Bio

Character name: Untitled (click to select a new character name)

Level: 8

Class: Null

Race: Human

Stats

HP: 220/220

MP: 150/150

Stamina: 300/300

Active effects: Null

Attributes

Strength: 12 (+16)

Intelligence: 6 (+2)

Dexterity: 10 (+7)

Endurance: 15 (+15)

Etheric Potential: 7 (+7)

Skills

Languages: Human

Acrobatics: Lv 3

Armed Combat: Lv 1

Creature Identification: Lv 1

Dark Vision: Lv 1

Dual Wielding: Lv 1

Sneak: Lv 2

Reckless: Lv 3

Available Points: 32

Level 8! Chloe punched the air. She'd finally made it past level 1, and not only that, she seemed to have skipped a bunch of levels after somehow completing the quest.

She beamed as she studied her naked body, noting that already she felt much stronger than she had. She stood up taller. Her thighs and arms were more muscular, and...were those *abs*?

Endorphins shot through Chloe's body as the sun beamed down on her. For the first time since she'd arrived in Obsidian, she felt truly happy.

She turned back to her character sheet. Not only had she gained several levels, but *finally* her attributes had been unlocked. She noticed a small Help icon and focused on it.

Attributes: Your attributes are the lifeblood of your character. Attributes remain locked during the first 5 levels of play while the system studies your style and generates attributes to further support your character. A maximum of 30 attributes form your base traits, with each additional level gained offering 4 attribute points that can be assigned to any of the 5 available branches. Additional points must be assigned within 24 hours of gameplay. Any unassigned points after that time will be randomly assigned to available traits.

For more information on each attribute, select the text.

Chloe found herself laughing at the assignment of points she had generated. She supposed it made sense that her biggest bonuses would be in endurance and strength, given that her Reckless ability had boosted those traits, although she couldn't quite work out where the additional boosts had come from.

It kind of sucked that her intelligence was considerably lower, but given that she had found herself in the very depths of an ancient cave with zero clothes on to the point where a deity had to take pity on her, she guessed that might have played some large role here. At least with...*32!*...available attribute points to spend, she'd be able to boost some of her attributes and make her character more balanced.

Hmmm...unless certain classes need particular traits to succeed? She figured maybe she'd wait a while before rushing to spend them all.

At least the rest of her stats seemed pretty even. The only thing she wasn't so sure about was what Etheric Potential meant. She focused on the text, but before she had a chance to read the notification, Kier-aFreya started talking.

"Etheric Potential is a person's ability to manipulate the etheric to cast spells. It's the magical realm that mages, wizards, and warlocks access to explore the limits of their powers."

Chloe blinked away the menu. "Hold on, how did you know that was what I would select on my screen?"

"Easy question to answer, really. I'm a part of you now. I can see everything you can see. Hmm...Let's have a look here... Got a few good skills here... Okay, base attributes don't show a lot of intellect in that noggin of yours..." The voice from the bracers gasped. "Wait a second... *You're a level 8?*"

Chloe stood up proudly, her hands on her hips. "Yep! I've just gained 7 levels thanks to finding you, my little emerald and gold sweethearts." She brought the bracers to her lips and kissed them in turn.

The next thing Chloe knew was a strange force brought the bracers back down to her side. She tried to raise them again, but they suddenly felt like they weighed fifty pounds each.

"Okay, Sweet Tits, rule number 1. *Never* kiss KieraFreya. If you think I'm just some sweet accompaniment to your armor, you have definitely misread exactly what the fuck is going on here.

"Secondly, you're saying that you were a *level 1* when you took The Deathwalk of the Gods? Something must be wrong there. A glitch in the etheric, or some kind of prank by the gods or something. Hold on a second..."

Without warning, Chloe's menu popped open. Her eyes found her activity log, even though she tried her hardest to look away. The system scrolled through it, all the way from her first encounter with the goblins, right up until the final notification of a quest complete. There was also a message Chloe hadn't had a chance to read.

Quest complete: Walk the Deathwalk of the Gods

You've done it! You've outwitted the trolls, swum the unforgiving lake, made it through the realm of fire, and emerged victorious through the fractal labyrinth of death. You've truly proven yourself—

#ERROR404

—a champion among champions—

MISSING_SEQ

REBOOT_POPUP

—Carry on adventurer Untitled, and soar to ever great heights!

Bonuses: 10,000 experience + Bracers of KieraFreya

Item obtained: Bracers of KieraFreya

You've found the lost bracers of a fallen goddess. Made from metals forged by the gods, these bracers are virtually indestructible, though some say that they have a mind of their own.

Bonuses: +5 strength, +10 endurance, +5 etheric potential

Rarity: Mythic

Chloe beamed.

The next thing she knew, the menu was gone.

"Hey!"

KieraFreya continued to muse, "So *you're* telling me that you just *happened* to stumble across the entrance to the Deathwalk of the Gods, and, even after seeing the trolls, you, a Lv 1 human with *no* armor, *no* weapon, and *no* clue, still went ahead and tried to run the trial?"

Chloe shrugged. "Yep."

KieraFreya chuckled, a dark laugh. "Well, I guess that explains your Reckless ability. So you didn't see the realm of fire?"

Chloe shook her head.

"You didn't swim the unforgiving lake?"

Another shake of the head.

"The fractal labyrinth?"

"Nope."

KieraFreya sighed, a small breath of air tickling Chloe's wrists. A strange feeling, really, given that the air was coming from *armor*.

Chloe giggled. "Hey, that tickles."

"So, to sum it up," KieraFreya said, clearly having a hard time processing what had happened, "Despite the ridiculously high-level dungeon that was created for the sole purpose of keeping a part of me trapped in the depths below the earth for thousands upon thousands of years—"

" Who'd want to keep you trapped—*ouch!*" Chloe shut up as her own hand rose to her face and slapped her.

"Don't interrupt. Despite all that, a Level 1 was dumped into the world with literally 0 experience and managed to find a way to survive the fall—with a little help from the gods—" KieraFreya scowled, "and *finally* release me from my prison in the darkness?"

A beat before KieraFreya burst into laughter. Chloe's arms rose, unbidden, wrapping themselves around her shoulders in a hug. It would have been the strangest thing, she thought, for a stranger to pass her in the woods now and see a naked woman with glowing green bracers hugging herself.

"Aha! Thank you so much...er, Untitled, for releasing me and allowing me the sweet scent of freedom. Finally, I can serve my ultimate purpose and restore myself to my former glory!"

"Untitled?" Chloe asked, taken aback by the excitement and yet still perturbed because her arms were moving of their own accord. "It's actually 'Chloe.' You can call me Chloe." She forced her attention to her bracers and found that, although there was some resistance, she was able to bring them back down.

"I'm sorry. I only have the ability to call you what the system has called you."

Chloe raised an eyebrow. "You can't call me by the name I've requested, but you're able to swear without setting off the censorship beeper?"

"What's the censorship beeper?"

Chloe took a deep breath and shouted, "MOTHER—" *beeeeeeep!*

Her shout rang around the clearing, the beeping of the sensor sounding like an alarm was going off. Several birds took flight from the tops of trees, their silhouettes darkening the sky for the briefest of moments.

When the echoes had stopped, KieraFreya snorted. "*What?* That's fucking absurd!"

"Showoff."

"Like, seriously. Why would swearing be censored, Untitled? It's, like, the basis of all languages!"

Chloe rolled her eyes. "I know! Now quit calling me 'Untitled.'"

"Change your goddamn name, then!" KieraFreya retorted. "The power's in your hand, Sweet Tits."

"Oh! But nicknames are fine— Argh! All right!"

Chloe flicked open the menu and selected her character sheet. She hovered over the name and highlighted the text. When no keyboard appeared, she thought about the name "Chloe," and the next thing she knew, her name had updated on the menu.

"There. Better?"

"Much better, Untitled. Much better." KieraFreya sniggered.

"Hey!"

"Oh, come on. You're really just going to go with 'Chloe?' You're dumped into a realm of infinite possibilities, of self-defined names of men such as 'Drake the Berserker,' 'Helen the Almighty,' and 'Zachary the Damned,' and the best you can come up with is 'Chloe?'"

"It's my name."

KieraFreya sighed. "Fine, little girl. As you were."

Chloe huffed, trying to make up her mind about the bracers. It was definitely nice *finally* having someone she could talk to, but already she was finding that part of the conversation was tiresome. One minute the bracers were as kind as sin to her, the next they were mocking her. She also didn't feel entirely comfortable knowing that deep inside, there was some force that was able to control her limbs and move her body and mind without her volition. She wondered if there was a way to control the bracers more effectively.

Chloe reached with one hand and tried to run her thumb under the bracers to loosen them around her wrists. She was surprised to find that she literally couldn't get any purchase whatsoever. She was even more surprised when her right arm pulled away from her left.

"Don't even think about it," KieraFreya said darkly.

"I was just adjusting them."

A snicker. "I know what that means. You were trying to remove me already. Well, good luck with that, princess, I'm in this for the long haul."

Chloe's heart quickened.

"The long haul? What do you mean?"

"Wow, your intelligence really is low, isn't it? Didn't you hear me earlier? I'm a *part of you now*. That's right. No shifting from these wrists. No escaping. No shoving me in a bag. You found a piece of enchanted armor, bitch, and you've started on your road to one of the most epic quests this game has to offer. Congratulations. You're now stuck with me."

A notification popped up.

Quest unlocked: A Fallen Goddess

The Goddess of Retribution, KieraFreya, fell from grace. Her form has been divided and scattered across the land of Obsidian. For eons, she has lain in wait, hoping for an adventurer brave enough and strong enough to unite her pieces of armor once more and restore KieraFreya to her former glory.

Find all [x] pieces of KieraFreya and return her to godhood.

Difficulty: 10/10

Rewards: 100,000 exp, + rare items (locked).

Accept quest: Y/N

"100,000 experience!" Chloe exclaimed, light-headedness washing over her. "100,000?" She immediately selected Y.

"That's right, little naked girl. Now perhaps you should focus on starting your journey of 1,000 steps by taking the first one toward getting yourself some goddamn clothes. I mean..." Chloe's wrists rose of their own accord until they were level with her chest, "as impressive as they are—and they *are* pretty impressive, as far as breasts in Obsidian go —you're far more likely to survive a stab wound if you've got something to cover your body. What were you, *born* into this world naked?"

Chloe slapped her head, unsure if it was a voluntary movement or another of KieraFreya's. She'd forgotten all about her clothes!

Chloe's mind flashed back to the clothing floating in the cave where the goblins were.

Would they even still be in the cave now that it was daybreak and the sun was high? Would the clothes still be there? What if there was a set time for how long a player could wait to collect lost items?

She started back toward the cave and paused. "Is it really only going to take me 1,000 steps to find all the pieces of your armor?"

Chloe's hand slapped her forehead once more, this time harder than she'd have liked. "No more questions, dumbass. Let's work on scaling that intelligence up before you open your trap again."

CHAPTER EIGHT

The sun peaked in the sky. By its position, Chloe guessed that it was around noon.

She strolled with a fresh note of confidence in her gait. Around the forest were vivid hues of green and brown, leaves dazzling in the sunlight. Forest creatures hopped and skittered around her. Squirrels, rabbits, foxes, a badger, and something that looked like a rabbit had had sex with a deer hopped around with large antlers on its head.

Chloe felt great. A smile was plastered on her face as she felt the rough material of her tunic and shorts again. Her sandals stopped the pine needles from spiking their way into her feet, and she was already growing used to the bracers, which had been close to silent since she'd left the cave.

The only downsides were the bloodstains on her clothing and the goblin stench that clung to her skin. It was laughable, really, just how easily Chloe had taken the goblins down. She hadn't even needed a weapon of any kind. She had the ultimate weapon attached to her wrists.

She had to admit she had been a bit surprised when her arms rose of their own accord. As Skud attacked with his knife, her arm had moved instinctively to block the attack, the metal bracers deflecting the blade. The next second, her right arm had grabbed the dagger from the goblin and returned the swipe at his throat.

Skud fell, his hands trying to stem the bleeding. A moment later, with the flick of a wrist, she had thrust the knife into the second goblin's chest. A swift punch in the face and the other goblin was down, yielding Chloe a modest 30exp per goblin and her first rudimentary weapon—**Rusty Dagger**.

Now she practically skipped along, heading nowhere in particular. She had tried to discover from KieraFreya if the bracers had a preferred direction, but it turned out the fallen goddess was as clueless as Chloe.

"Nope, not a clue," she had said as Chloe scratched her head at the cave entrance. "You think this would be a challenge with a difficulty of 10 if I knew where to find the rest of me?"

The trees began to thin as she walked farther. She stumbled across a babbling brook and took a long drink of water from cupped hands. A little farther downstream, she saw a deer lapping the water.

"This place really is beautiful," she mused.

KieraFreya scoffed, the first sound she'd made in hours. "You haven't seen the places I've seen, sweetheart. Sure, a baby deer in the sunny woods is cute, but I assure you that nothing lasts long in this world. It won't be long before…"

As if on cue, there came a mighty roar. Chloe recoiled, the sound familiar from her adventures in the dark the previous night. A moment later, the trees made way as a colossal bear appeared behind the deer, batting the poor creature with one paw and sending it flying in a grotesque display of blood.

"Point proven," KieraFreya said matter-of-factly.

Chloe studied the bear. Its black fur was in patches. One side of its bulk was covered in scars. Its eyes glowed a deep red. As it neared the remains of the deer and chomped the creature with its teeth, it turned its head toward Chloe.

Chloe used her Creature Identification skill.
Black bear.
"Well, that clears things up," KieraFreya quipped.

"Enough sarcasm from you. What do I do?" Chloe retreated slowly as the bear began to advance."

"*RUN, idiot!*"

"Right."

Chloe steeled herself, turned on her heels, and fled. The bear roared and sprinted after her.

"Now what?" she asked, trying not to worry about her stamina bar as she felt the drain from running. She was pleasantly surprised, however, to notice that she definitely felt more energetic than the previous night.

"Keep running and find a place to hide?" KieraFreya urged. "Whatever you do, don't get eaten. I've only just found a host. I mean, a partner for this journey. The last thing I want is to be farted out as bear shit and made to wait for you again in the woods."

Chloe made a mental note to address the "host" comment later, but for now, she continued running through the woods. She ducked around branches, turning sharply in all directions to throw the bear off the scent. In the middle of a copse of tight-knit firs, she found a series of large rock structures which she wove through, moving as randomly as she dared. Soon enough, the cries of the bear began to sound farther and farther away.

When she reached a small alcove cut into the side of a hill, she paused and took a breath. Her stomach rumbled, and her mouth was dry. She opened her menu and saw that she'd spent 75% of her stamina.

Hey, at least I have something *left.*

Not wanting to wait around too long, and wondering where the hell the edge of the forest was, Chloe pushed herself to her feet and made her way up the hill. Surely higher ground would yield some sort of advantage? For the first time since she'd arrived, she noticed that she had been walking on relatively flat land. This was the first gradient she had encountered, and surely that had to mean something?

The top of the hill was bare of trees, reminding Chloe of the heads of the boring drones who sat in her family's board meetings—executives who wore sharp suits and clung desperately to their fading youth by allowing silver rings of hair to crown their balding heads. How they would turn their nose up at her to see where she was now.

Shading her eyes from the blazing sun, Chloe scanned the forest—trees, trees, and more trees for nearly as far as the eye could see. From the north to the west to the south, she saw nothing but a canopy of green, falling and rising steadily until the world dropped off the horizon. To the east, there was a series of mountain ranges capped with snow and cloud.

Chloe brought her right wrist up to her mouth as if speaking into a walkie-talkie. "Any ideas?"

"You don't need to get so close, y'know," KieraFreya replied. "I'm a part of you. I can hear you even if you whisper."

"Does that mean you can hear my thoughts?"

A pause. "Hey, look. Smoke!"

Chloe looked in the direction her hand was now pointing and saw the thin ribbon of smoke rising lazily into the sky.

She wondered what the source of the smoke might be. Had she been asked the previous night, she might've just taken her chances and wandered in that direction without a care. Now, though...

Now she had learned from several goblin stab wounds in the gut that sometimes fire meant bad things.

Still, it was the only lead she had, so with a caution that would have been beneficial the night before, she stalked in the direction of the smoke.

Chloe peered through a thicket of bushes at the cottage. It was a dilapidated old thing. The windows were nothing but holes, the door hung off its frame, and vines wrapped around the structure.

"What a shithole," KieraFreya whispered, making Chloe jump.

"Will you *shut up*?" Chloe hissed, sticking the bracers under her arms. "We're supposed to be sneaking, remember? What if there's a monster inside making the fire?"

Skill increased: Sneak (Lv 3)

Incredible. You're a natural at this shutting-up-and-lying-low thing. Soon you'll be on a par with the elves, able to whisper without sound, undetectable by any creature!

For now, though, you're slightly quieter than you were before. Congrats!

Bonuses: +3 dexterity

(NOTE: Increases in skill override any previous bonuses gained from the skill).

Well, what do you know?

"Hmmpgphhmmrgh!"

Chloe rolled her eyes. She felt her arms struggling by her side and released one of the bracers. *"What?"*

"Can you *not* put me under there! I am the fucking Goddess of Retribution. You think I belong in those sweaty pits of yours—"

Chloe fought her arms, folding them tightly again. She wriggled and writhed, straining as her arms shook and pulled in an attempt to escape. Using every ounce of strength she had, she managed to hold them in place as more muffled utterances of disgust came from her pits.

"All you have to do is shut your..." Chloe thought for a moment, "mouth? Yeah, let's go with mouth. If you shut your mouth for long enough that I can talk to you, you'll have your freedom."

After another moment or two of struggling, Chloe's arms relaxed. Another second, and there was a muted, "Hmm...fine."

"That's better," she said, bringing her wrists closer to her face. A sweaty film decorated the ornate metal. Chloe flushed. "Oops, I see what you mean. It *is* super-hot out..."

Chloe waited for KieraFreya to jump in. When she didn't, she continued, "Okay, so are you going to help me on this mission of yours, or am I going to have to keep you cooped up in various orifices of my body until you learn to control yourself?"

Another beat of silence.

"Well?"

"Oh, I'm allowed to talk now?" KieraFreya hissed, her voice quiet as if she were talking to herself. "How could this possibly be? I'm *Kier-aFreya*, for Obsidian's sake. I used to rule from the heavenly thrones, and now I'm just a pet, strapped to a weakling's wrist, unable to even overthrow her body. What has become of me?"

To Chloe's surprise, KieraFreya began to cry—as much as an item of armor could weep.

Chloe took a seat, glancing nervously at the cottage for fear that something inside might hear them both. The shadow of something moved past the window.

She brought her bracers closer to her mouth.

"I've already told you—" KieraFreya snapped between sobs.

"I'm sorry," Chloe hissed. "Look, I'm really sorry. I won't do it again."

"You promise?"

Chloe considered this. "Well, as long as you don't do anything that might put us in danger, then, yes. I promise."

KieraFreya's sobs began to slow. Chloe waited patiently, eyes darting awkwardly from her wrists to the trees to the sky. She had never been great around crying people, and every iota of her instincts were telling her to comfort, hug, and show affection to the weeping person.

The only problem was, how the hell did you hug bracers?

Chloe brought the bracers across her chest and began to hug herself.

KieraFreya spoke up. "What're you doing?"

Chloe's cheeks glowed red. She glanced back at the sky, remembering that Mia and Demetri were probably watching her right now, bellies sore from laughter. She imagined bowls of popcorn falling as they fell off their chairs, watching Chloe try to comfort the tubes of metal that had melded with her body.

That is, unless they weren't already banging.

Chloe felt a bubble of laughter rise. In all the excitement of the last night and collecting her lost items, she had almost forgotten that she was in a game and there was a world beyond this one. Once more, she marveled at the ability of this game to create an experience for the player.

There came a clatter from inside the house, followed by a minor explosion. Streams of smoke fluttered out of the window and joined the chimney's column. Someone inside coughed.

"Argh… Son-of-a—" *beep*, came the voice from inside the house.

"It doesn't matter," Chloe said. "Come. Let's play detective and see what's going on."

"What's a detective?

CHAPTER NINE

It didn't take them long to discover what was making the noises inside the house.

Peeking through the window, Chloe saw one of the strangest men she had ever encountered. He wore a thin robe that shone purple and blue, he had a weak tuft of hair protruding from his chin, and he was so skinny that probably the slightest gusts of wind would blow him over.

"Oh, no. Oh, no. Oh, no," he whined as he whirled around the small kitchen. There were several pots out on the work surfaces, many of them tipped onto their sides as they spilled liquids of various colors. Above a fire, a larger pot was boiling, emitting small stars and sparkling as the liquid snapped, crackled, and popped. It was from there that the smoke was billowing.

"No, no. Not again." The man ran a hand through his long, thin hair. Peered at a small book, nodded in confirmation, and threw something small and black into the fire. "Mmhmm, that seems to stabilize—"

Another explosion. A shout from the man. Chloe ducked her head as he turned her way, his face a blackened mess. She did her best to stifle her laughter.

"Who goes there?" the man cried.

"I've got to get a look at this." KieraFreya chuckled, lifting Chloe's arm in the air. Chloe used her other hand to try to bring her back down, and the two struggled for a moment. Chloe's biceps strained to hold her other arm, managing to lower both arms as she strained and gritted her teeth, pouring every morsel of remaining strength into the move. She quickly flicked open her stats and saw that the maneuver had taken 10% of her stamina. Luckily, in the walk toward the house, most of her stamina had recovered.

Chloe smiled wickedly at her bracers, a bead of sweat dripping off her head when she heard the cough from behind her.

She turned, seeing the blackened face of the man hanging out of the window.

An awkward silence passed between the two as Chloe realized how stupid she must look. She was knelt as if praying, her hands palm-up.

"Hi," she managed.

The man blinked at her, smoke wreathing behind his head. "You're not a bear."

"No. No, I'm not."

"You're human."

Chloe nodded. "Yes, I am."

Another explosion came from inside the house. The man jumped and threw his hands over his head.

"Need a little help?" Chloe asked.

The man nodded. "Yes, please."

Quest unlocked: We didn't start the fire

Some idiot has lost control of his flames. Help him to put out the fire before the whole house burns to cinders.

Difficulty: 1/10

Rewards: 50 exp

Accept quest: Y/N

Chloe nodded toward Y and joined the man inside the house, fanning her way through the smoke. The whole place was a mess. Chairs were upturned, and the rest of the furniture was broken and rotting. She found a doorway that led to a small cellar and headed down the stairs, finding that the cool air soothed her throat. At the bottom of the stairs was a small hole bored into the ground, through which running water dashed under the house.

Managing to find a bucket, she called the man downstairs, and between them, they managed to ferry water upstairs to chuck at the blaze. Between their trips, embers leaped from the fireplace and landed on various surfaces, which burst into flame. A quick dampening with a water-soaked rug Chloe had found in the upper bedroom soon brought the fire and smoke under control.

Chloe placed her hands on her hips and looked around the kitchen as she recovered her breath. "No permanent damage, then?"

The man laughed, coughed, then laughed again. "Thank you so much for your help. I wasn't sure I was going to last much longer, let alone stop this house from burning to the ground.

Quest complete: We didn't start the fire.

Smart, cunning, quick wit, and intelligence to solve a problem. These were none of the things you used as you launched water on the fire and jumped head-first into a smoke-infested building. You somehow managed it, though. Hooray!

Difficulty: 1/10

Rewards: 50 exp

Chloe smiled as she read the notification of the increase to her experience.

"Woah, I just gained 200 exp." The man grinned, a far-off look in his eyes.

"*Hey!* No fair. I only gained 50, and I did half of the work."

"*You* had a quest unlocked too? What did it say?"

Chloe read out her initial quest log.

The man's face fell. "Some idiot? It doesn't say that, does it?"

"Sure does." Chloe smirked. "What did yours say?"

The man read his notification out, the quest titled Clean up your mess.

"This is a pretty smart system," he said, finding a clean(ish) towel and dabbing the char off his face. "Giving us two separate quests with different rewards for the same thing? I got bonus points in mine for acquiring help to complete the task."

"So it forces cooperative play?" Chloe scanned her notifications, not spotting anything about working with other people.

"I guess so. Which is ridiculously hard out in these woods, considering that there's barely anyone here, and it's stupid easy to get lost." The man stepped forward and held out his hand. "I'm Gideon, by the way. Gideon Fleetwood."

"I'm…" Chloe paused, remembering the fun KieraFreya had made of Chloe's name of choice. "Tamara the Incredible." Chloe puffed out her chest, adopting a superhero stance.

To her dismay, Gideon burst into laughter. Chloe glared at him.

"I'm sorry," he said between breaths. "That's one of the dumbest names I've ever heard. Have you *ever* played an MMORPG before? That's…that's…" Gideon clutched his stomach, tears falling from his face.

"Well, at least it's better than 'Gideon Eatwood,'" Chloe retorted. "I'd hate to think what you get up to in your spare time."

Gideon stopped laughing instantly. "Actually, it's 'Fleetwood.' As in, the Fleetwood Forest where you're standing now? Don't you know anything about this game?" Gideon grabbed the pot, checking carefully to make sure it had cooled down before kicking the back door open and flinging the contents outside.

Chloe felt herself at a disadvantage. Truth be told, she *did* know nothing about this game. This was a brand new game, or so she had been told, but this guy Gideon seemed to know a hell of a lot more than she knew about the mechanics and the lay of the land. Not only that, but she was certain he'd been practicing some sort of apothecary or magical arts in that house.

An idea struck Chloe.

"You seem to know an awful lot about this area." Chloe softened her voice, coyly twirling her hair. "I suppose that means you have a map of some kind, yes? Something that might perhaps help us get out of these woods?"

Gideon returned inside and placed the pot back on the stove. He sadly shook his head. "Not anymore."

Gideon's eyes lowered to the floor as he told Chloe about a party that had been traveling with him and how they had gotten lost in the woods. According to Gideon, he had managed to gain an early VIP tester pass to play *Obsidian* due to the ridiculous number of hours and followers he'd generated livestreaming his gaming conquests with his friends.

"I didn't even have to ask them. They called me, like, a day ago. Out of the blue." He flung out his hands like an explosion. "*Poof!* And here I am."

Gideon told Chloe he had come into the game with two other friends, Ben and Tag, and they had been exploring when they were attacked by the black bear and each scrambled in their own separate directions for safety. Gideon had trundled through the forest until he found succor in this cottage, and was now looking for better ways to arm himself against the elements.

"I'm only a level 3 mage, y'see?" Gideon fanned his robes out wide.

Chloe nodded appreciably. "Nice. And you were spawned with that to start?"

"Yep. Selected my class and character, and there you have it. Meet Mage Gideon Fleetwood." Gideon twirled and knocked over what appeared to be, an empty potions bottle. "I admit that my skills need a bit of work."

"I'll say," KieraFreya piped up.

"What was that?"

Chloe flushed, crossing her arms to cover her bracers. She had forgotten about KieraFreya for a moment and wasn't sure now whether it was the best idea in the world to let a stranger know she had found a mythical relic that had a personality and voice all its own.

"Nothing," Chloe said. "I'm actually jealous you got to pick your class and character. I was dumped into the game with nothing but these clothes. I didn't have a chance to customize anything."

Gideon shuffled awkwardly.

"What?" Chloe asked.

"It's nothing. Just…" He raised his hands. "You know what? It doesn't matter."

Chloe considered pushing the issue but could tell from Gideon's demeanor that he would much rather put a lid on that particular topic.

"Fine." She joined him in leaning against the work surface on the other side of the kitchen. "Well, since we're both stuck in this godforsaken forest, I don't suppose you'd be up for a bit of collaboration? Y'know, I scratch your back, you scratch mine?"

Gideon's eyes flickered to Chloe's chest, hovering a moment too long before finding her eyes. He gulped. "What did you have in mind?"

Chloe raised an eyebrow. "It seems to me that in order to get back to your friends, and for us to find this map so I can get out of these woods, we need to fix the local pest problem. What do you think about doing a little bit of bear hunting with Tamara the Incredible?"

Gideon scoffed, bringing a hand to his mouth as a notification popped up in Chloe's vision.

CHAPTER TEN

There was a knock on the door. Mia started awake, wiping the line of drool that had crept down the side of her mouth with her sleeve. She pawed at her eyes and rose to answer.

"Just a minute." She paused at the door. "Password?"

A muffled voice said, "Delta, kappa, delta."

Mia laughed, opening the door and allowing Demetri to sweep into the room. It was dark outside, the sounds of traffic disappearing when the door closed.

Demetri ruffled his hair and exhaled. He took his place in the leather chair where he had spent every available moment staring at Chloe on the screen. He had had to disappear for a few hours today to spend his time consulting the other Lagarde siblings, ensuring that fame, fortune, and success didn't inflate their egos too much.

Yeah, like that was a problem he could stop.

Demetri actually found it fascinating to watch Chloe go through the trials she was encountering in-game. Compared to her egotistical brothers and sisters with their scoffs and whines and petty little problems, it was almost addictive to spend time watching someone redevelop herself in a brand new world. He had to give it to Mia and Praxis Games. *Obsidian* could be a huge hit in the future.

Mia caught Demetri up on what he had missed, which was to say, she told him about Chloe's journey through the woods and the incident with the bear. Now they could both see Chloe live on the screen, working with this new character, Gideon, to prepare something in a large pot.

"Another NPC?" Demetri picked up a piping hot drink, side-eyeing Mia, who had changed into different clothes since he had left.

Now she wore a pair of leggings and a sweatshirt, and her hair was in a ponytail. He figured he should maybe take a leaf out of her book at some point. He was still wearing the same suit he had been since Chloe started her adventure.

Demetri raised his mug. "Thanks for this, by the way."

Mia waved a hand. "Don't mention it. And, no, not an NPC. A real person." A smile played on her lips. "You know what this means, right?"

Demetri shook his head, recoiling as he burned his tongue on his drink.

"We're officially live in beta testing. Praxis opened up the game to a selection of candidates, and now they're meeting for the first time."

When Demetri's expression remained blank, Mia explained that this was a necessary part of game testing. Chloe had been their first player and was the constant in the game, the first player to fully submerge themselves into *Obsidian* for an extended period of time. Meanwhile, approximately a thousand other players were now finding their way into the game, spawning in random locations across Obsidian's vast map and getting involved in quests, conversations, and battles.

"They told me that trials wouldn't start for at least another week," Mia said, curling her feet under her butt to warm them, "but I guess that they deemed the game stable enough after Chloe's playbacks that they just went ahead and got everyone involved."

Demetri watched as something exploded in the pot on the screen. Chloe and the other character were dancing around manically, Gideon waving a towel as Chloe wagged a finger in the man's face. "You mean they didn't tell you when they were going ahead?"

Mia rolled her eyes. "I'm a game developer, D. One of the lowest rungs of the ladder, although probably a shoo-in for a promotion, thanks to your powers of persuasion." She winked. "And probably an even bigger shoo-in considering that your baby Lagarde has already managed to exploit quite a big hole in the game's story development. No level 1 player should *ever* have been able to complete that task, especially the way she did."

"Right, I meant to ask you about that," Demetri said, remembering the question that had hounded his head as he had sat and listened to Henry and Hilary Lagarde drone on about the fact that one had stolen the other's Netflix password and for some reason the wi-fi box had decided to reset itself at a moment at which they were about to lose their investment. "Chloe was saved by Divine Intervention, right?"

"Mmhmm."

"And her bracers are a fragment of a god, correct?"

"God*dess*. What's your point?"

Demetri rubbed his chin. "How exactly does the god system work in Obsidian?"

Mia thought for a moment, searching some lost corner of her mind. "It was explained to me once in a storyboarding meeting about the root makeup of Obsidian's narrative, though, for the life of me, I can't remember much. I'm pretty sure I remember it being loosely based on the structure of the Greek Gods and Olympus. Y'know, brothers and sisters, incest and fighting. It doesn't matter what I remember anyway. The AI could have changed it all."

"What do you mean?"

Mia sat up, bringing her drink to her lips. She pressed a button on the remote and muted the TV as another explosion went off, this time causing the man to run around the kitchen with his hair on fire.

"Praxis created a gaming AI that can predict, create, and interpret a player's style of play, manipulating the world around it to create the challenges players face. Truth be told, only a few elements of the game are predictable. The rest is created by a super-advanced computer that has been fed enough information from fantasy roleplaying games over the last few decades to be able to create its own game. That means the gods, the rivers, the towns, the NPCs—they're all artificially created. There isn't a single developer who knows *everything* about Obsidian. That's what makes it so fun."

Mia's eyes were alight. In the dim, flashing glow of the TV screen, Demetri couldn't quite believe she was still as beautiful as he first remembered her.

He distracted himself by taking another sip of his drink. Now the TV displayed Chloe and the man sitting down in chairs in the living room while the man ate some food, possibly to restore his health. Demetri pondered Mia's words, wondering just how safe it was that there was no one on the planet in control of the storylines in this game.

"What if it's dangerous?" Demetri asked, his voice so quiet, Mia had to strain to hear.

"What do you mean? There's nothing harmful in that game."

"You heard her say it herself before she ran through that hidden crack in the wall. The pain receptors are too high, and you've just admitted that the game is sentient and can create its own narratives. What's to say the game won't freak out and suddenly send spikes through Chloe's chest? Who's to say she won't be imprisoned or tortured by corrupt dead men?"

Mia rose from her seat and padded over to Demetri, finding a place to sit on his lap. "Oooh, that's quite the imagination. Ever thought about writing for Praxis Games? *Obsidian* isn't the only game that we're working on at the minute," she said playfully.

Demetri blushed, unable to meet her eyes. "I've got an investment in that game too. If she suffers, I'll suffer. I'm out of a job if this fails."

Mia's hand found his chin and teased it toward her until their eyes met. "Believe me, I've got an investment in this, too. Why do you think I jumped at the opportunity to talk to you and see you again?"

Before Demetri could respond, Mia's lips were on his. The kiss was sweet. Tender. They tasted each other in the darkened room for an amount of time that seemed to stretch to eternity.

Demetri forgot all his troubles, losing himself in Mia. On the TV screen, Chloe and the man fist-bumped, then punched the air, clearly excited to have finished whatever the hell they had been working on.

83

CHAPTER ELEVEN

The smell of the damned thing was foul, a mixture of burned sulfur and her brother's farts. Even from across the clearing, Chloe and Gideon were forced to cover their noses against the stench from the pot.

They had been crouched for a while, biding their time. Waiting. Occasionally Chloe would scan the area, cocking an ear for any sign of the beast. She caught sight of Gideon and had to stifle her laughter.

Gideon *tsked*. "Will you get over it?" he whispered.

Chloe closed her eyes, trying to erase the image. Gideon's hair was in patches, there being a large bald area where the fire had burned away his hair.

"Seriously, will you—"

Gideon's demand was cut short by a colossal roar that sounded as though it was right next to them. As they ducked and peered through the bushes, they saw the bear emerge from the tree line.

It approached cautiously, nose in the air. Spotting the pot, it padded nearer, standing on its hind legs and letting out another roar. Several birds took to the sky. A tiny squirrel that had been foraging for food near Chloe skittered up the tree and disappeared into the foliage.

Satisfied that it was alone, the bear reached the pot and stuck its head inside. Its red eyes disappeared into the pot as its tongue came out and lapped the viscous amber liquid. At first, it seemed that the heat was still too much, but then the bear went in for several more mouthfuls. After about a minute, the bear plonked back on its behind, sitting in a way that seemed oddly human.

"Aaand three...two...one..."

As Gideon counted down on his fingers, the bear's eyes closed tight. The next thing they knew, the bear had folded over and was snoring loudly.

"Okay, warrior," Gideon whispered, body visibly shaking. "Over to you. Time to put the creature out of its misery."

Chloe moved into the clearing, her heart beating double-time. She advanced slowly, terrified that the bear would wake up before she made it to him. She held her dagger out in front of her and swallowed.

"Oh, hurry your ass up," KieraFreya hissed, forcing Chloe's arms forward. To Gideon, it looked as though an invisible cowboy had lassoed her arms and pulled her forwards. Chloe jogged to catch up.

"Hey, quit it."

The closer she got to the bear, the bigger it seemed. Its great bulk rose and fell with each breath. Chloe stood beside the bear, noting that its paws were the size of her head. She raised her dagger with both hands, prepared herself to strike, and—

A soft mewling came from somewhere in the woods. Chloe hesitated, spotting the three bear cubs as they crept out and wandered up to their mama. Even on all fours, the babies were at Chloe's hip height.

She turned back to Gideon, who was standing behind in the bush, gesturing her forward with his hands.

Chloe pointed at the cubs with an "Aw, but they're so cute" expression on her face.

Gideon mimed stabbing the beast before raising both arms and imitating a bear standing at its full height and tearing an animal limb from limb.

"Fine," Chloe spat.

She raised the dagger again and paused. The cubs had made it to their mama and now looked at Chloe with an inquisitive expression. The largest of the three moved toward the pot, putting both paws on the pot's edge.

"No, no, little cub. Not for you." Chloe dashed toward it, gently nudging the cub away from the pot. "Come on," she said, struggling against the cub's muscles. "That's for grown-ups only."

Gideon threw his hands in the air and joined her in the clearing. "Tamara, just dispatch the problem so we can collect the experience and go on our way. That bear's been tailing me ever since I got into this game. Just because it's got cute little fluffy babies doesn't mean we're suddenly safe!"

"He has a point, y'know," KieraFreya whispered.

"So that makes *me* the monster if I'd rather not dispose of three innocent cubs or their mother. I'm sorry, but this changes things, Gid. Can't we just run into the forest and find your friends?"

Gideon's nostrils flared. "Only if you like your chances taking on all four of the bears at some point down the line?"

"I'd rather that than—*ow!*"

While Chloe had been arguing with Gideon, the smallest of the cubs had approached and was now on its hind legs, reaching for her. Its claws were sharp and had left small bloody tracks down her hip.

Cut the little shit down before he cuts you, KieraFreya growled, her voice appearing in Chloe's head.

Chloe gasped. "What?"

"What do you mean, 'what?'" Gideon responded.

The bear reached for her again, its claws cutting deeper into the previous tracks. Chloe sucked in a lungful of air. Unbidden, her stats came into her vision.

KieraFreya snapped, *With every scratch, you're losing HP, Sweet Tits. Kill the bastards before they decide they want to kill you. You know that bears eat people, right? Take the dagger, shove it in the bear's skull, and collect the loot!*

Chloe blinked the stats away and was about to tell KieraFreya where to shove it when the bear cub bit her leg. She cried out and kicked the cub away, noticing now that the cub's eyes had turned the same red as its mother's. Meanwhile, the second cub was advancing on Gideon, and the largest had managed to take a deep draught of the potion and was now out cold, flat on its back.

The red-eyed bear cub turned to Chloe hungrily, teeth bared. A growl emanated from the back of its throat.

Chloe swallowed hard before realizing that her hands were acting of their own accord again. The hand that gripped the knife spasmed toward the bear, slashing and narrowly avoiding the bear's face as Chloe fought against her bracers.

Seriously? You're going to fight me on this? I'm doing you a favor, girl.

"No. I will not kill the innocent," Chloe said through gritted teeth.

Gideon, on the other hand, was busy moving his hands in a sequence of gestures he had picked up from his book. He muttered an incantation under his breath, finished his movements, and pushed his palms toward the second bear cub. His hands glowed a fearsome purple, and smoke erupting from his palms as a small fireball shot toward the cub…

Well, at that general area. The fireball missed the cub by a good foot and continued its travels toward the mother, hitting her stomach. Immediately her fur burst into purple flames.

Chloe's cub cried out in distress and lunged at Chloe. Instinctively, she brought her hands to her face. The bracers took the brunt of the damage, although a second later, Chloe felt teeth biting again into the chunk it had previously bitten. Chloe crumpled to one leg, too preoccupied with her own pain to notice the knife switch from her left hand to her right, then find its way across the bear's throat.

The cub roared, reared back, and came in for another charge. This time Chloe was ready. She dodged to the side, one knee still on the ground, and as the cub flew through the air, her dagger found the center of its back. She focused her intent and used **Creature Identification**, finding a surprising statement blinking back at her.

Black bear cub (Lv 5)
Health remaining: 21%
Another message appeared, which reminded Chloe that she really

needed to take a second to adjust her notification settings to prevent this type of shit in battle.

Skill increased: Creature Identification (Lv 2)

Great stuff, hero! Now you're able to view an increased amount of information on monsters, enemies, and even friends you encounter on your travels. Remember to use your powers for good, though. Or bad. We don't actually care.

Bonuses: +2 intelligence

(NOTE: Increases in skill override any previous bonuses gained from the skill).

"Great. A skill increase. Now could you move the hell out of the way so I can focus?"

"You know you can adjust your notification settings in the main menu— *Argh!*" Gideon shut up as the cub lunged at him. Before he knew it, the cub was chasing him in circles.

KieraFreya chuckled. "Your new boyfriend is a helluva soldier."

Chloe took another stab at the bear cub, watching as the health percentage bar lowered to 0. "Quiet, you!" A pang of guilt flew through her stomach, but when a wave of pain coursed through her leg, all of that guilt was forgotten.

Chloe spent the next few minutes chasing Gideon and the bear cub around the clearing. The bear was fast, but more than that, Gideon ran like an idiot. His arms flailed and his cries rang out. Eventually, Chloe managed to launch herself onto the back of the cub and distract it, and Gideon managed to hit the creature with a fireball from close range.

When the bear stilled, he took a knee and looked at Chloe's leg. "It's a basic spell, but we'll see what it can do."

His hands glowed bright yellow as he muttered something beneath his breath. A moment later, Chloe watched as the bite in her thigh began to heal. She felt the pain ease and let out a sigh of relief.

When Gideon was done, he smiled and rose to his feet. "Woohoo! Seems actually having the chance to use that on another player gains an additional boost to the skill! Thanks, Tamara."

Chloe rolled her eyes. "Okay, enough of this Tamara business. Just call me 'Chloe.'"

"Why?"

"Because that's my name. It's what I've set as my character's name. It's just my goddamn name, okay?"

Gideon looked startled until he noticed that Chloe was smiling. "Fine. If that's how you want it...Chloe."

Chloe opened her mouth to speak but quickly closed it again as she heard a sound that made her skin prickle. A deep, booming growl came from behind them. With sinking hearts, Chloe and Gideon turned around as Mama Bear began to stir. Her red eyes blinked stupidly as she pushed herself to her feet.

"Quick, Gideon, teach me your spell."

Gideon looked confused. "What do you mean, 'teach you?'"

Chloe's arms rose, slapping Gideon's head. She apologized, then glared at her bracers. "I mean, you must have learned the spells somehow. How can *I* learn them?"

Gideon pondered the question, eyes fixed on the bear, which seemed to now be realizing that her children had been vanquished. "Er, I guess...you just have to know the incantation. Know the words. It's...it's complicated. You're not a mage. *I'm* a mage."

Chloe scoffed. "I haven't specified my class yet. Who says I can't be a mage? Now, teach me."

With great speed, Gideon recited the incantation to Chloe and showed her the hand movements. For the first few times she tried to copy him, nothing happened. Then, with each repetition, she felt the familiarity of the spell grow.

Gideon's hands blazed with purple flame, creating an orb that he pushed toward the bear. The ursine stumbled, still fighting the effects of the sleep potion Gideon had concocted. His eyes widening at the circles of purple flame now blazing on the grass around him as each orb missed its target.

"You really need to work on your aim."

Gideon glared. "Shut up and keep practicing."

Chloe closed her eyes, thinking of the incantation and moving her arms. She felt power surge over her, a sense of warmth stirring her very soul. When she opened her eyes, she laughed because an impressive ball of purple fire hovered in the space between her hands. She aimed for the bear and threw the ball, but it dissolved just before it left her hands.

"Damn."

Gideon threw another of his own, this time hitting the bear's foot. The beast roared and began to advance. "Don't worry, mine did too that first time. It just takes practice."

"We don't have a lot of time for that."

Chloe concentrated again, this time creating a ball that felt sturdier. She threw it, and the ball sizzled the grass in front of the bear. It took a step back, uncertain, then crouched on its haunches and rushed at them both.

Chloe felt her wrists shake. She prayed that KieraFreya could control herself for just a moment longer. The last thing she needed now was another battle with the goddess.

"Now would be a good time to hit your target, fuckwad!" the bracers shouted.

The hurt was clear in Gideon's face. "I'm trying, okay?"

Chloe and Gideon gave each other one final look before synchronizing their movements. As the purple orb appeared in Gideon's hand, another appeared in Chloe's. She focused inside her mind, clearing all else she knew until she was living, breathing, and *embodying* the words to the spell and hoping that this time it would actually work. The bear streamed at them, its face twisted in rage.

And then it was gone.

Chloe watched in awe as the bear went up in flames, a great purple blaze toppling to the ground. The bear gave its final roar, skidding to within inches of where they stood, its great bulk sliding over the mud.

Gideon already had another fireball prepared, but he just let the thing fizzle out. He released a long breath, sweat dripping from his forehead.

"We did it," Chloe murmured as notifications popped up in her vision.

Quest complete: We can't bear it anymore

You've destroyed the foul beast that was stalking your fellow traveler. Perhaps, now that the creature is gone, he'll be able to bear going out in public once more. Get it? No. Maybe just paws for thought.

Bonuses: 250 exp

New spell acquired: Purple blaze (Lv 1)

Congratulations on learning your first spell! Now that you've taken your first foray into the realm of the etheric, you'll be able to call upon the mystical and the unexplained to aid you in the heat of battle.

Requirements: n x 20MP (where n is equal to the number of seconds taken to cast the spell)

Monster defeated: Black bear cub (Lv 5)

+50 exp

Monster defeated: Black bear cub (Lv 6)

+50 exp

Monster defeated: Black bear (Lv 10)

+100 exp

Chloe blinked away the notification screen and beamed at Gideon, throwing her arms around his shoulders and hugging him.

"What's that for?" Gideon said, blushing a little as she stepped back.

"We did it, silly. We beat the threat. We make quite a good team, you and me."

Gideon straightened his robe. "Does that mean you've already checked your notifications?"

Chloe nodded.

"Here." Gideon sighed. "Let me show you how to keep them from interrupting you while you're battling."

Gideon guided Chloe through the process. It actually turned out to be surprisingly easy, as if Praxis Games had anticipated that most players would want that function while they were in action anyway. It made Chloe wonder why they'd even bothered setting the display up the way they had in the first place.

Chloe stepped over to the bear and paused. "Did you want to do the honors?"

Gideon shook his head. "Ladies first."

Chloe touched her dagger to the skin of the bear to activate the looting process. As soon as the blade hit the charred remains of the skin, the bear began to dissolve into a fine ash that floated away in the wind. Chloe was pleased to see that it was the same way the goblins had disappeared when she had looted their bodies in the cave. When the remains were gone, only a small pile of treasure was left on the forest floor.

Or in this case:

Item obtained: Charred bear meat.

Eager beaver! You've already cooked this. Best chomp it down before it gets cold.

Bonuses: Recovers +50HP

Item obtained: Black bear pelt.

This pelt can be used in the creation of armor and wares.

Rarity: Uncommon

Chloe reached for the items, offering the bear meat to Gideon. "All yours. Until I can heal *you*, you'll need to rely on food."

Gideon chuckled, raising his hand palms out to Chloe. "Hey, as long as I've got my hands, I don't need anyone else."

There was an awkward pause between the two before Chloe burst into laughter for the first time in days, bellowing and clutching her stomach until it hurt. Gideon flushed deep crimson before letting himself fall victim to the laughter too.

Chloe wiped tears from her eyes and pocketed the bear pelt, noting a short message which informed her that her inventory was full. A quick scan of the menu told her that the half-stick she had pocketed in the cave was taking up her second item slot.

Huh. I guess I only have one item slot for each pocket until I can get some more gear.

Chloe was about to ask Gideon about his carrying capacity when she noticed that the third cub—the one who had drunk from the potion and passed out—was beginning to move.

Before Chloe could even open her mouth to warn Gideon, he had a glowing purple orb in his hand. He moved to cast the ball, then froze as two men crashed into the clearing.

"Fire!" a man—clearly an archer—said as he raised his bow and loosed an arrow.

The arrow found its mark in the cub's neck.

"Aaaargh!" a tiny man with a great brown beard roared as he charged at the bear, a wooden shield in one hand and a club in the other. He reached the bear and bashed its head with its club.

Chloe used **Creature Identification** and saw that the bear's health had dropped to 14%. With one final look at Gideon, who was smiling from ear-to-ear now, she cast her own ball and set the cub ablaze.

CHAPTER TWELVE

Chloe stepped carefully over a tangle of twisted thorns. Behind her, she could hear the men crashing and complaining as they laughed and joked, disturbing the wildlife and making quite a racket.

"Do you mind keeping it down a bit? The last time we brought attention to ourselves, an enraged bear and her three cubs came after us."

"*Ooooh,*" Ben Summers and Tag Murphy sang as more laughter erupted from them.

"Afraid, are we?" Ben said, winking at Gideon. Gideon gave him a weak smile but otherwise looked as awkward as ever. He didn't want to piss Chloe off, having now seen what she was capable of. He'd also been butthurt that she had learned (and mastered) one of his spells much more quickly than he could have dreamed of.

"Don't worry, darling. We'll protect you." Tag paused, kissing his dwarven muscles. "No monster can withstand *these* guns, baby!"

Another round of laughter.

Chloe rolled her eyes but paid no attention. She had gotten an idea of what she was dealing with the moment the bear cub's body had dissolved and Gideon had reunited with his fellow players.

They had hugged, beaming smiles on their faces, then spent the next hour or so sitting around a purple fire as they ate charred bear meat—which, though gristly, was surprisingly tasty—and caught up on their adventures.

It seemed that, since getting themselves lost in the woods, Ben and Tag had spent a good portion of their time tracking the bear, too. As the player with the highest intelligence stat, and with all the natural affinities of adopting the Elf race when he had spawned into the game, Ben had taken to studying the ground, identifying the patterns of the woods, and giving the bear chase.

Apparently, he had already managed to reach level 4 in his **Tracking** ability, and could now see, hear, and smell his way confidently toward targets which made no attempt to keep themselves hidden. Not only that, but he had gained several tiers in his **Crafting** ability—enough to have made his beginner-level bow and arrows.

Meanwhile, Tag had played the protector. While Ben had been grinding his skills up in long-range combat, the sturdy dwarf had kept them safe, managing to take down a low-level forest troll with a series of blows with a large rock he had found.

While Ben had shot from a distance, Tag had sped through the creature's legs, found his way up the troll's back, and caved its skull in from above. After the creature toppled, he had inherited its club, and now sported the object with pride.

They spent some time discussing Chloe's journey, marveling at her progression to level 8 so soon into the game. She held back on describing her journey through the Deathwalk, not wanting to give too much away—at least until she learned she could trust them.

When Ben and Tag pointed to her bracers, hungrily eyeing the objects, Chloe tucked them behind her back, noticing Gideon's curious stare as he sat with his mouth closed, warming his hands in front of the fire.

As the darkness fell, they had made their way back to Gideon's house to rest for the night. Ben, Tag, and Gideon logged off, while Chloe went to sleep in a comfortable corner of the room. By late morning, they had taken a glance at Ben's map and headed out toward a spot that looked like it had the best chance of some kind of civilization, agreeing that if they were to progress, they'd need to at least acquire better provisions.

As they made their way through the Fleetwood Forest, Chloe got a much broader idea of the type of wildlife and creatures that existed here. Rabbits abounded (which, Chloe discovered was Ben's and Tag's favorite delicacy and the reason they had managed to survive in the wild over the previous nights), deer ran through the trees, and occasionally a disgruntled badger or fox came at them, teeth bared, which they banded together to take down.

A couple of times, they overheard goblins stalking through the undergrowth and were forced to make the choice of whether to go around or take them down. When they spotted a group of three goblins, they worked together to dispatch them, gaining a nice handful of experience points and looting several bronze coins each, but when they passed a troop of around a dozen or so sitting around a large bonfire, they skirted the area as quietly as possible and continued silently on their way.

Or at least as silently as they possibly could, considering that Tag's version of tiptoeing was Chloe's equivalent jumping up and down on her bedroom floorboards in order to piss her siblings off.

"Damn, Tag. Can't you at least be a little quieter?" she'd urged once they were clear of the goblins—a few of whose ears had begun to go up as they detected the noise. "How are we supposed to make it to Oakston if you can't sneak quietly?"

Tag stuck his chest out proudly. "A dwarf's talents lie in other things. So what if we alert enemies? My tough skin and incredible strength will defend us from whatever predator comes our way." As he spoke, something small and black circled overhead, sweeping inches away from his face. He started backward, letting out a small yelp. "Argh! What was that?"

Ben rolled his eyes. "Relax, your incredibleness. It was just a bat."

Tag straightened his clothes and cleared his throat. "Yes. Of course."

They made steady progress throughout the day, pausing when the sun was at its highest for a break near the stream. Here, Gideon sat down quietly, practicing his incantations while Ben and Tag splashed water on themselves and cleaned their weapons.

After a lunch of rabbit and fox meat, Ben took to target practice with his bow and arrow, finding a wide trunk and etching a circle onto the wood. Tag lay in the sun, eyes closed, while Gideon sat and watched Ben. Chloe made her way over to Gideon and took a seat beside him, glancing down briefly at her bracers, which had remained suspiciously silent for a while.

"So... Your friends are...interesting..." She playfully nudged his shoulder.

Gideon nodded. "Yeah. They're made of good stock. I've played dozens of games over the years with them, and they've always been there for me. We've been through a lot together. Always the same classes and races, too, so they know their way inside and out of dwarves and elves."

"And what about you?" Chloe said, sensing Gideon tensing up already. "What class are you normally?"

Gideon met Chloe's eyes, his lips tight. After a moment, he sighed and lowered his head. "How could you tell?"

"Let's just say I presumed that if someone who had played *dozens* of games as a particular type of class could make as many mistakes as I've seen you make, then perhaps being a mage isn't your natural affinity."

Gideon blushed.

"I'm not being nasty," Chloe assured him. "If anything, it makes me like you more. At least there's someone else who's learning skills in the same way that I am. The last thing I'd want is to feel like the complete moob among the pros."

Gideon scoffed.

"What?" Chloe asked.

"I think you mean 'noob.'" He smiled, looking brighter already. "I've always played the warrior class. I love raising swords and charging into battle, getting right into the thick of it, y'know?"

"Then why didn't you choose warrior? Was it not available at the start or something?"

Gideon sighed again. "It was my brother's fault. A cruel prank, really. Truth is that when Praxis approached me to tell me that they wanted me to get involved in the game, it came with a pretty hefty fee. I didn't have the money to pay for it, so I begged my brother to loan me the money.

"He's loaded. He's a semi-pro musician who plays the circuit in New York. I really think he's going to make it big someday."

"But he's an ass, right?" Chloe chuckled.

"Yep. The biggest ass on the planet. He told me that he'd only lend me the money as long as I let him create my character. He even studied my old livestreams to check out the things I loved so that he could take great pleasure in giving me the opposite—everything from this ridiculous goatee to these flouncy purple robes to virtually 0 strength, and—the pièce de résistance—the mage class. It was all him."

"But you wanted to play?"

"*So* badly. I mean, come on!" Gideon gestured around the forest. "Look at this! I've played some pretty sick VR games before, but *this*? This just takes it to a whole new level. This is the kind of stuff I dreamed of when I was a kid pretending to be a noble warrior protecting queens. The smells, the sounds—it's *so* damn real. If I had the chance, I'd jump into a game like this and never let go."

Chloe nodded, taking in the sights around her. She felt a warmth inside her as she watched Ben retrieve his arrows from the trunk, several bullseyes among the couple dozen shots. Tag snored loudly, his chest rising and falling. Maybe her mind hadn't yet been made up about what would happen when they reached the village— whether she would remain with the group (if they'd have her) or take on the rest of her journey solo—but she certainly felt at ease with them.

And besides, working as a team definitely made taking down enemies a whole lot easier than her first few attempts.

When Tag eventually woke with a start, they packed their things and set off once more. Along the way, they heard danger in the woods but merely veered off in a slight variant of their direction to tread around the danger. Only once did they hear the whistling of an arrow, and they managed to take out the goblin archer before it could alert its group to their presence.

The trees provided adequate shelter from the sun, but all too soon, night began to fall. The temperature dropped in the snap of a finger, and soon they were treading their way through the overgrowth practically side by side. Chloe remained in the center, she being the only one of them who had made any progress with her **Dark Vision**.

She managed to miss the roots and tangles at the last minute but was unable to call out in time to keep Ben from catching his foot and falling on his face.

"At this rate, I'll have no HP left!" Ben growled, rubbing his nose and examining the blackened smear of blood. "Can you give a bit more warning next time, please?"

"I'm doing my best." Chloe sighed, squinting into the darkness where the leaves, vines, and tangles all looked like an indeterminate mess.

Skill increased: Dark Vision (Lv 2)

Guiding comrades through the darkness is a great way to gain experience in this ability. Now to determine whether you'd like to use your powers for good or evil.

Why not try tripping the little guy again?

Bonuses: +2 intelligence, +3 etheric potential

Chloe sniggered as she continued on her way and decided that she would likely use her powers for good.

For now.

The night wore on. Soon enough, they could see glimpses of the moon overhead between the boughs of the trees. The group's stamina began to wear down, and the longer they continued, the more the group began to complain.

After nearly half an hour of Tag's whining, Chloe spun on her heels and drew them to a stop.

"Look, enough whining. We must be nearly there, surely. Show us that map."

Ben unrolled the map. It was the first time Chloe had looked at it directly, and the instant her eyes connected with it, she noticed a flashing notification.

Chloe brought up her display, and suddenly she was looking at a clear picture of the whole forest, an identical image of what Ben was seeing in his hands. Chloe saw little markings across lines of tree and footpaths, as well as names and titles of rivers and streams. Around the edges of the forest, the map was black, but here she could see all the ins and outs.

The minute she moved her eyes away from the paper, the map disappeared.

"Well, that's a handy little feature," she mused, returning to the map.

Judging by the small Xs on the page, which they assumed were them, it looked as though they still had several hours of walking ahead of them.

Tag moaned and plonked his ass to the forest floor. He looked exhausted. "I give up. I can't go on much longer. Let's wait until morning."

Ben raised an eyebrow. "It's not like you to give up so soon. What's the matter?" He rested his hands on his knees and spoke as if addressing a baby. "Is Mummy calling for wittle Tattykins to have some din-dins?"

Tag turned away, arms folded. "It's roasted pork."

Ben, Gideon, and Chloe burst out laughing, doing their best to stifle their noise as they heard something howling out in the wilderness.

Gideon wiped a tear from his eye as the laughter faded, eventually saying, "Now might be a good point to rest. Look, we're fairly sheltered, so we can cover ourselves in foliage to protect us from being spotted. It might not be great, but at least it's something. We can pick up tomorrow and go the final leg of the journey."

"Yeah, maybe we'll actually find something *useful* in the woods." Ben took a seat beside Tag.

Gideon followed them to the forest floor. "Aren't you joining us, Chloe?"

Chloe, who had been staring into the darkness, sure that she'd seen something glimmer out there, turned her attention back to the guys. "Nah, you go ahead. I will keep watch while you guys rest."

Tag mumbled appreciatively. "Thanks."

"Don't you have things to do in the real world, Chloe?" Ben asked, settling down and creating a small pillow out of leaves and grass.

Chloe gave a weak smile. "Not for me. I'm more of a night owl anyway, so if I can do my bit and keep you guys intact until you return, I'm more than happy to help out."

"She's a keeper," Tag said, winking at Gideon and nudging him with his elbow.

Gideon's mouth flapped, but no words came out.

They were soon asleep, snoring gently in the darkness. Chloe watched them, still half-expecting their avatars to disappear the moment they closed their eyes.

It seemed a strange function of the game that the characters would remain exactly where they were even when they weren't being controlled. She supposed it added realism for players still in-game, in that attacks in the dark caught people by surprise, though she imagined that it would suck to discover that you'd died while you were logged out and had respawned miles away from wherever the hell you had been.

Chloe took a seat, chewing her cheek, wondering where the respawn point would be if a player got attacked while AFK.

(Un)luckily for her, it wouldn't be too long before she found out.

CHAPTER THIRTEEN

The first sign that something was wrong was a series of hushed whispers in the dark. The second was the sound of bodies being dragged through the brush.

Chloe woke with a start, not remembering the moment she had fallen asleep.

"Wake up, idiot!" KieraFreya shouted, causing several dark figures to snap to attention. Chloe caught glimpses of starlight on silver and the glimmer of eyes all around her. She tried to stand up but felt the hands on her legs as she was tugged over the ground, her head falling back and hitting the soft forest floor.

"Let go of me!" Chloe said through gritted teeth. She wriggled and kicked with her other foot, turning her head to see Gideon's lifeless form bumping along beside her.

The figures ignored her, tightening their grip on her leg. Chloe closed her eyes and began to summon a purple fireball.

There were gasps of alarm as the fireball grew. She could see their faces now, silhouetted in purple—several bulky men and women with masks covering half of their faces. They looked terrifying. Tribal tattoos decorated what was visible of their skin.

Chloe pushed the fireball out at the exact same moment her leg was dropped and the jolt sent her fireball in the wrong direction, illuminating its path through the darkened trees before setting the area ablaze.

Seizing the opportunity to move, Chloe jumped to her feet. A man lunged at her and she side-stepped, already feeling KieraFreya's pull on her wrist as it moved toward her knife.

"No," Chloe growled. "They're just humans. We can't just kill them."

KieraFreya's voice came into her head. *If you don't kill them, how long do you think it'll be before they kill you?*

Chloe considered this in the briefest of moments. Already she could see Ben and Tag being dragged way up ahead, their silhouettes only visible thanks to the purple flames that several figures were already rushing to put out before the fire spread. Though a number of the figures had swords, few seemed to be *using* them.

The man rose from the forest floor, grasping Chloe's leg. She kicked him away, fighting once more as KieraFreya put her energy into making Chloe draw the dagger. Before she knew it, the blade was in her hand.

No! Chloe thought, shouting at the goddess in her head. *I said NO!*

When KieraFreya replied, it was with a force that Chloe hadn't felt before. An overwhelming sense of strength rushed through her. *MORTAL! I am the Goddess of Retribution. These shitstains have stolen your friends and hounded you in the night. Retribution is due for their acts. Slay the man. Slay them all! Let honor and valor stand tall in the world, and let the weak burn...*

Chloe felt her hand dragged down toward the man, his eyes sparkling in the moonlight. The pointed end of her blade came down slowly since Chloe was still resisting the move.

When it was just an inch away from the man's eyeball, something hard hit the back of her head. A moment later, she felt the warm trickle of blood down her back.

And then all was dark.

"My lady sails over the shoreline
My lady sails over the sea
My lady don't buy me no red wine
My lady won't buy me no bree
For I've got a lady who hates me
She's covered top to toe in her sin
But I've got a lady who—BEEPs—me
Like she knows that the world will soon end."

Chloe's ears tuned in to the most beautiful voice she had ever heard. At first, the song was muffled as she came out of her unconsciousness, but as she became aware of the room around her, she allowed her eyes to shut and take in the sultry tones of the musician. As the singer continued, the dulcet tones of a lute were introduced.

"Just give me all of your ten pence
And I'll not return you my change
For ladies can carry resentment
'Til the familiar soon becomes strange
But I've got a lady who loves me
As much as she hates to admit
For the ladies who love and who hate you
Are the best ones at riding the di—"

"That's enough!"

Thank God for that, Chloe thought, her mind now active enough to actually read between the lyrics of the song.

She teased open her eyes, immediately finding herself feel nauseated as she discovered that she wasn't lying down, as she expected to be, but was actually upright, arms spread wide and handcuffed to the wall. She blinked stupidly as firelight dazzled her eyes and the room came into full focus.

She was in a wood cabin with a semicircle of people gathered around her. In the center of the room was the small fire, casting dancing shadows on those gathered around the walls. Chloe scanned the group, seeing that their bodies were decorated with tribal markings, and immediately her mind flashed back to the moments before all had gone dark.

"Where are they?" she said weakly, tugging at her bonds. "Where are my friends?"

Chloe looked at a large woman who had appropriated the middle of the semicircle. She was naked, except for a loincloth covering her downstairs area. Her hair was split into two braids that fell down her back. She looked blankly at Chloe, then pointed to the side of the room.

"We're right here," Tag said blankly, as if it were the most obvious thing in the world. "Didn't you hear my song?" He sat on a chair, elevated above the rest of the group.

Beside Tag were Ben and Gideon. Ben sat cross-legged next to the chair, while Gideon was slumped against the wall, looking all kinds of confused. A tribesman with a low-set brow stood next to Tag, a lute in his hand.

Chloe shook her head, then winced as the headache rocked her brain. "What's going on—"

"At last, she awakes!" a voice to her right said. A man stepped into her field of vision. Twice as tall as the others and with a body that rippled with muscle, this man would have been a sight to behold in her real life—the type of man she turned pages in magazines to get a glimpse of. His jaw was sharp, and his face rugged. She found herself flushing in his presence.

"Warrior maiden," he boomed, voice echoing around the room. "You have been accused of the attempted murder of one of our people. Now that you are able to respond to these accusations, how do you plead?"

The man was surprisingly well-spoken. Chloe closed her eyes and tried to understand the situation.

"Murder? But you...*you* kidnapped us. I mean..." She stared confusedly at Gideon, Ben, and Tag, "You ambushed us, and I... Okay, what the—" *beep* "—is going on?"

As the beep sounded, all of the tribespeople threw their hands to their ears, their eyes screwed up in pain. The larger man pointed a finger her way.

"This woman threatens death upon our own and now dishonors the gods! May they smite her where she stands!"

Reaching to his side, he pulled out a long gleaming sword, rearing it back as if to strike.

A second later, Tag had kicked his chair back and jumped across the room to stand in the man's way with his hands held up to his face. "Woah! Hey there, buddy. She's not an enemy, I assure you." He met Chloe's eyes, looking more awkward than she had ever seen him. "Honestly, we know her. We've been traveling through the woods together, and...she's...she's good people."

The man slowly lowered his sword. "Good people?"

Ben appeared at Tag's side. "Yeah, I can vouch for her. Good people."

Chloe turned to Gideon, who reluctantly got to his feet and trotted over. He could barely walk, his knees were knocking together so badly. "I'll vouch for her too."

The man turned around to the crowd and began speaking in some unknown language filled with guttural clicks and phlegm-y noises. The woman who was sitting in the middle of them all remained silent while the others chatted among themselves.

"What the hell is going on?" Chloe whispered, only loud enough so her comrades could hear.

Tag spoke out the side of his mouth. "Just keep your mouth shut and we'll get you out of here. Did you really try to kill one of them?"

"They were trying to steal us away," Chloe breathed. "I was trying to protect us. If it hadn't have been for Kier—" she paused as she realized the mistake she was going to make. "I was trying to protect us."

Eventually, the man returned his attention to Chloe. He signaled for Gideon, Ben, and Tag to move aside. The man stared at Chloe for a long moment before snapping his fingers. At the sound, another man, much skinnier than the first, stood up in the crowd.. Chloe recognized him instantly.

"My eye saw your blade." The man spoke slowly, as if each word was pulled from some dark recess in his brain.

"You were stealing my friends."

"We protect them," he said. "You and your friends sleep in forest. No protection. Bad idea."

Chloe had been ready to retort, but now it all seemed to click into place. Not once had she seen any of her captors draw a sword. they had not intended to bring harm to the group. The entire time they had been trying to *protect* them.

Surely there might have been a better way.

"Your friends are from the blessed, yes?" the larger man asked.

Chloe's brow creased. "The blessed?"

"Those who are birthed from the stars, blessed with the light of the gods. They sleep a deeper sleep but have a number of lives untold to others. Those who are blessed with the power of rebirth after the final darkness comes? That is them, yes?"

"I suppose." Chloe shrugged. "If that's the case, then I am also of the blessed."

The man whom Chloe had attacked snorted. "No, Mantari," he said, motioning to the larger man. "Stupid woman tries to trick us. We have been told the stories. We have seen the prophecies of the blessed coming to our lands. The blessed sleep the deep sleep, and are undisturbed. You were awake when our people come. You not blessed. You are Enpeecees like us all. Your life just as fragile as our own."

The larger man—Mantari—loomed over Chloe. "Brother Cijay is right. You have been proven to be a liar and trickster. We are not as blind as we appear to your deception. For the greater good of the village, you must be given back to the earth."

Mantari drew his sword once more. Ben, Tag, and Gideon tried to step in, but while they had been talking, several more tribespeople had stood up, and now held them back. "For the greater good of our people, I sentence this deceiver to the final death."

Chloe's eyes widened as she struggled against her bonds. She felt KieraFreya's power vibrating through her wrists.

Do something, bitch!

"No! I assure you and all of your people that I am of the blessed. I am a child of the sky. Please, spare my life, and I will honor your grace by offering protection to your people."

Mantari grinned wickedly. "If what you say is true, then this death will not matter all that much. If you lie, well then, we have saved our village from a great threat."

After a great sweep of his sword, Chloe felt pain roar through her entire body. She struggled to breathe, watched as rivulets of blood poured down her body, and then gasped as, moments later, a notification appeared.

Wup-wup. You're dead.

Wow, you really killed it in there. Just kidding! They really killed you. Maybe make sure you get a proper read of the situation before you go around trying to stab people, eh?

-50n experience (where n equals your character's level)

-1/2 your equipment

Time to respawn: 2 hours

CHAPTER FOURTEEN

"What the hell *was* that?" Chloe shouted, throwing her arms in the air in frustration as she plonked back into the white room's chair. "And that message? I *didn't* try to kill anyone. It was *you*—" Chloe stopped mid-sentence as she realized that, where she had expected her bracers to be, her arms were now bare.

"Oh."

She slumped back in her seat, trying to process what had just happened. It hadn't been her fault that she had nearly stabbed a man. She had fought against the armor with every ounce of her energy, but she could definitely understand how that might have looked to the people on the other side.

Without thinking about it, she rubbed her wrists, surprised by their smoothness. "That friggin'... *Rargh!*" Chloe shouted in frustration. The last thing she wanted to do was wait another 2 hours to respawn back into the world. For all she knew, that could be another 4, 6, or 8 hours before she landed in the game again. In that time, any number of things could have happened. The guys could have left without her. The tribe could have killed the guys. For that matter, *where* the hell was she going to respawn?

The telephone rang, scaring Chloe half to death. She had forgotten it was there, the game world already seeming more real to her than she could ever have imagined. She was taken aback by how passionate she felt about the journey. She wasn't even mad at the tribespeople. She understood their angle. She had just wanted to prove to them that she could help. That she was one of the good guys.

It was that friggin' goddess who needed to answer for her actions.

Chloe picked up the phone, diving into a twenty-minute rant about what had just happened before she even allowed the person on the other end of the line to speak. When she paused to take a breath, Mia asked, "Are you done now?"

"Where's the doc?" Chloe asked.

"You realize he can't be your permanent babysitter, right? He still has a job to go to. Lagardes to fix. It can't be all about you." Her words were playful, no malice in them.

"You've made a helluva impressive game in there," Chloe said, reclining in her chair and closing her eyes. Instead of darkness, she could see the tribe in that room. Gideon, Ben, and Tag. The whole gang.

"When we said we were going for full immersion, we certainly meant it. Do you have any idea of the programming hours and skills that have gone into that game?"

Mia dived into her own speech about the mechanics of the game and the developmental history, relaying elements of its construction as Chloe listened quietly, interrupting only occasionally to ask questions and prod Mia in certain directions.

When Mia trailed off, Chloe said, "I know you mentioned in our first chat that you wouldn't be able to help me, but is there *any* chance you could break your own rule and answer a question for me?"

Quiet on the other end of the line. Contemplation. "It depends on what that question is."

"Well, after finding KieraFreya's bracers, I received the quest to unite all of the pieces of her armor and restore her to her former glory. The only problem is, I have *no* idea where to start. Is there *anything* you can think of that'll help me along the way?"

Another pause while Mia arranged her thoughts. "Do you want the good news or the bad news?"

Chloe considered this. "Bad. Always start with bad. That's what Mum always used to say."

"I can't help you with your quest. Not only am I bound by contract to not reveal anything that might sway an adventurer's quest, but I also have no idea. The game's AI is intelligent, able to construct its own plots at will. You saw it yourself with yours and the wizard boy's—"

"Gideon's."

"Firefighting challenge. You received different things. Even if I had some inkling, the likelihood would be that as you played, the world would shift and adapt around you and the lines would change."

Chloe exhaled loudly, folding her arms. "What's the good news, then?"

Without warning, the computer screen on the desk switched on and turned to a web page that showcased a number of pictures of various shrines and altars. There were close-ups of broken ruins and carvings of powerful men and women in clouds and of strange, fabled creatures of legend.

"Cool trick," Chloe said with awe.

"Thanks." Mia chuckled. "The good news is that the land of Obsidian is based entirely on legend and myth. Most, if not all, of Obsidian's NPCs are well-versed in whatever theology the AI has set for them. Dotted around the land are a series of shrines and ancient structures built to honor the gods. My first suggestion would be to start there. Discover the truth behind the myths and set yourself on that path. That's what I'd do, at least."

There came a knock on the door on the other side of the phone.

"Oh, hold on one minute," Mia said, her hand now muting the mic. She heard a muffled, "Who is it?" before Mia returned to the receiver. "Sorry, Chloe. Pizza's here. I've got to go."

As Mia placed the receiver back down, Chloe was sure that she heard Demetri's voice calling in the distance.

Chloe tried to dial back, realizing at once that she didn't have a phone number for the pair.

As the countdown clock ticked toward her respawn, she browsed the net, looking for any hints or tips from players now in-game. The good news was that there were the beginnings of forums, where clearly players had arrived and had managed to get themselves killed. The bad news was that there were literally zero references to the name "KieraFreya" or any of the Obsidian gods to be found.

Chloe rested her eyes while leaning back in the chair, wondering why Mia would hang up before Demetri could talk to her, and how in the hell she was going to learn to control that goddamn parasitic goddess.

CHAPTER FIFTEEN

When Chloe respawned, it was to the sounds of screams.

She had expected to be greeted by the whispering woods, able to hear the rushing wind and see nothing but green, green, and more green. Instead, she saw huts and cabins, the tribespeople staring at her with mouths open. Several men in particular were giving Chloe more of a look than she appreciated.

She glanced down, feeling the cold air on her stomach.

"Oh, for… Not again," she said, noting that she was shirtless once more. She raised her wrists and was both happy and a little pissed that KieraFreya's bracers were still firmly affixed to her.

Welcome back, mistress, KieraFreya crooned. *I didn't expect to see so much of you again.*

Before Chloe could respond, a woman that Chloe recognized from the assembly shouted, "The blessed…she has returned! Someone call the chief."

Chloe was grabbed from behind and marched across the village toward a hut that was at least three times the size of the others. The roof was thatched, and a column of smoke rose from the chimney. She didn't even bother to struggle.

The chief's quarters were modest. Most of the hut was taken up by a meeting space with chairs, benches, and an open fire. Mantari was sat proudly in a large chair up a short set of stairs, and he was deep in conversation with a man who had open claw marks across his chest.

Mantari's concern for the man faded the minute he met Chloe's eyes. He rose suddenly and muttered something to an advisor, who led the injured man away. Walking briskly to her, he grabbed Chloe's shoulders.

"So it is true. You *are* one of the blessed. I am...I am so..."

"Don't even bother saying the words," Chloe said, anger in her eyes. "Do you have any idea how much it hurts to die in this stupid realm?"

Mantari ignored her scorn, signing and snapping his fingers at a couple of tribespeople at the back of the hut. They rushed out of the room without a word.

He motioned the men to release Chloe and headed out of the door. He signaled for Chloe to follow.

He led her around the village, taking many packed-dirt paths and trails. The sun was beginning to rise, turning the sky a beautiful orange, and calmness engulfed the place.

Mantari walked at a brisk pace, Chloe struggling to keep up. As he passed villagers, he nodded and waved, until finally, he spoke up.

"My apologies once more, blessed one. This village has been here for almost a dozen generations. What started as a humble cabin soon expanded into what we see before us now."

Several young children ran through the village, chasing a collection of butterflies as their giggles trailed behind them. Mantari ruffled a little girl's head as she darted past him.

"We of the Oakston tribe are a gentle folk. We live in the woods, we die in the woods. We keep our presence quiet and ensure that our borders are protected. There are dangers in this world that even we are unable to fight against, but as long as we keep each other protected, our little corner of the world can remain hidden and safe."

Chloe smiled as a tall woman with dark locks combed the shaggy hair of a small boy. The boy's father emerged from their hut—Chloe recognizing the man as the one she had almost left eyeless in the forest—and grinned at them both and kissed the woman before tickling the boy's sides. He stood up and paused as his eyes met hers, then lowered them back down and disappeared inside.

Mantari looked down at her. "I know there is no way to take back the death, and a thousand apologies will not erase the hurt we inflicted upon you, but you must understand the threat you posed to our people. I will always place my people before a stranger, and if the situation occurred a second time, I would do it again. I wonder if that's something that you can understand?"

Her mind flashed back to the bear and its cubs. Had it not been for their attack upon her and Gideon, she would have left them at peace. Sometimes conflict is forced upon you, even if you in no way intended to create it.

Chloe nodded, her eyes fixed on the entrance to the hut.

Mantari placed a hand on her shoulder, guiding her away. "Come. Let me show you more."

The village was a lot bigger than Chloe had first estimated. There must have been at least a hundred individual buildings crowded together in the woods. Some were bunched in larger clearings, while others used the trees as part of their structures.

There were places to store foraged food, rudimentary smithies, a woman who dealt with medicinal herbs and practices, trading outlets with makeshift market stalls, and even a place to pen and keep livestock among the residents,

Chloe quickly became friendly with Mantari, asking questions about the tribe and the people they met along the way. Although she encountered several more men who stared at her chest, she started to become numb to their attention, noticing that half the women here were topless themselves. After a certain point, she began to walk more proudly, her chest held high as she shook hands and spoke to the children.

Toward the end of her tour, Mantari led Chloe into a room she instantly recognized by the handcuffs pinned to the wall. Mantari called this room the "Room of Judgment." Chloe liked his style.

And there, against the wall, were Chloe's shirt and dagger. She kept the stick for sentimental reasons, although she really didn't want to use the storage slot.

On her way back outside, she heard a voice she recognized. Tearing herself away from a laughing Mantari, Chloe burst into a hut which housed a large fire and from which dozens upon dozens of tribespeople were busy collecting their breakfasts, a selection of chopped fruits and dried meats.

She shuffled through the crowd, drawn in by the sweet sound of music. When she reached the far corner, she folded her arms, her face stern.

Tag was in the zone, hand on chest, a mug of something frothy that spilled on the floor with each swing of his other arm. Ben was beside him, struggling with a lute that sounded as if it was out of tune, occasionally glancing at the tribesman at his side who was playing with his eyes closed.

Gideon sat with his legs crossed and a drum on his lap. One hand rested on his leg, the other occasionally bashed the drum with a stick.

Chloe cupped her mouth, speaking loud enough to be heard above the din. "Since when did the three musketeers become the Jackson 5?" she said, one hand on her hip.

Tag stopped singing and choked on his drink when he took a sip. "Well, it took you long enough."

"Do you take requests?"

Tag let out a laugh and jumped off the stage, wrapping his arms around Chloe's waist. "We missed you, girly. What took you so long?"

Ben, deciding to abandon his efforts with the lute, rose to his feet, and nimbly jumped down to join them, hugging Chloe when he got to her. Gideon tossed the drum aside and stepped carefully down, stopping nervously in front of Chloe.

She reached out and pulled Gideon toward her, wrapping him in her arms as his ears flared red. "Aw, you silly git." She ruffled his hair with her fist. "What do you mean, 'so long?' I thought it would take even longer to find my way here. You know I spawned in the center of town, right?"

Ben nodded sagely. "You found the respawn site, then?"

They made their way to a spare table, but Tag looking back with envy as another from the tribe took the stage and began singing.

Chloe frowned. "Respawn site?"

Gideon nodded. "Yeah. The tribespeople must have dragged us over the spot by accident on the way into the game. Didn't you notice that strange triple-layered star scratched into the floor?"

"I'll be honest, I had bigger worries on my mind," Chloe retorted. "In case you didn't notice, I literally died back there. My first thought on appearing in the middle of the village was whether my bladder was empty enough to stop me from pissing myself before they all jumped on me and sent me back to the white room."

"And did they?" Gideon asked earnestly.

Chloe clicked her tongue. "Yeah. They *all* jumped on me, and I'm in the white room as we speak."

Gideon seemed to realize what he had said and looked abashedly at the table.

The four adventurers made their way back outside to look for Mantari. When they found him, the man was in the middle of a conversation with two burly men who had large swords strapped to their waists. Their faces were serious.

"Is there some kind of problem," Chloe asked, leading the pack and stopping next to the men.

Mantari finished speaking in the native tongue and the two men left. "Nothing my warriors can't deal with."

Chloe heard a small sigh from Gideon.

Mantari spread his hands wide. "So, what do you think of Oakston? How are you finding our humble little village?

"It's a little basic," Chloe teased. "I could really do with a shower and a cosmo, but I'm guessing that since I didn't see a single working toilet in this place, you also don't have running water?"

"Or basic cable," Tag grumbled from behind.

"Our way of living is modest, and our people are fair. If you want to stay awhile, I can take you to the chief to assign you temporary abodes. While we sometimes allow visitors to recover and rest in our village, full-time residents must choose a talent among the people and contribute to the village. Everyone works or has a contributing skill in Oakston. That is the way of our tribe."

Chloe's eyebrow raised. "Hold on. You're telling me that you're not the chief?"

Mantari shook his head, kindness in his eyes. "Not me."

Ben and Tag looked at each other, confusion on their faces. "Then who is?"

Mantari chuckled. "Follow me."

The sheet-covered entrance to the chief's quarters flapped shut behind them as they made their way into the room where Chloe had initially found Mantari. The chair where he had been sitting was empty, but the fire still roared. There were sentries posted around the room, still as statues.

"This way." Mantari waved them into a room off the side to where they could hear water splashing around. As they ducked through an entrance, Chloe's first instinct was to laugh.

She brought a hand to her mouth, doing her best not to look at Ben, Tag, and Gideon, whose mouths were all now wide-open.

In the center of a small room was an immense wooden tub of sorts. Five women surrounded the tub and held small jugs, which they dipped into the water and poured over one of the largest women Chloe had ever seen. She recognized her instantly as the woman who had sat in the middle of the semicircle, but she now had her eyes closed and appeared to be deep in thought as the women bathed her. Water cascaded down her skin, joining the suds in the tub as they rhythmically took turns pouring as if in some kind of odd dance.

Wall-mounted torches lit the room with a strange glow, making the whole ordeal rather hypnotic.

Mantari bowed his head and uttered a quiet series of clicks and vowels.

The woman's eyes remained closed, her body unmoving. Not a word came from her, but somehow Mantari seemed to receive a message.

Another nod. Another guttural communication.

Mantari turned to face them again.

"The chief has approved your stay. Let me show you to your quarters."

As they headed back out of the tent, Gideon hovered a moment longer than the rest, unable to take his eyes off the giant chief.

CHAPTER SIXTEEN

Mantari set Chloe and the guys up in a modest hut halfway across the village. As they walked there, Mantari explained that the chief, Makkah, was the last living heir of the founders of the village and possessed powers that couldn't be explained.

While he didn't go into great depths on what exactly this meant, Ben and Tag seemed eager to probe and ask more questions of the man.

"So she can perform magic?"

"Can she summon dragons?"

"Can she teach me how to Dougie?"

Mantari laughed and waved their questions away.

Their new abodes were on the edge of the village, so they could hear the sounds of the forest after they reached their assigned rooms. Although he was the smallest, Tag was quick to claim the largest room. Since no one could be bothered to argue, Ben, Gideon, and Chloe chose quarters across the hall from each other. Chloe took the smallest, figuring she had no need for a larger room, considering she hardly had any equipment and didn't plan on using the bedroom all that much anyway.

Besides, it's best to keep the employees happy before they set out on their missions. We want to keep their morale boosted and all that, Chloe mused, taking a second to lie back and close her eyes.

She jackknifed in bed, looking suddenly disgruntled. *Woah, where had that come from?*

"Did you just call your companions 'employees?'" KieraFreya asked silkily, speaking up for the first time in what seemed like hours.

"Great timing, oh wise goddess. I thought I'd finally lucked out and your spirit had fled my armor."

"It's *my* armor, remember?" KieraFreya hissed. "I rather thought the last thing you would have wanted was to have to answer a thousand questions about how and where a player of such a low status as yourself managed to find enchanted armor in the first place. You wouldn't want to raise even more questions upon your arrival into the village, oh *blessed* one."

Chloe knew KieraFreya was trying not to laugh.

"Oh, bite me," she said, then something pinched her arm. "Ouch!"

KieraFreya chuckled. "You asked for it!"

"Look," Chloe said, lowering her voice as her eyes darted to her door. She was sure that she heard footsteps outside her room. "I'm still pissed off at you for what you did back in those woods. What were you *thinking,* to try to kill an innocent man for no apparent reason?"

"No apparent reason? In case you didn't notice, they were dragging you and your friends away. The only information we had in that situation was that you were all in danger. Sometimes you need to attack first and ask questions later. This world is dangerous, and filled with people willing to drain you as soon as look at you."

"I've known women that like to do that to men." Chloe smirked.

"If you're not ready and willing to kill to protect yourself and your companions, you're not going to make it very far in Obsidian."

Chloe's smile faded, and her brow creased. "Well, I have done pretty well so far. I managed to find you, didn't I? I've managed to get the other guys here. I've managed to gain favor with the village leaders."

"Oh, yeah," KieraFreya said sarcastically. "You're doing so well, dying...how many times is it already? 5? 6? Let's take a quick look at your character sheet, shall we?

Bio

Character name: Chloe (*click to select a new character name*)

Level: 7

Class: Null

Race: Human

Stats

HP: 220/220

MP: 150/150

Stamina: 300/300

Active effects: Null

Attributes

Strength: 22 (+16)

Intelligence: 6 (+4)

Dexterity: 20 (+9)

Endurance: 25 (+15)

Etheric Potential: 9 (+8)

Skills

Languages: Human

Acrobatics: Lv 3

Armed Combat: Lv 1

Creature Identification: Lv 2

Dark Vision: Lv 2

Dual Wielding: Lv 1

Sneak: Lv 3

Reckless: Lv 3

Available Points: 0

Chloe studied the sheet, trying to work out what was different. "Hey! My available points are gone!"

KieraFreya clicked her tongue. "You couldn't even find two minutes to assign your points to better attributes? I've seen some unbalanced sheets in my time, but this is ridiculous."

Chloe deflated. "I was going to put more points into etheric potential and intelligence so that I could start working on my magic. Then I was going to have a proper look at what was on offer." Chloe made a mental note to remember to assign points in the future. She might have felt stronger, but she didn't feel wiser. "Hold on, I've lost a level too?"

"Comes with the pain of dying. You lose items *and* experience, Sweet Tits. This world is tough, although it does *everything* within its power to try to help the blessed avoid dying, and there you are offering yourself out as a human pincushion. If you want my advice, work on acquiring more items and *finding my armor.*"

Chloe considered KieraFreya's words. The last time she had died, she had been at level 1 with barely any experience, so the punishments had hardly seemed like punishments at all. Now that she was rising in the ranks, she agreed that the last thing she wanted to do was start to go back down again. If she wanted to progress and make her way through the game, she would have to start playing by the rules, at least until she could advance further with her quest.

"Very well," Chloe acquiesced. "Now for the million dollar question: what do we do about *you?*"

"What about me?" KieraFreya asked.

"Well, if we're going to play by the rules and try to make some sort of progress toward your other bits, I'm going to need you to play along *with* me."

"I'm not sure I understand your meaning."

Chloe slid her hand down her face. "I mean, *you* need to listen to me, okay? The last thing I need when I'm in the middle of a combat situation is to have to battle *you* as well."

KieraFreya scoffed. "When have I *ever*—"

"Outside the cave, when I was attacking the bear, in the middle of the woods when you tried to drive a knife through someone's eye..." Chloe interjected.

"Point taken."

"The point is, I can't keep moving forward if we're not going to work as a team. You have to trust me, and, in turn, I will trust you." Chloe's face softened. "You *did* help me out with those goblins, which was great, and I thank you for it. But this is *my* adventure. So, what'll it be?"

Chloe could've sworn she heard KieraFreya mumble something that sounded like, "Sure, we'll see," but when she prodded her, the goddess simply said. "Sure. Agreed."

Chloe smiled at her bracers. A second later, her cheek warmed as her own hand slapped her across the face.

KieraFreya burst into laughter. "One last one for old time's sake."

Chloe opened her mouth to retort, then thought better of it.

The village was a hub of activity throughout the day. The higher the sun got, the more people came out and went about their daily activities. She saw people walking past with fish impaled on long sticks, women whittling away at poles in order to make basic spears, children frolicking and running through the streets, and a great deal of cooking and crafting.

Chloe made her way as best as she could toward her destination, finding herself lost a handful of times. She had never been the greatest with directions, so when she stumbled across a tall, thin man who was in the middle of sketching something on a pale piece of bark, she stopped and asked for help.

The man pointed in many directions, his English not the best in the world.

Chloe paused for a moment, wondering if it was correct to call the language "English" in this game. For all that she knew, she was speaking Taiwanese and the game translated for her.

After a short time, Chloe noticed that the man had stacks of scrolls and sketches in his tent. Chloe spotted one that looked remarkably map-like and pointed to it.

The man wandered over, grabbed the scroll, and waved it at Chloe.

"I'm sorry, I don't understand?"

Quest unlocked: Crossing the language barrier

There are many in the Oakston village who can speak your

language. There are, however, also many who can't, and this might quickly become tiresome for you.

Unlock new quests and interactions in Oakston by either learning a new language or finding an interpreter. The rewards you gain will be based on the choices you make.

Difficulty: 2/10

Reward (Interpreter): 100 exp

Reward (Learn a language): 1,000 exp, +3 intelligence

Accept quest: Y/N

Chloe exhaled loudly, waving the man away. "I'll be back shortly," she said, re-reading the notification and leaving the bewildered man behind.

A split quest. Now Chloe had to make a decision. She sauntered through the village, thinking hard about which way she should go. On the one hand, she could make this *super* easy and find herself an interpreter—Mantari sprang to mind, but Chloe figured interpreting might be a little below his station—but it would mean a very basic reward.

On the other, if she managed to somehow *learn* the language, she'd bulk up her experience *and* gain additional intelligence. Considering that the AI had auto-assigned her points and left her thirsty for more intelligence and etheric potential, maybe the additional work would be beneficial.

You've got to think, Chloe. Time is money. Money is time. Chloe blinked as the voice of her father came unbidden into her head. She imagined him, sleek silver hair combed back, at the head of the table in the boardroom. *Sure, you could gain the additional experience and attributes, but would you not be better off spending your time on more profound quests than talking to peasants? You've got to weigh the alternatives to determine which will pay the biggest dividends.*

Chloe shook her head, erasing the image of her father. She wasn't sure if she was more annoyed that he had appeared uninvited or that he was right. She could spend hours, or possibly days, hunting around the village and picking up the language from the willing, but would that really be the best use of her time?

Chloe scoured the village for Mantari, but he was nowhere to be found. Just as she had given up searching, she rounded the corner of a hut and bumped into someone, their shoulders colliding.

Chloe span, surprised to see that it was Cijay. "Sorry!"

Cijay's skin went bright red as he realized who he'd bumped into. A mixture of feelings coursed through Chloe as the memory of Cijay pointing her out and calling her a liar came flooding back. Now that she was closer to him, and as he stared wide-eyed at her, she recognized something incredibly familiar.

"It was you!" she said suddenly, pointing at his chest. "You were the one who was dragging me through the forest."

Cijay gave an awkward laugh, looking as if he was weighing what his chances would be if he were to sprint away into the crowd. He decided against it, saying, "Oh blessed one, I am so sorry. I meant no harm. I protect people."

To her surprise, Cijay folded to his knees, arms outstretched and clawing for purchase on her ankle.

A wave of guilt washed over her then. She looked down at the man with pity, wondering how she had been able to strike this much fear into the heart of a person who wasn't even real. Moreover, she was surprised by just how much guilt she felt about the entire situation. Her. Chloe. The girl who used to take great delight in watching little kids tripping at the mall.

Chloe went to one knee and raised Cijay's head by tipping up his chin. "It's okay, Cijay. I forgive you. You couldn't have known."

KieraFreya's voice cut across her thoughts. *Cut his throat. Kill him. Retribution must be ours. It's his fault we died.*

No, Chloe said, eyes closing momentarily. *I died. You were fine. His honor is intact because his intentions were pure.*

To her annoyance, Chloe's hand began to shake. She clenched her fist and thought, *We had a deal!*

Her hand stopped shaking, although she felt as if the goddess had let go reluctantly.

"Thank you," Chloe said out loud.

Cijay rose to his feet. "No, thank *you!*" The next thing Chloe knew, his arms were around her shoulders. "If I can do anything to repay your kindness, please let me know."

Chloe went to wave away his words, thinking that he had done enough—that their debts had been paid—when an idea suddenly struck her.

"Cijay. You speak my language!"

Cijay nodded. "Most of it. I'm still learning."

Chloe grinned. "In that case, I don't suppose you would be willing to do me a favor? You know, an eye for an eye?"

Cijay's hand immediately rose to his eyes. "No! No, blessed one. *Anything* but my eyes."

Chloe gasped, realizing what she had said.

CHAPTER SEVENTEEN

Chloe grew fond of Cijay very quickly, discovering that the key to unlocking low-level quests and missions was in being able to cross the language barrier.

Cijay spent virtually every moment by Chloe's side. After receiving a blessing from Mantari and the silent chief, Mukkah, he was granted permission to work solely as an interpreter and advisor for one of the blessed ones.

Chloe completed her language quest, earning an entire map of the village from the tribesman. In purchasing and *owning* the map, for which she paid a single bronze coin, she discovered that she was now able to draw on the map whenever she wanted without having to hold it on her person. In the same way that Ben's map had displayed in her vision, she could see every street and hut the village had to offer, labeled and titled with symbols and useful services she could access.

Over the next few days, Chloe steadily acquired new quests, managing to make her way around the village and acquiring the basic levels of a handful of skills she hoped would make her journey into the wilds for KieraFreya's armor much easier in the future.

From the whittling women, she learned the art of **Crafting (Lv 1)**, helping the villagers work through a handful of requests that had become backlogged over the last few weeks. As a reward for her work, the head whittling woman parted with a small **Leather Satchel (basic)** that Chloe hooked over her shoulder, impressed when she opened her items menu and saw that her carrying capacity had grown from 2 items to 16.

Chloe followed the foragers on one of their daily treks into the wild, discovering a waterfall and large pool filled with fish. There she earned her first level in **Herb identification, Swimming,** and **Fishing,** with one particular forager taking a liking to Chloe and gifting her a **Fisherman's Rod** (Tag had laughed until he cried the evening she had arrived back at the village and told her friends this fact). She also earned a skill in **Cooking** that night when she helped the women prepare the fish over a log fire.

Not only that, but Chloe managed to regain her status as a level 8, beaming as the bright flare and wave of good feeling soared over her and lifted her off the ground.

Occasionally, she'd bump into Gideon, Ben, and Tag (who seemed virtually inseparable), though for the most part, Chloe went out on her own. She did join the guys and a handful of villagers one night when a tribesman ran into the eating hut and called everyone's attention to a pack of wolves that had been stalking the area and had just been detected sniffing around the village's borders.

Without hesitation, Chloe, Gideon, Ben, and Tag looked at each other, resolve in their eyes, and left their drinks and food behind them. Chloe informed Cijay he would no longer be needed that day and the man exhaled a deep sigh of relief.

"Thank you, Chlo-E."

Chloe winked, giggling at the fact that even after several attempts at trying to teach Cijay how to pronounce her name properly, he still couldn't quite get the nuances of her language.

The wolves were taken down with an ease Chloe couldn't imagine. She had almost forgotten that the other guys would also be honing their skills as well and was impressed when Tag pulled out a horn and blew a long, proud note. A mystical blue haze fogged around the defenders of the village, and a notification popped up for all players involved.

Call of the Valiant: Your comrade has blown the note of battle, uniting all fighters and raising spirits.

+2 strength, +2 endurance

Time remaining: 1minute 46 seconds

Ben cheered, drawing back his bow and loosing two arrows at once, both of them finding their marks in one of the wolf's sides. He fist-pumped, drew another duo of arrows at lightning speed, and shot again before turning to Chloe and saying, "Hey! Chloe. Can you spot me?"

Chloe looked around for Ben, but he was nowhere to be seen. She could hear him laughing, but in the darkness of the woods, he was invisible. A moment later, she saw a shimmer of movement against the trunk of a tree and threw a rock in that direction.

"Ouch!"

"Impressive cover," Chloe said, pointing to her eyes. "Night vision —" *beep*.

Ben laughed, shaking his head. "Such a filthy mouth."

Chloe brought her wrist to her mouth. "Okay, new deal. The next time I want to swear, you have to fill in the blanks for me. I'm tired of this censorship business."

Meanwhile, Gideon charged past all the tribespeople, shouting at the top of his voice. He dived on top of a wolf, his hands charged with lightning. As they met the wolf's skin, the creature's hair stood on end, the electricity working its way around its entire body. Gideon only managed a quick "Wahoo!" before the lightning reached him and his whole body convulsed.

"For God's sake, Gid," Ben called. "We've told you a thousand times, keep back. Use your powers at range. That's how you play the mage!"

Gideon slid off the wolf as it hit the ground and kept twitching as the remnants of electricity traveled through him. A moment later, his hands lit white as his body began to heal itself.

"I just want to be at the heart of the action," he whined, yelping as a wolf leapt at him and bit into his shoulder. For the briefest of moments, his hands glowed purple.

"We said no fire, Gid! It's too dangerous in the woods."

Gideon bared his teeth, rolled onto his back, and held the wolf at arm's length. Its jaws snapped in his face, saliva dripping onto his cheeks.

"Naw, the little pup is hungry," Tag bellowed, leaping to a surprising height out of the bushes and smacking the wolf on the back of the head with a large hammer, an item he had acquired from the village's smith. A loud metallic sound rang around the forest and the remaining two wolves turned to flee.

Several tribespeople sped after them, but they were down before they could reach them. Ben replaced a couple of arrows in his quiver and nodded at Chloe. "This **Night Vision** is great, eh?"

"Who said that?" Chloe winked.

When dawn broke on the sixth day of their stay at the village, Chloe was awoken by a knock on her door.

"Who is it?" she croaked.

After no reply came, she rose from her bed and opened the door. A boy who was likely in his teens held out a note and Chloe took it.

You have been summoned.

You've made quite an impression with Oakston's chief. Meet her at her hut across town to accept a permanent position in the Oakston tribe.

Chloe lowered the note. The boy was gone. A notification blinked at her.

Quest unlocked: One of us

The chief has summoned you to her chambers to accept a permanent position as part of the tribe. The tribespeople of Oakston may be basic, but there is opportunity for growth and development here. Learn from local experts, hone your skill under the tutelage of others, and make Oakston your home.

Difficulty: 1/10

Rewards: 5,000 exp, Title unlock (Oakston Villager), New language (Tribal: Primitive).

Chloe took a deep breath.

This was unexpected. She had made her way to the village purely on the off-chance that she would be able to help her character progress. That much had happened, for which she was incredibly thankful (despite the rough time she had gone through in her initial meeting with the tribe).

Now the chief wanted Chloe to *join* them? *Permanently?*

She wasn't even sure what that meant in game terms. Would that mean she had to swear a blood oath, slice her wrist over a fire, and commit to the tribe forever, unable to leave the boundaries of the village without hitting an invisible wall, or worse, triggering an automatic death.

A tiny part of Chloe wished she'd paid much more attention to Blake's run-throughs of *Relic Hunter*. Perhaps then she'd have some kind of clue.

Making her way across the hall, Chloe knocked on the door of the person she had learned to trust the most since landing in Obsidian.

Gideon's eyes showed surprise as he opened the door and invited Chloe in.

Chloe handed him the note, allowing time for Gideon to read the words.

"Well, that's a kick in the face." Gideon grabbed a note of his own that was off the side and handed it to Chloe.

Your time is nearly up

The Oakston tribe has enjoyed hosting you and your team for the past 6 days. However, it was agreed that your visit would be temporary. You must vacate your rooms and leave the village by sundown tomorrow, especially the small guy. He has eaten more than 4 people's share of our food.

Chloe brought the note down, doing her best to keep a straight face. Gideon was the first to break, laughing and falling back on the bed as Chloe joined him.

"Really? You get invited to stay forever, and we all get our asses kicked to the curb?"

Chloe shrugged. "I guess what they say is true. Girls *are* far superior to guys at everything!"

Gideon nudged Chloe, and they both fell back on the bed. They stayed there, lying side-by-side, Chloe's hair fanned out behind her head.

Chloe stared at the ceiling. "What do you think I should do?"

"What do *you* think you should do? I've never seen an offer like this in any other game. I have no idea what the consequences or bonuses will be if you choose to stay."

That was less than helpful.

Chloe chewed the inside of her cheek, contemplating both sides of the decision.

"I think," Gideon mused, "what you need to consider is what you want to do next. Me, Ben, and Tag were looking at our next steps anyway, and Ben has identified a mountain on his map, just over the rise of the hill to the north, that looks like it might host some pretty decent dungeons. That's where our strength has always laid, in raiding crypts and digging up treasure. Well, before I became...y'know..."

"A—" *beep* "—poor excuse for a mage?"

"You mean 'piss-poor?'"

Chloe's lips tightened and her eyes went wide as KieraFreya spoke in the quiet room.

Gideon raised his head. "Er, what was that?"

"Nothing," Chloe said sharply, placing her hands beneath her back so they were muffled by the mattress. "Nothing. I, er, I said..."

"Something just *swore* in-game."

Chloe shook her head. "No, don't be silly. You must have misheard. I said—"

Chloe's hand shot out from behind her back. "Oh, I'm sorry. Did I speak out of turn? You *did* tell me to fill in the blanks the next time you swore. That was our deal, was it not? Are you telling me I've done badly again by following your orders, *Your Highness*?" Unprepared, Chloe couldn't stop herself before her wrists moved of their own accord and she began spanking her own ass. "Have I been a bad, bad girl? Should I be *punished*?"

With a great burst of willpower, Chloe moved her hands away and shoved them into her armpits. There they continued to writhe, emitting a series of muffled utterances.

Gideon stared, mouth agape, and pointed at her wrists. "What the..."

Chloe sighed. "It's kind of a lot to explain."

CHAPTER EIGHTEEN

Gideon exhaled. "You have *got* to be the luckiest son-of-a—"

"KieraFreya, do the honors, please."

"I'm not a dancing monkey!"

"Do. The. Honors. Otherwise, you're going back into my pits."

KieraFreya sighed. "Bitch."

"Thank you." Chloe nodded. "Gid?"

"In the whole realm."

Chloe grinned. "Yeah, something like that."

She had told Gideon everything about KieraFreya. About stumbling across the cave, the hidden entrance, and the arrival of her first quest in the form of the Deathwalk. She had laughed out loud as she recounted the tale, realizing now that she was in the comfort safety of the tribal village how ludicrous it all sounded. A level 1 had conquered a high-difficulty dungeon, lived to tell the tale, and inherited mythical armor that could talk and was unaffected in her language capacities by the system.

"Level 1 to 8 in one mission." Gideon sighed, unable to take it all in. "Your attribute points must be completely out of proportion with your level."

"What do you mean?"

Gideon explained how usually in play, as players leveled up and found their playing style, they'd inherit items from quests and learn a whole host of skills that would bulk up their character to suit each level. However, since Chloe had jumped 7 levels from one quest in which her only treasure acquired were a pair of bracers and a rusty dagger, this meant her attribute skills were *much* lower than anyone who would have been an equivalent level 8.

"I'd imagine that by level 8 I'll have honed a few of my skills to level 5 or 6, with my intelligence and etheric potential hovering around 60 or 70 with my bonuses. What are you on?"

"My highest is endurance, which is around 40 points."

"Well, that's why we're here, I guess. To find bugs in the game, eh?"

"I imagine there are still a fair few bugs to find," Chloe said as the pair skirted the borders of the village. Chloe had wanted to get out of the small abode for fear of others listening in on their conversation.

Gid continued, more to himself, "I mean, there're bugs, and then there's full-blown error reports. I thought I was lucky just to have been in the first cohort of players, but you take it to a whole new level." His eyes sparkled. "I wonder if I could find any bugs out there that boost my level and give me mythical treasure too?"

"Not the way you shoot, genius," KieraFreya quipped.

Gideon glared at KieraFreya, then deflated.

"She's probably right. I'd need the extra boosts from points."

Chloe placed her arm around Gid's neck, resting her head on his shoulder. "Don't pay any attention to her. She may *think* that she's all-knowing and powerful, but she forgets that she's strapped to *me*. Talk about a fall from grace, huh, KieraFreya?"

The bracers pinched Chloe's wrists.

"Ouch! Fine. Let's both be nice, shall we?"

"So, this quest. You have to unite all of the pieces of Kifarna's armor to fulfill the requirements?"

KieraFreya growled, "It's Ke-erra-Fra-ya. One word, no space. Dumbass."

"Yep. That's about the size of it. The only problem is, I have no real idea of where to start." Chloe remembered Mia's words. "My only hope, as far as I can figure, is to search for some kind of shrine or altar. Something that will give me a leg up with the deities of Obsidian."

Gideon tapped his chin. "Shrine. A shrine..." His eyes lit up. "There's a woman...or man...or...I don't know, one of them. They call him 'the shaman.' He's feared by many in the tribe, so he has his own little place in the woods past the outskirts of the village."

"How do you know this?" Chloe asked.

Gideon wracked his brain. "It was just something I overheard one night when Tag was hogging the stage. I ducked out the back of the tent to get some air and enjoy the starlight when I saw him standing at the edge of the woods, eyes glinting. At first, I was ready to sound the alarm, thinking it was some kind of creature until I asked a villager and they dragged me inside real quick."

Gideon rubbed his hands nervously. "Apparently he can speak to the gods. Uses their powers to heal and curse."

Chloe pulled up her map, and, sure enough, there was a mark in the tree line around the village. She could understand how she had missed it before since the house was nothing more than a tiny mark with a strange sigil over the top.

She grabbed Gideon's hand. "Come on!" she urged excitedly.

Gideon resisted, freeing his hand from Chloe's. "I can't. I really should be getting back to the guys. We promised that we'd get in one final quest with the villagers before we were no longer welcome to stay here, y'know? Gain some experience that could be useful for dungeon-raiding."

Chloe nodded. She understood but had to admit that it felt a little sad leaving Gideon behind, given all that she had just shared.

"Sure thing," Chloe said. "Just promise me something, will you?"

Gideon mimed zipping his lips. "I won't tell a soul."

Chloe beamed and kissed his cheek. "I know you won't."

With that, she sped into the trees.

The shaman's house was difficult as hell to find. Chloe navigated through the forest, occasionally blinking up her map to check her progress and make sure she was on track. The damn marker seemed to move every time she pulled up the display—either that, or the forest was shifting around her.

When she finally approached the hut, she almost walked straight past it. Whereas the Oakston huts were built in such a way that they were unmissable when one was up close, the shaman's hut was a complete tangle of leaves, foliage, and brush. It was a covered top to bottom in vines and blended in perfectly with the trees around it.

Chloe made her way toward the entrance, feeling a strange chill creep along the forest floor and prick her skin into gooseflesh.

"What's the matter? Not *scared,* are you?" KieraFreya teased.

Chloe puffed out her chest and went to knock on the door. Before her knuckles connected, the door swung open.

"Efficient," KieraFreya whispered.

"Shut up," Chloe hissed.

The inside of the house looked like an abandoned mess, accurately reflecting the outside. It was hard to tell where the greenery on the walls ended and the tangles on the ceiling began. Several vines sported blooming purple flowers that hung like bells across the ceiling. There was a horrid stench of decay and rot around her, and Chloe tugged her shirt up to cover her nose, only realizing then how bad she herself smelled. She chose the lesser of two evils and kept the shirt over her face.

"Hello?" she called, pacing from room to room. No answer came.

Strange, Chloe thought, bringing up her map again. She zoomed in, and, sure enough, her marker was over the house with the sigil on it. *This has to be it.*

"You realize nobody actually told you that this is the shaman's house, right?" KieraFreya pointed out, pulling up the map again for Chloe. "See? It doesn't even mention the shaman here. You just assumed it would be here, and you know what happens when you assume, right? It makes an *ASS* out of *U* and—"

KieraFreya stopped short as a notification blinked. Chloe opened it.

Quest unlocked: Where's the shaman?

You have quite the inquisitive mind. You've found the shaman's house, but the shaman is nowhere to be found.

Use your powers of detection to track down the shaman before the poisonous gas from the Deathbell flowers that has been filling your lungs sends you into your final slumber.

Difficulty: 4/10

Rewards: 500 exp, final slumber potion recipe

Instinctively Chloe grabbed her throat, now tasting the air as it went down her windpipe with every breath. Sure enough, upon inspection of her Activity Log, she noticed that her health had taken several large hits in the immediate past. There was an initial message about the poison, followed by a new notification every few seconds that informed Chloe she'd lost more health.

Uh-oh! You've been poisoned.

You have ingested the infamous scent of the Deathbell flower.

Effects: Poison debuff. -5HP for every 10 seconds that you breathe it.

Duration: Poison lasts an additional 15 minutes after vacating the poisonous vicinity.

Uh-oh! You've been poisoned.

Clear the vicinity or find an antidote!

-10HP

Uh-oh! You've been poisoned.

Clear the vicinity or find an antidote!

-10HP

Uh-oh! You've been poisoned.

Clear the vicinity or find an antidote!

-10HP

Uh-oh! You've been poisoned.

Clear the vicinity or find an antidote!

-10HP

Uh-oh! You've been poisoned.

Clear the vicinity or find an antidote!

-10HP

Uh-oh! You've been poisoned.

Clear the vicinity or find an antidote!

-10HP

Uh-oh! You've been poisoned.

Clear the vicinity or find an antidote!

-10HP

Chloe pulled up her character sheet, checking the state of her health.

<u>**Bio**</u>

Character name: Chloe *(click to select a new character name)*

Level: 8

Class: Null

Race: Human

<u>**Stats**</u>

HP: 150/220

MP: 150/150

Stamina: 142/300

Active effects: Poison debuff (ongoing)

<u>**Attributes**</u>

Strength: 22 (+16)

Intelligence: 6 (+5)

Dexterity: 20 (+13)

Endurance: 25 (+15)

Etheric Potential: 9 (+8)

<u>**Skills**</u>

Languages: Human

Acrobatics: Lv 3

Armed Combat: Lv 1

Cooking: Lv 1

Crafting: Lv 1

Creature Identification: Lv 2

Dark Vision: Lv 2

Dual Wielding: Lv 1

Fishing: Lv 1

Herb Identification: Lv 1

Sneak: Lv 3

Swimming: Lv 1
Reckless: Lv 3
<u>**Available Points:**</u> **32**

Chloe quickly did some mental arithmetic, working out that that with 150HP remaining—

Uh-oh! You've been poisoned.

Clear the vicinity or find an antidote!

-10HP

—*Fine!* 140HP remaining, that gave her just under 5 minutes to find out what the hell was going on and identify some kind of antidote before she died of the poison. If she didn't find the antidote, it wouldn't matter how quickly she found the shaman. With the active debuff effects currently on her, even if she cleared the vicinity, she'd still have to battle to keep her health above 0 until either the villagers healed her or she drank enough potions to outlast the debuff.

Chloe whirled, searching for something—*anything*—that might provide some sort of clue. Remembering her **Herb Identification** skill, she focused on the deathbells.

Deathbell (plant)

Emits a poison that can be made into potions.

"Great. Well, that's as useful as…" Chloe stomped her foot.

"What?" KieraFreya said, snapping to attention. "Did you want me to say 'shit?' Or 'fuck?' Or how about 'fuckity-fuck?' Let's be honest, this ventriloquist blaspheming isn't really working, is it?"

Chloe glared at her bracers. "Well, forget the swearing, then. Any ideas for surviving this poison? I'd really rather not die if I can help it."

"Are you sure? You are very good at it."

Chloe threw down her wrists and ran through the house, doing her best to ignore the blinking notifications as her health drained from her.

After a full lap, she turned on her heels and looked longingly at the exit.

It was there that something caught her eye.

Nestled behind the thick stem of a vine, Chloe saw markings on the wall. Without thinking, she drew her knife and hacked at the plant, revealing a series of lines that snaked around the room in all directions. She followed the first, hacking and slashing at the plants until the line veered off from the others, swirling and whirling around on the walls.

Chloe growled when the line reached a dead end.

She followed the next one, making her way halfway across the room before she met yet another dead end. After a quick cry of frustration, a check of her health revealed that she was now down to just 60HP.

As quickly as she could, she followed two more trails. One worked its way into a hole in the floor, clearly set up as a misdirection, Chloe realized that after a rat poked out its head and bit her finger, taking an additional 4HPs with it. The second curled back on itself instantly, Chloe now beginning to feel woozy and light-headed.

Chloe looked at the dozen remaining trails and recited a rhyme that she'd used hundreds of times over the years when she wasn't sure what decision to make or which way to go.

"And my mother said that you." Chloe pointed at a thick line with thorns decorating the art. "Are." Another line, thin and sleek. "It!" she exclaimed, ignoring the warning notification that she was almost out of health points. She sprinted around the room, dragging the knife along the walls and finding that the trail led through the door and into the next, then the next room.

The trail made its way to a broad wall that was thick with vines. Chloe coughed into her hand, small spatters of blood appearing on her palm. Her eyes felt heavy. KieraFreya said something, but the words turned to cotton puffs.

With a last burst of energy, Chloe cut the vines, which melted away to reveal a shimmering white portal. Without conscious thought, she closed her eyes and fell forward, her body disappearing into the white liquid pool of light.

CHAPTER NINETEEN

The moment that Chloe's head fell past the portal, she felt sick.

Not sick-from-poison sick, sick as in the whole house literally cartwheeled alongside her as she emerged on the other side.

Chloe placed her hands out in front, managing to break her fall before her face hit bare wood. If she had missed, the damage surely would have sucked up the last 6HP she had remaining.

Shit. 6HP left and a poison debuff.

Chloe scrambled to her feet, realizing that she was soaked from head to foot. She blinked in the blinding light that poured in through the open windows, her vision affected. The room was still swimming, and she was so disorientated and confused that for a moment, she couldn't find her bearings.

A warm humming greeted her ears as she ran from one side of the room to the other, calling for help as she looked for some kind of antidote that might do the trick.

"The blessed ones should learn that panic is the ultimate breeding ground for the poison of a Deathbell flower," a gravelly voice crooned. "When panicked, the blood flow becomes more rapid. When blood runs fast, the poison speeds to catch up."

"Who's there?" Chloe called. "Show yourself!"

"I am here. All one must do is calm oneself to see."

Chloe's chest rose and fell with desperate breaths. She stopped in her tracks, continuing to take rapid breaths in through her nose and out through her mouth. The walls were bright white, reminding her of the room she went to when she died. After a few more breaths, her heart began to slow. Surely the poison had taken her, and she was back in the white room?

She turned, looking for the phone and computer. Instead, she saw a strange-looking man sitting cross-legged on the floor. He had a hookah beside him, the pipe trailing from his mouth and smoke rising in purple coils.

"You narrowly survived, child."

"Who are you?" Chloe asked, her nose recoiling at the stench of the greasy hair tied back on the man's neck. He sported the tribal tattoos of the villagers, only his were thorny and dark.

"I am the one you seek, Chloe. The shaman of the Oakston village. Tell me what it is that you wish to find?"

He motioned for Chloe to approach, and she took a seat in front of him.

Chloe told the shaman that she desired to know more about the gods. She wanted to walk a holy path and connect with those above in any way she could. The shaman listened patiently the entire time, occasionally puffing on his hookah.

When Chloe was finished, she waited patiently for a response. She looked around the house, wondering if this was the same house she had entered when it was covered from top to bottom in vines. The shaman was slow to respond.

"Here, child. Taste this."

The shaman offered the hookah to Chloe. She held the pipe near her mouth. "What will this do?"

The shaman stared at her, as still as a gargoyle.

Chloe slowly placed the pipe in her mouth and took a long draft of the smoke. It caught in her throat, and she coughed.

The shaman smiled. "See?"

Unbidden, Chloe's menu opened to her character sheet.

Bio
Character name: Chloe *(click to select a new character name)*
Level: 8
Class: Null
Race: Human
Stats
HP: 36/220
MP: 150/150
Stamina: 158/300
Active effects: Null
Attributes
Strength: 22 (+16)
Intelligence: 6 (+5)
Dexterity: 20 (+13)
Endurance: 25 (+15)
Etheric Potential: 9 (+8)
Skills
Languages: Human
Acrobatics: Lv 3
Armed Combat: Lv 1
Cooking: Lv 1
Crafting: Lv 1
Creature Identification: Lv 2
Dark Vision: Lv 2
Dual Wielding: Lv 1
Fishing: Lv 1
Herb Identification: Lv 1
Sneak: Lv 3
Swimming: Lv 1
Reckless: Lv 3
Available Points: 32

"You… You healed me?" Chloe said softly.

The shaman shook his head. "Do not forget, child. I was the one who injured you in the first place. Do not so easily forget the wrong-doings of those who have brought suffering upon you."

Told you, KieraFreya thought.

Shut up.

"But why the big charade? Why put me through these hurdles just to allow me to sit down with you?"

"You said it yourself, child. You search for that which is beyond the realm of difficult. To determine how badly you wanted what you seek, is it not wise to test a person's mettle?"

Chloe supposed he had a point. This strange man with powers unlike any she had seen so far in Obsidian must have to protect himself in order to survive out in the woods and deflect requests from those who were weak-willed.

"Now, about your request," the shaman said, shaking Chloe from her thoughts. Her head felt light and cloudy. "First, you must understand that all requests come with a price. Payment must be received before you can accomplish your task."

Chloe looked up and saw that the shaman was no longer in front of her, but was now sitting upside-down on the ceiling. The smoke also moving in the opposite direction to what gravity should have allowed. It dropped from ceiling to floor, tickling her nose. Chloe sneezed and suddenly found herself falling on her head. She twisted at the last minute, managing to crash onto her side.

"Well, that was unnecessary," she wheezed. "What did you do that for?"

The shaman chuckled, revealing a crooked set of rotten teeth. He took another draft of his hookah and exhaled the smoke into Chloe's face. "Tell me, child. What price are you willing to pay for your destiny?"

Chloe was surprised to see that there was already a crowd gathered as she parted the sheet covering the door and made her way into the chief's hut.

Faces beamed at her. Faces she recognized from her last week at the village. Faces of the men, women, and children she had grown familiar with and would consider friends. The atmosphere was lively. Warm. The fire in the center was even larger, and the warmth of the hut almost made Chloe reconsider her decision.

"Ah, our guest of honor is here!" Mantari said, rising to his feet and sweeping his arms wide. "Let us welcome Sister Chloe to our midst!"

Chloe worked her way to the front of the room, noting that Gideon, Ben, and Tag were sitting toward the front, toasting their hands at the fire. As it was their last night in the village, Chloe imagined that they were taking advantage of the luxury of warmth before heading off on their adventures.

Chloe took a knee in front of Mukkah, Mantari taking his place at her side.

Mukkah looked exceptionally blobbersome at that moment. Her girth spilled over the sides of her chair, and her loincloth cut tightly into her sides. Her breasts spilled down her stomach, finding a place to rest on her knees, and her eyes were sunken pits in her face.

Mantari addressed the crowd. As he spoke, Cijay interpreted his words for those in the group who were unable to speak the modern tongue. "Sister Chloe has been extended an invitation to join our gracious ranks in the village of Oakston. A fine specimen of woman, she has grabbed a place in each of our hearts this week, and it is with honor that we welcome her to become one with our tribe. Though Chloe has yet to specialize, she brings a fountain of gifts to the Oakston people, and we look forward to seeing how she might fare in our mighty ranks."

"Sure, she fits in, but did you forget about the person that Cleveland's local paper termed 'The Voice of our Generation?' I guess there's no place for a new singer here," Tag grumbled, swaying a little as he hiccupped into his cup.

"Your graciousness," Chloe said, speaking directly to the blob of a woman. "It is with deep appreciation and thanks that I received the honor of an invitation to become one of your own. Only a week ago, I was lost and alone in the forest, with no one to call a friend, and now..." she indicated the crowd, "now I have been blessed with companionship beyond my wildest dreams."

There was a round of applause. Mantari beamed at Chloe. Mukkah simply stared. She might as well have been made of stone. Wobbly stone.

Behind Mukkah's chair, Chloe was sure she could glimpse the shaman's gleaming eyes hovering in the shadows.

"However..." Chloe continued, bringing a hush back over the crowd. She swallowed hard, unsure of what would happen next. "It is with great regret that I choose not to take up this honor, but rather choose to continue to pursue my own adventures, discovering more of what this great realm has to offer."

A great many mumbles rippled across the tribespeople. Cijay hesitated before translating her words, meeting Chloe's eyes and only continuing after she offered a curt nod.

Mantari stepped toward Chloe, that same smile on his face that lit up the room. "Chloe, Chloe! Are you quite sure you're making the right decision? Think of what we're offering you here."

He spun Chloe around and directed her gaze to a table at the far side of the room that she had missed upon entering. The table had a selection of items neatly displayed and centered around a gleaming silver sword. There was a leather cuirass, leather trousers, a dark set of leather greaves, and more. Beside the table sat a woman with a tattoo needle and a pot of dark powder.

"As a warrior of our tribe, you will receive the finest garments to protect you during your efforts. You will be appointed to the rank directly below me and keep our people safe. Not only that," here Mantari turned as if he may have been speaking out of turn, "you'll receive full roaming privileges. You may leave the boundaries for short periods of time, and return each night when the sun is at its lowest. You'll be one of us, now and forever."

Chloe tore her eyes away from the offering. "I thank you a thousand times over, Mantari. Mukkah. My answer is still no."

Tag rose unsteadily to his feet. "I'll take her place!"

Ben pulled Tag back down and rolled his eyes. "Not so fast, little one. You're on our team." A ripple of laughter emanated from around them.

Mantari's face stiffened. "Very well. If that is your final choice, you must understand it." His voice grew deep. Chloe noted the hurt in his eyes, as if he were speaking to a naughty child. The same look her mother and father gave Chloe when they sat at the end of her bed after a late Friday night out.

"That is your decision?" Mantari asked, confirming once more.

There were a few whispers in the crowd of "No" before Chloe nodded. "That is my decision."

Chloe ignored the rapidly blinking notification, having expected it to flash instantly—the announcement of the failure of her quest to join the village. She decided to save that little nugget of information for later.

"Very well." Mantari signaled several of his men. "Then it is time for our guests to make haste and leave."

The tribesmen appeared around Chloe, but her gaze remained fixed on Mantari. She heard Tag protest as more men came to accompany them in their departure. Ben and Gideon did their best to quiet him down.

"Thank you," Chloe said. "For everything."

As she moved to leave, Chloe heard the oddest noises behind her, like a giant grub or earthworm crawling through gravel. There was a strange coughing choke, and as Chloe turned, she saw that the great blob that was Mukkah had begun to move.

Mukkah struggled with her limbs, her minuscule tongue poking out of her mouth with each hacking cough. Between choking sounds she uttered half-words, pointing to Chloe with pudgy fingers.

"What is it?" Mantari asked, kneeling by her side and taking her hand affectionately in his. He snapped his fingers, and a tribeswoman appeared with a cup of water.

Mukkah swallowed the contents in one go, liquid dribbling down her chin and into the folds of her body. She began to settle down, her breathing returning to normal. She leaned closer to Mantari and whispered in his ear.

Mantari's eyes widened. "Chief Mukkah, you can't be serious?"

Another hacking cough sent sprays of saliva across Mantari's cheek. He wiped them away with one hand and listened once more. His eyes met Chloe's, and for a long time, he was still.

"Chief Mukkah would like to thank you for your service," Mantari said, not quite believing his own words as he rose back to his feet. "As a shining example of the blessed, and as an adventurer who has taken the sword to the final death and come back again without showing a sign of anger or a desire for vengeance, we of the Oakston tribe bless *you* with these items of the warrior as a token to remember us by and aid you on your travels."

Chloe's eyes lit up, her composure gone in a second. "You have *got* to be kidding me?"

"Nope," Mantari said, finally smiling at Chloe. "It is the greatest honor the tribe has ever bestowed. No other warrior outside our tribe has taken the armor and weapons and braved the world."

He moved closer to Chloe, placing his hands warmly on her shoulders. "May you be a representative of the Oakston tribe out there in the wild. Bring honor to our name."

Chloe fought back the tears that brimmed in her eyes.

Mantari leaned closer and whispered, "And don't tell anyone where our village is, please." He winked.

Chloe scanned the crowd, who were now on their feet, applauding. Tears were shed. Cries were shouted. Hugs were given. Chloe made her way to the back of the room and touched each individual item, not even bothering to read their statistics but beaming as each item faded and disappeared into her inventory.

The tribe crowded her, squeezed her, and said their goodbyes as the sentries waited patiently to accompany them to the village's borders.

Chloe couldn't stop smiling, never having felt more welcome in her life anywhere than she did here. She had a moment where she wondered if she had made the right decision, then she found Gideon's eyes through the crowd.

She nodded at him.

Gideon added his own applause and nodded back.

CHAPTER TWENTY

The forest was dark, the village of Oakston now long behind them. Chloe walked on, determination in her strides. The faded ghosts of her final goodbyes with the team behind her.

That had been the hardest part—saying goodbye to the team she had quickly become fond of. It was a whole different ball game saying goodbye to the NPCs than it was to players who existed in the real world.

While the NPC goodbyes had pulled on her emotions, her good-byes with Gideon, Ben, and Tag damn near tore her heart out.

"Are you sure you don't want to come with us, Chloe?" Tag giddily hiccupped as he raised a skin of what he'd brought from the village to his mouth. "Adventure and treasure await."

"We could use talents like yours," Ben added. "The more of us, the merrier."

Chloe smiled but once again refused, explaining that she needed to follow her own path. She had her own agenda and quests to fulfill, so she had to ride this train solo, even if that meant taking on the dangerous wilds alone.

She hugged each of them in turn, delivering smooches to their cheeks. When she got to Gideon, she pulled him aside from the others, stirring their curiosity as they wolf-whistled and chuckled.

"You take care of them, okay?" Chloe said sternly.

Gideon rolled his eyes, a weak smile on his face. "Come on. You know they'll be looking after me, right? I can't do this mage stuff. I'm a warrior."

"Then you should *learn*." Chloe reached into her bag and pulled out a dog-eared tome as thick as her wrist. She handed it to Gideon.

"What's this?"

"A gift from the shaman. Combat magic from ages past. I had a quick look through it, but I thought this might be right up your alley."

"From the shaman?" Gideon asked, awe in his voice. "Is it...safe?"

Chloe shrugged. "I honestly don't know. I guess we'll both find out soon enough just how trustworthy the old monster is, won't we?"

Gideon smiled, pocketed the book, and hugged Chloe. They held each other for a long moment, relishing the warmth of their bodies. KieraFreya, hovering near Gideon's ear, whispered, "If you tell a single soul about me, I'll find you, and I'll cut you."

They pulled apart, fear striking Gideon as Chloe reprimanded the bracers. "Ignore her. She can't do anything I won't let her do."

"We'll see about that—" KieraFreya's voice cut off, now buried in Chloe's armpits.

They laughed, looking warily at Ben and Tag to check they hadn't seen or heard anything they shouldn't. Ben was too busy spinning a very drunk Tag around to notice anything.

"Keep in touch," Gideon said at last.

"And you."

Gideon gestured toward Chloe. "No, seriously. Keep in touch. Pull up the notification."

Chloe focused on the notifications and saw a message appear.

Gideon Fleetwood would like you to be his friend.

You've made quite the impression. Add this character to your list of people who'll cry at your funeral.

Accept: Y/N

"Now you just need to modify the friend settings and allow

communications from me, and we can message any time we want." Gideon beamed.

"That's... Gideon this is amazing."

"Well, it's not *that* amazing," he said modestly. "Nearly every game has this function. And don't go thinking it's like a phone call, because it's not. Just open your notifications, and you might see messages from me from time to time."

"Sweet!" Chloe fist-pumped the air. "What about the others? Should I get their information too?"

They looked back at the pair. Ben was doubled over in fits of laughter while Tag hurled his guts all over the floor.

Gideon raised an eyebrow. "Maybe just get their information and forget about *their* messages."

Chloe nodded her agreement.

Now Chloe made her way through the dark woods, guided by a small glowing orb of light. The wisp had been a gift from the shaman, a guiding beacon to direct her to her next destination. But as she made her way onward, narrowly avoiding falling into yet another bog, she began to doubt the wisp's intentions.

"Yo, dude? Can you give me a little warning please?" Chloe said, her foot hovering over what she now saw as a menacing black pool. The whole area teemed with them, with only thin grass paths between the water to safely navigate.

The wisp floated patiently and waited. Chloe felt a slight note of doubt creep into her mind, wondering if she had done the right thing by trusting the shaman and the vision he had cast in Chloe's head.

"You know that this could all be a trap, right?" KieraFreya piped up. "For all you know, this wisp is going to take us miles off track to a respawn point surrounded by a thousand immeasurable dangers. You'll die repeatedly—and painfully—until you get sick of the realm altogether and eventually leave."

Chloe paused and tapped her chin. "Well, I guess I'll have to endure being a fragment of myself surrounded by immeasurable dangers until a strong-willed, empowered female eventually finds me a thousand years later, and I use *her* as a host to accomplish my tasks. Sound familiar?"

KieraFreya sighed. "Mmhmm."

"You know I'm doing this all for you, right?" Chloe hopped over a small puddle, her foot almost losing purchase on the landing. She managed to regain her balance. "The woods, the bear, the village, the shaman, this freakin'… Would you do the honors?"

"Shithole?"

"Exactly! It's all for you and your mission. So maybe think about that the next time you're thinking of spewing venom."

KieraFreya pondered her words. "You're a liar."

"*I'm a*…excuse me?" The wisp began to veer right. In its faint light, Chloe could make out the shadows of creeping vines dangling loosely off great weeping willows.

"You heard me. You say that you're doing all of this for me, but you're not, are you? By completing this quest, you're doing something that has never been done before. You'll be gaining a shit ton of experience, *and* there are bound to be extra rewards involved. You think what you're doing is selfless? Well, honey, it's the most selfish act I've ever seen."

Chloe stopped in her tracks, her foot splashing mud. "Oh, yeah?"

"Yeah!"

In a fit of desperate rage, Chloe worked her fingers beneath the edge of the bracers. She tugged and pulled, spittle flying from her lips, but there wasn't even the slightest bit of give. Her anger working through her, she gave up pulling and instead bashed the metal of her wrists together, the clanging sound carrying far off into the night.

The whole time KieraFreya simply laughed, fueling Chloe's anger all the more.

"Simple human. Just because my mind is trapped in here doesn't mean I can feel pain. All you're doing is hurting yourself."

Chloe stopped and lowered her wrists. She pulled up her Activity Log and saw that KieraFreya was right. Her stamina bar had taken a big hit in her fit of rage.

"I'm sorry," Chloe said, catching her breath. "I don't know what came over me."

"You should be," KieraFreya teased.

Chloe threw her hands in the air. "You're impossible, you know that?"

"Once again, you're wrong. Nothing in this realm is impossible." KieraFreya guided Chloe's hand, pointing her to the water ahead. "Take those, for instance."

Chloe's face fell. In the darkness, she could see the silhouettes of creatures gliding through the water. She squinted at them, using **Creature Identification** on the shapes.

Bogland Crocodile (Level 7)

151HP

Bogland Crocodile (Level 6)

136HP

Mutant Bogland Crocodile (Level 9)

213HP

Chloe was pleasantly surprised by the additional information. She opened up her menu and saw several updates that lifted her spirit.

Congratulations! By using two skills in tandem, you have gained additional boost bonuses to your skills.

Skill increased: Creature Identification (Lv 4)

You can now view the HP of your opponents with a simple cast of this skill. Watch their health decrease in the form of a progress bar as you hack and slash your way to victory.

Bonuses: +6 intelligence

(NOTE: Increases in skill override any previous bonuses gained from the skill).

Skill increased: Dark Vision (Lv 4)

The night is fast becoming your mistress. Dark shapes become more refined, night terrors lose their fuzz, and oh, the pranks you can play as you dissolve into the darkness and lead your friends astray.

Bonuses: +5 intelligence, +8 etheric potential

(NOTE: Increases in skill override any previous bonuses gained from the skill).

Great! Always handy to have a boost just before a battle.

Chloe took a calming breath and closed her eyes. She focused her will and summoned **Purple Haze**, and a fireball appeared in her hands. She grinned, glad to finally have the chance to practice again with this spell, considering that she had been unable to in the dry woods around the village.

"Eat fire!" Chloe shouted, chucking the purple ball at the encroaching crocs. The ball headed straight for the big guy in the middle, who ducked under the water at the last moment. The ball of fire sizzled and steamed as the water extinguished it.

"Aw, nuts."

The lower-level croc to her left came onto land, snapping its jaws hungrily, a low growl emanating from its stomach. Chloe drew her sword and struck at the beast, the blade catching the end of the croc's snout.

It reared back in pain. Chloe watched with a satisfying smirk as its health bar dropped, losing around 10%.

"Aha," she said triumphantly, missing the croc that had crept up beside her on the other side and now snapped at her ankles.

Chloe jumped just in time, landing on the croc's snout with a sickening crunch. She stabbed her blade through the side of the croc's face.

The reptile thrashed beneath her, sending her toppling backward. She landed in wet mud and struggled to stand. She heard the first croc coming at her from the other side and quickly took a few steps back.

She looked around briefly for the third croc—the one the identification had labeled as mutant—but he was nowhere to be found.

Chloe spotted the second croc and raised her sword to attack, but she was knocked off her feet as the first croc charged her from behind.

On the ground now, she struggled to see what was going on. She raised an arm and felt as a croc attempted a bite, catching its teeth on her bracers. There was a sickening ringing noise as the croc roared and several teeth came out.

"Damn, girl. You're tougher than I thought," Chloe muttered.

KieraFreya replied. "No comment."

Taking a deep breath, Chloe rolled backward and put some distance between her and the crocs. She glared at them, tucked her sword back into its sheath, and began making movements with her hands.

Words came without understanding to her lips. She poured her willpower into the spell, electricity pooling around her hands. With a cry of triumph, she slammed her hands into the wet forest floor, sending the bolts out in all directions as the water conducted the electrical charge.

She watched the health bar of the croc she had stabbed fall to zero before she fell to the ground, the wet patch that she was standing in receiving a fair amount of voltage. Even KieraFreya screamed.

Chloe cut off the electricity, twitching for a couple of seconds in the same way she had seen Gideon do with the wolves. She hadn't really expected the spell to work, given that she had only seen the mage perform it once, and although it now hurt like hell and her health bar had lowered by a good...40%, she was quietly impressed by the damage it had caused.

Craning her head off the mud, she saw the second of the lower-level crocs coming for her. Behind him, dark bubbles pierced the surface of the water and the mutant croc re-emerged, anger in its eyes as it stood up on its hind legs.

Chloe quickly drew her sword. With the croc right on her, she didn't have time to get the blade into position, so she smacked its cranium with the hilt, watching the final portion of the health bar drop to 0.

"Boop," Chloe mumbled posthumously.

Now Chloe turned her attention to the standing croc. It was a disturbing image, really. She'd seen crocs walk on two legs in cartoons as a child, but she had never imagined how disturbing it would look in real life.

Not real life, dummy. This is a game, remember?

The croc leered darkly over its snout, keeping its distance and remaining in the water. Its body was malformed, with strange lumps all over it. Incredibly long claws glinted on its front paws, and the spikes on its back were much longer than they should have been.

One pleasant surprise was that the brute had lost almost 30% of its health already, though. That was nice.

"Come at me, bro," Chloe urged.

"Why do we assume it's a boy?" KieraFreya sassed. "It has no genitals. It could be a girl. Sexist cow."

A coy smile played on Chloe's lips as she advanced on the croc, her mind flashing back to the first time she had flown solo in battle with the goblins and how much had changed for her now. She felt confident. Strong. Able to take on whatever faced her.

Chloe brought her sword back for the swipe and—

The croc slipped back into the water. Chloe was now waist-high in the muck.

"He tricked us," she said, suddenly turning to return to the closest piece of land.

"No, he tricked *you*," KieraFreya said as the sound of splashing came from behind. The next thing Chloe knew, there were powerful teeth in her leg.

Chloe cried out in pain and kicked back with her other leg. Although she was sure crocodiles couldn't smile, she was certain she would see a small grin on his snout.

The croc retreated as Chloe got her leg free and slipped back into the water.

"What do I do?" Chloe asked, wracking her brain to work out if it was better to run or continue the fight. If she ran, she'd lose out on valuable experience. *Plus*, given that crocs were sort of built for this type of land, she wasn't quite sure she'd escape.

A cursory glance of her stats showed that she had 132/220HP left, with 78/150MP left after casting her fireball and electricity—*wow, that took a fair chunk of power from the etheric*—and 111/300 stamina.

She'd have to pull herself together if she was going to make it out of this one.

Chloe scanned down her list of skills and an idea struck her. She reached into her satchel and pulled out the **Fisherman's Rod** from its depths, marveling at how such a large item could be stored in such a small bag.

Working as fast as she could, she pulled out some basic bait that the tribespeople had given her on her day of foraging and cast the rod into the water. Waiting in tense silence, it was only a few seconds before the line went tight and she felt the pull of something in the water.

"Got you now." Chloe chuckled, winding in the line, confused when a gleam of silver emerged from the water and the shape of a large, flat mudfish flew toward her.

"Ummm…" was all that she managed to say before the much larger shape of the croc appeared, leaping into the air with incredible agility. The large moon behind him silhouetted his graceful figure. His jaws clamped shut on the mudfish. Chloe felt her line grow even tighter as the hook caught on the croc's mouth. She gave the rod a hard tug, throwing the croc off-balance and sending it splashing upside-down into the water just a few feet in front of her.

Chloe triumphantly pumped her fist as she watched the croc's health drop another 10%. A small red droplet appearing by the health bar, which Chloe assumed meant that she had inflicted some kind of bleeding debuff.

She took one step toward the croc, rod forgotten, sword once again drawn, ready to go for the heart on the exposed belly…

But the croc was too fast. Again it came for her, teeth finding their mark around the armor on her waist. Chloe felt the teeth sink into the leather, the pressure of the jaw closing taking her breath away. She saw the start of white flowers bloom in her vision as the fishy stench of the croc's breath filled her nostrils.

Chloe cried out, struggling to raise her sword. In a desperate flash of inspiration, she muttered her incantation, performing the movements with one hand, and when small bolts of lightning appeared in her hand, she gently slapped the blade of her sword, focusing her willpower on making the bolts travel through it.

The sword exploded in a thousand bolts, the electricity contained within the length of the blade. Chloe's face smiled darkly in the glowing blue light as the croc's eyes widened, his teeth lost some of their pressure, and the sword found its way into the back of the croc's throat.

The beast's body went rigid as it throbbed with electricity. Chloe squeezed her eyes shut, prepared for the electricity to take the rest of her health as it traveled back up her body. To her surprise, the voltage stayed mostly within the blade.

Chloe was released, her body collapsing to the mud. She landed on her damaged leg and slumped backward, lying in the wet mud as she heard the dying gurgles of the croc.

She stayed there for a while, wanting to loot the crocs' bodies but not ready to make a move until some of her stamina had recovered. She watched the night sky as stars wheeled overhead and meteors flew across it. Eventually, she blinked her notifications up and smiled when she saw the current ones.

New spell acquired: Volt Shock (Lv 1)

Thunderbolts and lightning, very, very frightening! You can now summon the power of electricity to inflict damage upon your enemies. Find creative, unique ways of using this skill as you develop and grow.

Requirements: n x 30MP (where n is equal to the number of seconds taken to cast the spell)

Monster defeated: Bogland Crocodile (Lv 6)

+150 exp

Monster defeated: Bogland Crocodile (Lv 7)

+150 exp

You've unlocked a new skill: Dual wielding (Lv 2)

Many don't understand the diversity of battle styles that dual wielding has to offer. Some stumble across this by chance. Like you. You're a chancer, right? Now you can combine magic and the physical in battle. Boop!

Bonuses: +2 dexterity

You've unlocked a new (unique) skill: Experimental (Lv 1)

Your mind works in mysterious ways. In the heat of the moment, you choose to take the path less...well, never traveled. Continue working on this skill and your experiments will become more and more successful and less likely to backfire with each level gained.

Bonuses: +1 intelligence, +1 dexterity, +1 endurance, +1 etheric potential

Monster defeated: Mutant Bogland Crocodile (Lv 9)

+500 exp

Level increased! You are now level 9

Congratulations! Through fire and water, earth and air, you have gained enough experience to ascend to the next level.

+4 attribute points

(Attribute points must be assigned within 24 hours of gameplay. If unassigned after 24 hours, any remaining points will be randomly assigned.)

Chloe felt her body lift, hovering an inch or two off the floor. She felt warm, she glowed, and the pain in her leg and chest subsided almost instantly.

She smiled smugly, watching the stars and listening to the sounds of the forest creatures for just a moment longer.

CHAPTER TWENTY-ONE

Despite the ongoing struggle against the sticky mud of the bog, Chloe's smile stretched from ear to ear.

With her level 4 **Dark vision**, she was able to navigate a lot more smoothly than she could have imagined. Even in near darkness, she could see through the trees ahead, keeping an eye out for danger. The wisp floated in front, conveniently reappearing not long after the crocs had been taken care of.

Chloe had given the wisp a sharp talking to, but she wasn't sure that the floating orb understood her words. She had looted the crocs, inheriting 2x croc claws, 2x croc meat, and 1x mutant croc meat. That last item had come with a warning beside it, detailing that consumption of the item was at the player's own risk.

Chloe decided to pocket the item anyway and checked her available slots, pleasantly surprised to see that the items that came in multiples automatically stacked in one place.

Leather Satchel
Carry slots remaining: 10/16
Available Items
2x croc claws
1x fisherman's rod

2x croc meat

1x mutant croc meat.

1x rusty dagger

1x tiny stick

She had then closed the Inventory and glossed over her character sheet, nodding appreciatively at the collection of skills she had attained, and the increases that came with level 9 status. She remembered that her attributes had been locked until level 5 and wondered if there might be some kind of upgrade around level 10 that would make her life easier. KieraFreya, unsurprisingly, offered no additional help on the matter.

<u>Bio</u>

Character name: Chloe *(click to select a new character name)*

Level: 9

Class: Null

Race: Human

<u>Stats</u>

HP: 250/250

MP: 180/180

Stamina: 330/330

Active effects: Null

<u>Attributes</u>

Strength: 22 (+16)

Intelligence: 6 (+13)

Dexterity: 20 (+15)

Endurance: 25 (+16)

Etheric Potential: 9 (+14)

<u>Skills</u>

Languages: Human

Acrobatics: Lv 3

Armed Combat: Lv 1

Cooking: Lv 1

Crafting: Lv 1

Creature Identification: Lv 4

Dark Vision: Lv 4

Dual Wielding: Lv 2
Experimental: Lv 1
Fishing: Lv 1
Herb Identification: Lv 1
Sneak: Lv 3
Swimming: Lv 1
Reckless: Lv 3
<u>**Available Points:**</u> **4**

Musing over the available options, Chloe dumped 2 of her available points into intelligence, and the remaining 2 into etheric potential, anxious to make a quick decision before she once again got swept up in the game and forgot to assign them. There was still a long way to go to even out the imbalances from the system's stupid auto-assignment choices, but at least she was making *some* progress toward balancing her attributes.

Still, with a strength of 38 and an endurance of 41, she supposed there were worse problems she could have. At least she wasn't the same weakling who had managed to get herself killed by low-level goblins.

As the night wore on and the dark of the night began to lighten, the footing shifted from damp, squooshy bogland to firmer ground. After a while, Chloe noticed that the ground began to slope up and, looking back the way she had come, she realized that the slope's gradient was increasing.

The wisp led the way with not a single word. Even KieraFreya remained oddly silent on the journey. After another stretch of forest, Chloe began to feel light-headed. Her calves started to burn from the constant climbing. Rocks and boulders appeared around her, breaking up the dense foliage.

"Are we...nearly...there yet?" Chloe was panting, sweat trickling down her brow. She could feel the moisture beneath her armor and felt a little sorry for KieraFreya. The goddess could not feel pain, but could she feel and smell the sweat that was peppering Chloe's body?

Eventually, the trees gave way to a small clearing with an outcrop of rock that jutted out like a great shelf against the incline. Chloe climbed her way up and took a seat on the rock's edge, from there able to scan the vast forest and see how far she had come. A thin layer of morning haze hung lazily over the canopy, dappling the light from the pink and orange sunrise into a thousand magical shards.

Birds flew low over the canopy, occasionally disappearing into the leaves. Chloe listened to the caws and cries of the morning animals, her breath taken away by the view.

Things sure hadn't been like this at home. All her life, Chloe had been a city-dweller, born and raised with the weight of her parents' legacy on her. She had lived in several houses and moved to several luxury condos, and had always thought that she had loved city living. The bustling streets, the neon signs, the nightlife, people-watching from skyscrapers and several-dozen-story restaurants.

But now…

Now Chloe took a deep breath through her nose. The oxygen filled her lungs and gave her an energy she wasn't sure she had ever felt before. All of this in front of her—it was *alive*. It was magical. It was all natural. If she could take a snapshot in her head of what happiness was, she was sure this would be it.

After a quick bite of some cooked croc meat (courtesy of her **Purple Blaze** spell), Chloe picked the stray bits from her teeth and continued following the wisp up the rock face.

There were several ledges similar to the one she had sat on and enjoyed the view. Now the journey began to feel more perilous, with the gradient ever-increasing. A couple of times, as the wisp floated lazily up, Chloe was forced to use both her hands and feet to climb. Rocks came loose as she fought for purchase, and before she knew it, continuing to climb began to seem like an incredibly dangerous option to take.

The air was thinner up here, too. Chloe squinted after the wisp who, by now, was getting harder and harder to see. When she looked up, she saw the burning purples of the sky beginning to turn to blues.

"Where the hell is he taking us?" she mumbled to KieraFreya as she shinnied across a rather precarious ledge and found a safe spot to stand.

KieraFreya was slow to answer. "Why do you presume that it's a 'he?'"

"Oh, no. Not this again."

"I'm just saying, it shows your inherent sexism when you assign gender to non-gender-specific entities."

"Force of habit, okay?" Chloe retorted. "Where I come from, that's how people have spoken for years. Cars and boats are 'she,' guides and waiters are generally 'he' unless otherwise specified. That's just how it is."

"What's a car?"

"It doesn't matter."

KieraFreya scoffed. "Well, I guess that just shows how primitive your homeland is. We're pretty progressive here in Obsidian."

Chloe paused, staring at her bracers incredulously. "Progressive? The people here wipe their asses with leaves. I'm wearing *leather* armor. The entire patriarchal structure of the Oakston tribe is a laughable allegorical nod at what *my* civilization has spent centuries eradicating to allow men and women to have equal rights."

KieraFreya chewed on this. "You realize that using the Oakston *tribe* as your example of a base culture of Obsidian is entirely redundant? I'm sure you have dozens of colonies in your land that live in the way that Oakston does. And 'equal rights?' Pah! I refer you to my original point."

Chloe thought about that for a moment, then growled. She hated being proven wrong, and even more so by an enchanted piece of armor. She kept climbing, glad to see that her stamina had regained some of its points after the small rest.

"There really are other cities here?" Chloe asked, grunting as her latest handgrip crumbled and fell away. She stretched toward another.

"Of course. If you think Oakston is the epitome of living in Obsidian, you have yet to come across any of the great cities. Nauriel, Hammersworth, Killink View—the world is filled with civilization and culture. Just because you found yourself in the ass-end of nowhere, doesn't mean that this is all there is. You should widen your worldview, babe. You've barely scratched the surface."

Chloe imagined it now—fantastical cities like those she had seen in films. Great metropolises filled with many different cultures and races. She remembered that Blake used to spend *hours* in the cities of *Relic Hunter*, searching for quests, looting boxes, picking pockets, and acquiring items. It seemed like cities were the places to be if you wanted to level up fast.

Chloe pulled herself over a steep ledge, then rolled onto her back to catch her breath. "And how does someone find any of these cities? All I've seen so far are trees and rock. Oh, and a cave. Can't forget the cave."

When KieraFreya didn't respond, Chloe sat up, not quite believing just how far they'd climbed. She looked down at her wrist and said, "Hey? You still there?"

Her wrist raised by itself, turning her body and pointing Chloe toward where the wisp was hovering in front of a tall stone door. Ornate carvings decorated its front, detailing scenes of people, light, battles, and peace. At the zenith of the doorway was a modest carved statue of hands in prayer, a complex carved bracelet around the wrists.

Chloe stood up, mouth open in awe. She slowly moved closer, her tired feet dragging as she went. The wisp met her at the doorway, stopping just in front of her face.

"Just when I was beginning to doubt you." Chloe reached forward and tried to pat the orb, but her hand went straight through it. "Oops, sorry."

She advanced on the door, putting her hand against the cold rock. She pushed gently, but there was no movement. Another push, then a shove, and it wasn't long before Chloe was shoving against the door with her entire body weight, her shoulder against on the rock, then her back as her feet slipped and skidded on the ground.

"How the heck am I supposed to get in? You haven't brought us *all* this way just to have us fail at the last hurdle, have you?"

As if acknowledging her words, the orb floated over to a small basin Chloe hadn't even noticed. The bottom of the basin was dark, as if some deep-colored liquid had stained the bowl long ago.

Chloe looked at the orb for further explanation. Instead, the orb drifted into the bowl and spun around several times, then disappeared.

"Huh?"

Chloe pulled up her notifications, noticing an alert trying to get her attention.

Quest unlocked: Donate yourself for entry

You have reached the fabled "Seat of the World." Legend tells us that in order to gain entry, one must first donate a piece of themselves as a tribute to the gods.

Rewards: 50exp, entry to the Seat of the World

"The Seat of the World, huh?" Chloe mused. "Do you know anything about this place?"

Chloe waited for a response but garnered nothing from KieraFreya.

"Trust you to go silent when I need you." She sighed.

She ran a hand around the surface of the bowl, determining that the stain was clearly from long ago. She hunted for a lever or button of some kind and tried the door a few more times, then resigned herself to dealing with the basin.

"Well, we've come all this way." Chloe reached for her sword and ran the blade over her palm. She winced as the skin opened and blood dripped. She squeezed her fist tight, and several drops of blood fell into the bowl.

Chloe stepped back, ready for something dramatic to happen—for the doors to swing open of their own accord, or maybe a voice to call to her and guide her home.

When nothing happened, she scratched her head and wandered back to the basin.

"You know it's not blood they're asking for, right?" KieraFreya said, finally weighing in. "The quest said 'donate a piece of yourself.'"

"Yeah, so?"

"The gods require something bigger."

Chloe's skin went cold. "You don't mean..."

"Mmhmm," KieraFreya confirmed. "Chop-chop, Sweet Tits." She chuckled. "Excuse the pun."

Chloe stared back at the door, then, resolving herself, brought her sword to her hand. *A single digit wouldn't hurt, right? Just one finger. Would that be enough to please the gods?*

As she closed her eyes and prepared to slice, she heard the grating of stone on stone. She noticed that the blood from the basin had disappeared and now dark red lines of flowing liquid coursed around the etchings on the doorway, making the place come alive. The carved hands pulled apart with a deep grinding sound, and dust drifted to the floor. They rotated until the palms were outstretched, pointing toward the valley.

Then, as suddenly as it had started, it stopped.

Chloe stared into the darkness of the cave, heart pumping.

"You nearly had me chop off my finger," she growled, lips barely moving.

"I wanted to see how far you would go to complete my mission. Turns out, farther than most. I'm impressed. Now, chop-chop, little lady. You've got some goddess parts to find."

CHAPTER TWENTY-TWO

Demetri smiled into the darkened room, feeling calmer than a buddha in a health spa.

Working his ass off as a psychologist for years had taken its toll on the man. He spent day in and day out discussing people's problems and helping them come up with workable solutions. Add that to the volume of time and work required to balance the world-renowned Lagarde family and its odd private appointments, as well as serving his other clients, and Demetri had little room to manage his own life.

Sure, he made use of the Lagardes' facilities—the heated pool, the spa, the gym. He was even lucky enough to be able to write off most of his expenses through the family's accounts, so he made a fair living doing what he did. But did that really make up for companionship? Did that leave room for a social life?

Did that leave *any* room for love?

Demetri understood that love was an abstract concept; he was a scientist, after all. But he was also open to the notion that changes in bio- and neurochemistry created the base feelings and desires that many believed in as 'love.' Even so, that didn't stop the butterflies fluttering in his stomach. An aviary of feelings and emotions that hadn't surfaced in years now kept him awake as he watched her sleep beside him, eyelids fluttering on that beautiful alabaster face.

Demetri smiled and closed his eyes, remembering the warmth of her body on his. Remembering through a tipsy haze the taste of whiskey on her lips as they enjoyed a tipple while watching Chloe's adventures on screen.

That was the first time they had made love. Chloe had been scouring the small tribal village, the name of which escaped Demetri now, looking to increase her character's experience and skills. The villagers had mentioned something about being blessed, but he could hardly remember what that meant. He'd been too wrapped up in the softness of Mia's skin at the time. Her breath on his neck. Her legs around his waist.

And so it had been for every waking moment he could spare recently. Demetri's day consisted of meetings and sex, sex and meetings. Every spare moment was spent either thinking about Mia—the one who had gotten away—or being with her. They ate together, they slept together, they showered together. Hell, a couple of times Mia had popped out of her small apartment and met Demetri outside the Lagardes' condo, waiting on the ground level with a bag full of his favorite things.

Demetri rested his head on his arm and thought back to their days in high school. She had been just as pretty then. He had been even nerdier, his glasses often hanging off the end of his nose. They had spent a summer together at camp, growing close in the way teenagers do when they're away from the schoolyard and familiar things. He realized now that the entire social structure changed the minute the students were dumped into a new place.

That was what had triggered his interest in the human psyche, he supposed—watching the popular kids befriend the social outcasts after discovering they were bunkmates. Watching the pretty girls speak to the rejects as if they were just people. If it hadn't been for camp, Demetri never would have spoken to Mia in the first place.

Which also meant that Mia would never have broken his heart.

That was what cemented it for Demetri. It hadn't been so much the social changes and the observation of how much fun could be had outside the schoolyard as much as it had been the reinstatement of the hierarchy when summer ended and they returned to school.

The bullies found their red flags again. The nerds found their hideaways. Summer friendships were shattered in a moment, and camp romances soon dissolved.

All it took was one comment, one single callout from Julia Hendricks—Mia's best friend at the time—to say that single syllable that made teenagers cringe.

"*Oooooh!*" she had started when Demetri had waved at Mia by the water fountain.

His eyes met hers.

Her eyes met his.

He waved.

She turned her back.

Nothing to be done.

Now, though…

Now he watched her sleep, listening to her snores. Had it not been for the fact that Mia had approached him with the opportunity for Obsidian, would she be lying here now?

He doubted that very much.

Did he, at that particular moment, care at all?

Not one iota.

Water dripped from the ceiling to the floor, repetitive drops that produced their own music within the chamber.

The place was bigger than it should have been, a great dome of carved rock with patterns and sigils hewn into the walls. A large number of torches lined the round room in perfectly spaced increments, blazing with Chloe's purple fire and casting a mystic glow around the place.

In the center of the room was a large throne, also carved directly from the rock. The floor was covered with dust and webs, and the chamber echoed with every step Chloe took.

She stood before the throne, eyebrow cocked.

"It's a chair."

KieraFreya mumbled her agreement. "A big chair.

"A big chair carved from rock."

Chloe scanned the room, looking for any indication of what to do. The way into the chamber was nothing more than a long tunnel with smooth walls. There were no other entrances or exits that Chloe could see. There was simply a big chair and a plethora of images around her.

"Cool," she said quietly. "Only one thing to do, I suppose."

Chloe placed her foot on the first step and stopped.

"Wait," KieraFreya said, tugging Chloe's arm back

"Naw," Chloe soothed, patting her bracers. "Finally, you've grown a conscience. You *care* about me. How sweet. But you really don't need to worry. What's the worst that could happen?"

Another step, and KieraFreya tugged her harder. She stumbled down to the main level.

"What are you *doing*?"

"I just want you to be cautious," KieraFreya replied. "If something appears too easy, it's likely there's a reason. Didn't your parents ever teach you that?"

Chloe rifled through her memory bank. "There's always a catch?"

"Right."

"Well, I don't see any other option, and we've come this far, so..."

Another step.

Another tug.

Chloe slapped her forehead, sliding her hand down her face. "Look, if we die—"

"We end up back at that village, remember?" KieraFreya said more sharply now.

Chloe froze.

"That's where your last respawn was, *princess*," KieraFreya continued. "Remember? If you die here, you'll be forced back miles and miles through the woods, and you'll have to start your journey all over again. Is that what you want?"

Chloe considered the goddess' words. That was the *last* thing she wanted. Now that she felt as though she was actually making good progress toward some kind of goal, she definitely didn't want to be flung all the way back across the map.

"Fine. What do you suggest?"

KieraFreya considered the matter, and when no ideas struck her, she sighed. "Just...be careful."

"I always am." Chloe winked. "I have to admit, I like this side of you."

"Don't get used to it," KieraFreya growled.

This time when Chloe took the stairs, she moved more slowly. Her ears were pricked, her eyes scanning the room for danger. At the top, she investigated the seat, finding nothing but smooth stone, and climbed on top. She sat down, facing back toward the entrance...

And waited.

And waited.

And waited a little more.

"The Seat of the World, huh? More like the Seat of—"

Chloe's words were cut short as a blinding light exploded from the ceiling. It was as if a sunroof had opened and now allowed the daylight to flood the cave. Chloe shielded her eyes, trying her best to see what the source was, but couldn't hold focus without it being painful.

A great booming voice began to speak.

"O mortal one who has discovered and summoned the great channel of the gods, tell us, do you have your one request?"

Chloe's hair flew into her face, and her ears hurting from the volume of the voice. She felt a great presence around her suddenly, as though immense beings were speeding around the edges of her vision. She could sense clouds and hear curious chattering voices in the background, but most of all, the sheer *power* that overwhelmed her. For the most fleeting of seconds, she had the sensation that she was nothing more than a tiny insect in a land of dinosaurs.

"Forgive me, O great ones?" Chloe said sheepishly. "I'm afraid I don't understand what you ask of me? I am but a traveler looking for adventure in this realm."

"You mean to say that you have come unprepared for your bequeathing? Mortal, the gods do not hang around for indecisiveness, nor do we appear at will. As punishment for your insolence, our offer has been withdrawn, and a tag placed against your character as a time waster and a nuisance of the—"

"Oh, give it a rest, pea-brain!" KieraFreya called, rage in her voice that Chloe had never heard before. "You think you're *sooooo* high and mighty up there in your ivory tower!"

There was a moment of silence, during which the only things Chloe was aware of were the beings flying and swooping outside the light.

The voice returned, softer this time. *"KieraFreya? Is that you?"*

"In the flesh...kind of...you son-of-a-bitch! Why don't you cut this 'mortal' some slack and just allow her a minute to ask a friggin' question? Aren't you gods supposed to be all-loving and kind? Oh, wait, I forgot. That's to everyone except your family, right?"

Chloe stared down at her bracers in disbelief. *Had she really just said that to a god?* She supposed that since KieraFreya was a goddess, it might not have been as much of an issue. Still, the venom in every syllable was alarming.

"KieraFreya, I've waited so long to hear from you—"

"Save it, pube-beard. I don't want to hear it. Grant this bitch her request and let us get on our way. I don't want to tie up the line for any longer than I have to."

Another pause, this one heavier and much longer. Eventually, the voice said, *"As you wish."*

Chloe twiddled her thumbs, waiting for some kind of instruction. When none came, she said, "Oh. Er, okay. I need some help completing a quest and...well, I've got no—"

"It is done."

Chloe took a large inhalation of breath as the world went black. A second later, she was looking down at the landscape from the height of a bird, soaring through clouds, diving over mountains, sweeping across oceans. The images came in strobe flashes.

A thriving city with people. A great gray tower of marble penetrating the sky. A wide-open ocean strewn with great blocks of ice and snow. Lava spewing from the mouth of a volcano in a land ashen and black. A field of wildflowers falling down a well to the caverns below, walls glimmering like a thousand stars...

Image after image assaulted her almost physically. The light rimmed her vision. She felt KieraFreya's presence on her wrist. Felt the bracers vibrate as the next barrage of images came.

A breastplate shining gleaming with emeralds and gold. Gauntlets rotating and hovering in a shower of sparkles. A cuirass. A gardbrace. Greaves. The list went on and on, individual components of armor of the same ornate style as the ones that Chloe's wrists sported. Snow-capped mountains, caves, and volcanoes formed the backgrounds.

The vision turned. Now Chloe could see them all—the monsters of Obsidian. Flashes of enormous trolls, dragons, great beasts with many limbs, tentacles, leagues of fires, crypts, daggers, boobytraps, and more.

As suddenly as the visions came, the light vanished. Chloe dropped back onto the great throne, her ears ringing. The silence of the room was a stark contrast to what she had just experienced.

Chloe pulled a bracer up to her face, panting slightly. "A friend of yours?"

"I don't want to talk about it," KieraFreya croaked back.

Feeling like now might be a good time to hold back on teasing KieraFreya and respect her wishes, Chloe acknowledged her notifications and saw a pop-up that made her eyebrows raise.

"Huh?"

Map updated: Click to open

Chloe opened the map. She had expected to see the Oakston village appear in all its glory but instead found that she was staring at a large expanse of land primarily shaded in black. Thin gold detailing defined various different regions and lands, and in the lower west quadrant was a tiny area that was available for viewing.

Chloe focused on that area and the map zoomed in, revealing the Oakston village. She focused again and the map zoomed out.

Chloe gasped. "*Sweet!* This is the entire map of Obsidian from corner to corner."

She inspected the map slowly, able to view only the most basic information. She could see the small pyramid-like structures that detailed mountain ranges. There were thin strips that looked like they might be rivers or roads. Dotted around the map were little symbols of hands in prayer.

Chloe zoomed in on one such symbol, seeing the legend QUEST: A FALLEN GODDESS written in tiny letters above it.

Chloe brought a hand to her mouth, realization finally dawning on her. Considering she hadn't had a chance to finish her request to whatever god they had just spoken to, he had been spot-on in providing exactly what Chloe had been after.

"You realize what this means, right?" she said, clapping her hands excitedly.

Even KieraFreya seemed gratified. "We've got a starting point."

It was then that the earth began to shake and the rocks began to crumble.

CHAPTER TWENTY-THREE

"Oh, why can't we go just *one* journey without encountering any danger?" Chloe whined, searching all around for an escape route. Already the tunnel back to the outside had caved in.

"There!" KieraFreya pointed, indicating a small dark indentation where some rocks had come loose.

Chloe sprinted toward the hole, hands above her head for protection. She spat out dust, the particles stinging her eyes as she heard KieraFreya cry out above her.

Chloe stepped aside as a huge boulder fell, almost squashing her flat. She picked up her speed, then crouched and skidded across the floor, sliding smoothly into the hole just as the entrance was blocked, leaving them in complete darkness.

Rocks continued to tumble in the original room. They waited for a good while in the darkness before the last rock fell and all went still.

"Great plan, genius," KieraFreya quipped. "Now what?"

Chloe squinted with her **Dark Vision** but could hardly make out anything other than a tiny tunnel ahead of them. It was small enough that a person would have to crawl on their stomach to have any chance of making it through.

Chloe tested the rock blocking the entrance, but it didn't budge.

"Guess we go this way."

KieraFreya protested but Chloe ignored her, managing to get down on her stomach. She began crawling along the floor earthworm-style.

The tunnel stretched on for what seemed like miles. At some point, Chloe managed to tune KieraFreya out, continuing her painfully slow progress. Her stamina began to decline as she crawled, but she figured the tunnel must lead *somewhere*. Otherwise, what was the point of its existence?

Time stretched. The darkness cloaked them. The idea came into Chloe's head to try her **Purple Blaze** spell, but with her arms pinned by her sides, she found that there was no way to cast the spell so that she could see. She wasn't sure what the consequences would be for failing a cast, but she sure as hell didn't want to find out while she was shinnying through a tiny tunnel.

At one point along the way, a little while after KieraFreya finally seemed to grow tired of talking, Chloe hit a fork in the path. She paused and closed her eyes, taking a deep breath. A gentle stream of air was coming from somewhere, and, holding her face to the tunnels, she felt it kiss her right cheek.

Right it is!

As she manipulated her body, Chloe saw the notification blink. She pulled up the menu and saw a message from Gideon.

Hey, Chloe! How's it going? I bet you're out there kicking ass right now!

Me and the guys found the sickest dungeon. We managed to take down a small army of skeletons between us and got massive gains from it. Right now we're taking a quick break in the main chamber. I'm sitting on the skeleton overlord! Lol.

Anyway, thought I'd check in. Missing having you with us.

Do what you gotta do.

Gid

Chloe's heart warmed. She clicked Reply and stared for a good few minutes at the display, wondering how the hell typing worked in this game. She thought about a keyboard, but nothing came up. Then she got another message from Gideon.

Oh! And in case you were wondering, just talk to type. There are no instructions about that. Might be a bug that Praxis will iron out later.

Chloe rolled her eyes, making a mental note to mention that to Mia the next time she got a chance.

Hey Gid! Great to hear from you. This message function is pretty sweet. Can't believe I didn't discover this sooner, not that I had any friends to add. LOL!

Can't believe you're already conquering dungeons. You should check that book of spells for possession or resurrection spells and make the skellies fight for you. That'd be SA-WEET!

My journey is going well. Y'know, found a shrine, spoke to a god, yadda-yadda, now stuck in the world's smallest crawl space in the pitch-black.

Just another day in the life, eh?

Hit me back when you're out of the dungeon and keep me posted on your progress. If we ever end up nearby and you don't tell me and I find out, I will murder you.

(In real life, not the game. I know where you live.)

(Or do I?)

Chloe

Chloe blinked away the messaging screen and took a breather, allowing her stamina to regenerate some. She closed her eyes and let sleep take her, waking up a short while later, pleased to see that her stamina had worked its way back up to around 80%.

With a deep sigh, Chloe continued crawling.

It felt like the tunnel would never end. With each shuffle down the tunnel, she felt like she was being forced into the belly of the mountain. Her muscles ached, and her skin was getting sore. But eventually, feeling like the great poop of some forgotten beast, she slid out of the tunnel and plopped onto a cold stone floor.

Chloe groaned. "They should really work on making the rocks a lot softer in this game since they've got *real* players who feel *everything*."

"Soft rock." KieraFreya chuckled. "Good one."

Chloe rose to her feet, stretching and dusting herself off. It felt great to stand again. Several bones popped and cracked as she straightened herself out.

"Now to work out where the hell we are."

"What is this 'hell' place you keep talking about?" KieraFreya asked. "I'm assuming it's something bad?"

Chloe shook her head. She'd forgotten that idioms and places from her own world might not necessarily translate into Obsidian. She cast **Purple Blaze**, containing the spell in her hand as she lit up the cave and began walking.

"It's a bad place. Basically, many of my people believe that when you die, you can go one of two ways, depending on whether you've lived a good or a bad life. If you've been good, you go to live with God in heaven. If you've been bad, you spend your life with the Devil in hell."

"Only two gods? Life must be *super* simple for you."

"Kind of," Chloe replied, hissing as she watched her MP quickly fall as she maintained the spell. "There's a lot more to it than that."

"Do tell."

Chloe made a note of where she was heading and extinguished her purple ball, choosing to rely on her **Dark Vision** for the most part as she continued.

She explained to KieraFreya that there was more than one belief system in her world. She talked about Christianity and Buddhism, Judaism and Islam. She spoke mostly of her own experience with her Christian friends, and about how many in her world chose to determine their own morality and the basis of repentance. That there were some who lived evil lives with moral intentions, and others who lived with no morals but were actually kind of good.

When asked how many gods there were across all of the belief systems, Chloe shrugged.

"Dozens. Hundreds. I don't know."

KieraFreya laughed darkly. "Your world sounds stupid."

"Well, how many gods are there here?"

"You think I don't have better things to do than to keep count of the gods? There are a lot of us, but we vary in our strengths. We have gods of peace, love, music, war, retribution—of course, I had to get myself in there—and so on. Then there are those who serve the darker purposes. Death, ghosts, mischief, disease etc. Our dark ones serve in the realm of the Dark, and the former live in the realm of the Light."

"Sounds fascinating," Chloe said absentmindedly, spotting shafts of light up ahead. She jogged onward, careful not to go too fast over the damp floor for fear of slipping.

"Always nice to talk to you," KieraFreya grumbled.

"I'm sorry, but look…"

They were in an enormous cavern, the walls of which were so far apart that Chloe couldn't see them. The ceiling was high, only detectable by tracing the eye up one of the many stray beams of sunlight that stretched all the way to the floor, illuminating motes of dust and making them dance as though they were fireflies.

Chloe ran forward, pausing under a thick beam of light. She felt the warmth on her skin, only now realizing how far into her bones the cold and damp had sunk.

"What is this place?" Chloe brought up the map.

She found her tiny avatar on the map a short distance from where the map highlighted her last travel point. She considered traveling back for just a moment before shaking her head, wondering whether it was a real possibility now that the rocks had crumbled and blocked the room. What if she went there and found she was trapped forever in that room?

To her dismay, although she had felt as though she had been shinnying through that tunnel for ages, the cursor was not that far away. She had barely moved at all. And, of course, the map didn't show depth, so she had no idea just how far under the mountain she was.

Well, aside from the sunlight above. But even then, she couldn't be sure.

Chloe looked around the cave, not wanting to leave what little warmth there was. She saw the next column of light around 20 yards away and jogged over, pausing there to scan for anything else other than stalactites and stalagmites stretching and clawing to reach each other.

Another hop, skip, and jump to the next beam of light. Nothing.

After a few more of these, Chloe stopped, cocking her ear. Something was rumbling coming somewhere deep in the cave.

She made toward the sound, driven onward by her insatiable curiosity.

"Oh, sure," KieraFreya piped up. "Go straight *toward* the strange sounds you find in the middle of a mountain. Why would you consider going the other way if possible danger presented itself?"

"Shut up," Chloe hissed, ignoring the goddess' words, wanting to find out more.

Eventually, she reached the cave wall, finding a small passageway lined with cobwebs, seemingly undisturbed for years. Using her sword, she quietly slashed at the webbing, trying not to groan in disgust as the sticky threads tangled around her blade. A few times, she had to use her hands to shift some of the stray threads that would otherwise have found their way into her hair.

"Eww…" she whispered. The rumbling was louder now, and some of the webbing was sticking to her hair. "Man, how am I going to get this out without shampoo?"

"We have that here," KieraFreya quietly informed Chloe.

"Really?"

"Yeah. *Schampu*, the Goddess of Beauty."

"Huh?"

"I'm fucking with you. Keep your head in the game. We're almost there."

Chloe blinked open her messaging app.

"What are you *doing*?" KieraFreya hissed.

Chloe ignored her.

Yo! Gid!

Small note. Well, kind of a request. If you manage to find cleaning products on your travels, let me know. Got sticky white

stuff all over my hair and I'm not sure how I'm going to manage to get this all out.

Peace!

Chloe re-read the message, suddenly realizing the mistake she'd made by sending that particular wording to a *boy*.

Spiderwebs! I meant to add that the sticky white stuff is...oh, never mind.

KieraFreya *tsked*. "Real smooth."

"Armpit?"

A sigh. "No."

When Chloe reached the end of the spiderweb-infested tunnel, she cautiously poked her head around the corner. She was glad to see that there were several more shafts of light, but her heart fell when she saw that the walls of the tunnel ahead were lined from top to bottom in coffins both open and closed.

Some had their lids half-open, others had cracked after years of decay. There were a number of skeletons on display, laid to rest with hands on their chest and gold coins over their eyes. The rumbling was louder, and Chloe now recognized the tones and rhythm of snoring.

"What do you think it is?" she asked her bracers. "What kind of creature makes noise that loud when they snore?"

"Have you heard yourself when you sleep?"

"Not helpful."

"Not trying to be."

Chloe stepped out of the tunnel, aware that each footstep, despite her level 3 **Sneak** skill, made enough noise to reverberate down the passageway and back to her. She trod as lightly as possible, a sinking feeling in her stomach that she was now being watched. When she was in line with the first set of coffins, she was sure she heard cracking around her, but when she looked, all of the dead lay still.

Another few steps and she was in line with the second set of coffins. These ones were mainly open, with a pair of skeletons on either side. The gold of the coins glinted as she passed.

KieraFreya, can you hear me?

That question seems a bit redundant. You know we've spoken like this before, right?

Just checking. What's the value of a gold coin?

KieraFreya thought for a moment. *One gold piece is worth more than your life.*

Chloe stared at the two coins winking at her from the skeleton's eyes. *That valuable, huh?*

Chloe chewed her lip, fighting an inner battle. She wanted to find her way out of this stinking cave, but if she could make a couple of bucks along the way, surely that would help her later in the game. She thought about arriving in the first city she'd reach with several dozen gold coins, able to instantly buy housing, purchase the greatest weapons, and have great influence over the development of the city.

Perhaps she could deposit some of the coins in the local bank, or find a series of small businesses to fund and earn her interest so that she could further develop the city for good. Surely she had enough knowledge from her life in the real world to be able to work with the medieval attitudes of Obsidian?

Chloe shook her head, once again realizing that she had fallen into Lagarde mode. It was a strange feeling, really. Not once in the real world had she ever considered using her money wisely, investing and becoming a venture capitalist. What *was* it about this game that made her start to care?

Well, in for a penny, in for a—

Chloe reached out and nabbed the two coins. The skeleton's skull was dry. Flaky. A trail of dust was interrupted where her fingers had touched.

"Ew, ew, ew," Chloe muttered, rubbing the skeleton dust on her cuirass. She hesitated for a moment longer, studying the skeleton for any signs of movement.

When none came, Chloe breathed a sigh of relief.

Turning quickly on the spot, she tried to let out a small scream but found that her windpipe was restricted as she stared into the necrotic face of another skeleton.

Chloe's heart dropped as she watched several more skeletons rising from their beds, bones cracking and popping as they started toward her.

CHAPTER TWENTY-FOUR

Chloe learned very quickly that against the dead, fire was better than electricity.

"That... *That!*" Another fireball leaped from her hand, finding its mark on the rib cage of a skeleton.

All around her, she saw purple. The first few fireballs had helped Chloe escape the clutches of the dead that held her. Her sore neck throbbed as she rubbed the painful area, only to find that the hand was still attached.

"That wasn't what I meant when I said I needed a hand," Chloe muttered, summoning another ball and setting another skeleton ablaze.

The real shocker had come when Chloe had gone to cast a fireball, only to find another skeleton behind her. The arms had reached out from behind, grabbing her body and twisting her around at the same time she had thrown the ball.

The fireball had missed its target but found a great knot of webs on the higher reaches of the wall. Within seconds the flames had traveled up and down the passageway, meeting several ancient torches and finding a home as the torches lit. The fire continued to travel onward to a depth unknown.

Chloe ducked under another set of arms, her breath coming in short bursts, her face streaked with grime. She sprinted to the far wall, trying to perform a quick count. She made it to seven before she had to act again and found herself running up the passageway, following the trail of torches.

"All of this for a couple of gold coins. Now I know how Aladdin felt."

"An ex-boyfriend of yours?" KieraFreya asked.

"Forget it."

The passageway was long, the walls lined with even more of the coffins. Skeletons awoke as she passed, and the farther she ran, the more certain she was sure that she was hearing voices. Or, more specifically, *a* voice that echoed several times around the tunnel. It wasn't until she rounded a corner that she saw the source of the sound.

The passageway opened to a small room. Raised steps led to a dais where a hooded figure stood before a lectern, arms raised on either side as rhythmic words tumbled out of its mouth. A white glow shone around either hand as it leaned over the dusty pages of an ancient tome.

"Ahoy!" Chloe shouted, unsure of what else to do. The skeletons came up fast from behind.

"Ahoy?" What the hell are you, the captain of a ship?

The figure looked up, pulling back the folds of its hood to reveal a face so old and rotten that it took Chloe's breath away. She performed a quick **Creature Identification.**

Necrotic Black Mage (Level 15)

496 HP

Chloe exhaled, her shoulders slumping. Her MP was low, and her health had taken a hit. She also felt the effects of sprinting down the passageway since her stamina displayed that a hefty chunk was gone.

"Any ideas?" Chloe asked desperately.

"Throw fire at it? That seems to be the one arrow in your quiver."

Beep— "you."

The black mage's eyes locked with hers, and Chloe felt his power.

She focused on her own incantation, summoning another fireball between her hands, and launched it at him. Her heart dropping as the mage waved his arms and the fireball faded into nothing more than steam, rolling off a forcefield around him.

"Well, I guess it's back to good old armed combat," Chloe said, drawing her sword.

She charged at the mage, who merely leered back at her with its rotting jaw. The mage muttered some new words, hands turning to a putrid green. The next thing Chloe knew, the walls of the space were crumbling as bony arms punched through the rock and more skeletons crawled out.

Chloe sighed, not liking her chances here. She bent her will on using the last of her MP as she placed her palm flat against her sword and caused the blade to erupt into purple flames. She smiled with satisfaction, having been unsure that would work the same way the electricity had in the bog.

Chloe sized up her enemies now that the others from the tunnel had caught up. She was surrounded on all sides by the dead.

"Come at me, bro."

KieraFreya coughed. "Sexist."

"Shut up."

With a mighty roar, Chloe raised her sword and hacked at the first skeleton that came her way. She caught its neck at just the right angle, and the creature crumpled to the floor.

Keeping the momentum of her swing, she stood on the spot, stretched the sword out with both arms, and spun. The blade whirled around the room, leaving a bright trail of purple flames as the sword hit skeleton after skeleton. They came in waves, Chloe managing to take down several dozen before she became so dizzy that she had to stop.

The room whirled around her. She tried to steady herself and aim, but now found that every swing of her sword *just* missed its target. Stupidly her mind went to Gideon's message about his conquest with the dead. She imagined what it might be like if Gid, Ben, and Tag were here right now.

A smile played on her face.

That sure would be a lot more fun than this.

Chloe blinked, trying her best to fight the dizziness. Though she had made a dent in the skeleton population, there were still a dozen or so to defeat—not to mention the mage.

The mage!

The puppet master.

Surely that would be the trick to defeating the dead? The skeletons behind the wall hadn't risen until the mage had done...whatever the hell he had done.

Chloe dropped to the floor as several skeletons reached for her throat. Crawling as fast as possible, she ducked between their legs, emerging by the crumbled walls. Chest squeezed in, she skirted the confused skeletons and found her way to the dais, secretly pleased that the hooded mage hadn't changed his focus and that she was now out of sight behind the folds of his hood.

Chloe took a steadying breath, held her sword aloft, and lunged at the mage. Her teeth bared, she gave a great scream as she envisioned the sword plunging through the robes and into the mage's back.

She was just inches away when she suddenly froze in mid-air. The mage reached glowing hands up and lowered its hood again, neck turning a semicircle on its spinal column, eyes bright with etheric power.

"Er, call it a truce?" Chloe chuckled nervously.

Without another word, the mage flung his hands at Chloe, and the full blast of his power hit somewhere in the region of her stomach as she was forced back into the wall.

Chloe raised a pounding head, staring into the glowing eyes of the mage. There was pain somewhere deep inside her, and her sword fell limply to her side.

The mage advanced, hands raised. The remaining skeletons also came at her. She was surrounded on all sides—

—except one...

Chloe managed to pull herself to shaky feet. She psyched herself up, preparing for the run, ready to make a dash through the gap and dodge around the skellies. Surely if she just headed back the way she had come, she could find another way out? She could outlast them all. Hide. Find a way to heal herself before they found her again. She'd made it out of stickier situations than this, surely?

It was at that moment that Chloe spotted the small message icon in the corner of her sight. A small note from Gideon just waiting to be opened by her. She felt that familiar warmth grow inside her as she thought of her comrades, imagining what it would be like if they were with her now. Tag bowling the skellies over like ninepins and firing arrows to distract the mage from afar. Gideon caught in the midst of battle, hands glowing, giving the black mage a run for his money.

It would be a different story right now. It would be a *whole* lot different. The skellies' numbers would shrink, the mage would be toast, and they'd all be laughing as they healed each other's wounds, looted the corpses, and found whatever treasure remained.

Chloe knew what to do then. It was all so clear and simple. Obsidian, this…game, was built around leveling up and teamwork. It was designed around multiplayer adventure, and here she was trying to take on the world on her own. She had always felt lonely. Always been the odd one out. Even around her deliciously beautiful and shallow friends, Chloe had never quite fit in, which was something her family had made a point of highlighting whenever they could.

The mage advanced on Chloe, the gap closing.

Chloe wanted her friends there now. *Needed* them. It was all so clear. If she was to stand any chance of making her way through this game and fulfilling the legendary quest on which she had been sent, she needed to work with others. She would have to admit defeat and ask for help to get through the tougher times this game would offer.

But how to find them now? They had gone off on their own adventure. They had set off from Oakston and—

Chloe stared up at the ceiling and exhaled. If there was any way to work her way back to them, this was likely going to be it. She wouldn't find them by hiding. She wouldn't find them by running away from danger. There was only one way to get back, and as risky as it was, it was the only option Chloe could see.

Gritting her teeth and preparing for the worse, Chloe stared into the glowing eyes of the mage. She lowered her head and charged into the throng of skeletons, making her way toward him. Her battle cries echoed around the room.

When Chloe was just a few feet away, the mage's hands pulsed once more. He lifted Chloe and threw her against the wall a final time, taking the last of Chloe's health as her lifeless body fell to the floor.

Wup-wup. You're dead.

Congratulations. You tried to brave the big, dark world of Obsidian alone. Few solo travelers fare well there or chance taking on dungeons by their lonesome, but you? Well, look what just happened.

-50n experience (where n equals your character's level)

-1/2 your equipment

Time to respawn: 2 hours

CHAPTER TWENTY-FIVE

Demetri was already awake when he heard the soft notification from the TV screen in the other room.

He hesitated before rising, his arm trapped under the crook of Mia's neck. Her skin was soft, and her chest was slowly rising and falling in the moonlight. He considered waking her, then thought better of it, admiring how peaceful she looked when she was asleep, sleeping being something she rarely seemed to do.

In the short time since they had reconnected, Mia had always been awake by the time he got home and was nearly always up before he had thought of rising. She didn't have the zeal of an insomniac, but she certainly seemed to prefer sleeping when the rest of the apartment was quiet.

And since Chloe was getting along so well in the game, there had been little to interrupt them as they laughed, cuddled, kissed, and reminisced over the lost decades.

In fact, Chloe had been getting along *so* well in the game—according to Mia, anyway—that Demetri had had few worries over the last several days. His time was spent with his clients, then with Mia whenever he could get away.

At first, he had been concerned for Chloe's welfare, the experimental game seeming to be a lot tougher than anything he'd seen before. But now that she had friends and was spending time grinding in the village, there was little concern. She was glowing, her mind working hard to overcome the trials of her former life. When they went into her pod for preventive maintenance, her real body was smiling as her eyelids flickered as though she were in a deep sleep.

Which he supposed she was.

Wheedling his arm out, Mia shifting at the disturbance, Demetri crept into the apartment's living room and took a seat in front of the TV. The screen hurt his eyes—bright white light in a dark room—and it took him a few seconds to adjust.

"Chloe!" he said in a hushed whisper, the phone pinned between his chin and shoulder. "What brings you back to the land of the living?"

"You're kidding, right?" Chloe replied, an incredulous look on her face. He watched her on the screen, reclining in that chair, feet on the desk as usual.

It was strange speaking to Chloe through the TV when he knew her body was just a few feet away in the other room.

"No?"

"You mean you didn't just watch me get blasted by a mage and mauled by skellies?"

Demetri picked up a candy bar and undid the wrapper, shoving the candy into his mouth whole. "What's a skelly?"

Chloe explained her entire situation in the room, Demetri's eyebrows going up as she gave specific detail on the skeletons and their decaying appearance, his nose crinkling as she described their smell.

"Sounds gross," he replied. "How far is that dungeon from the village, then? Oaks...ville?"

"You mean 'Oakston,' Doc. I haven't been in the village in over a day or so. They booted me out."

"Why? They *loved* you? They called you 'the blessed!'" Demetri wracked his brain, remembering Mia's recounting of what was happening in the game. The last he could remember, she had been in that strange room with the villagers gathered around her.

"Loved me? Eventually, they did." Chloe scoffed. "I'll still never forgive them for killing me. Not really."

Something in Demetri's tone must have alerted Chloe because she added, "Doc, they stabbed me in the gut to test whether I was telling the truth about who I was. I died and came back to this room. Had a chat with Mia. She gave me advice about searching for shrines or holy places to start on my quest properly. Didn't she tell you?"

Demetri wracked his brain, trying to remember any nugget of information he might have missed. Maybe Mia had told him, and he had just forgotten. She must have done so. Surely somewhere between their daily bedroom tumbles (well, it wasn't always in the bedroom), she must have mentioned something about Chloe suffering another death and them talking one on one.

Demetri screwed his eyes shut, silent on the line. Try as he might, there was nothing. A small prickle of doubt appeared in the back of his mind. Surely if she *had* told him, he would have remembered. Chloe was the daughter of his biggest client. Hugo and Helen Lagarde had trusted Demetri with their daughter's life and well-being. He would have remembered something like that.

Which begged the question, why the hell hadn't she?

"Doc? You there?"

Demetri started. "Yeah, sorry. It's late here, and I'm not quite awake."

"Everything all right with you two?" Chloe asked.

"Fine. I've just remembered, she did tell me. Yes."

"Doc?"

Demetri brightened his voice, talking a bit too loudly. "Yes, nothing to worry about. Just keep focusing on yourself for now. In the best way possible, it's been nice that we haven't talked as much lately. You've had quite a run over the last few days." He heard Mia shuffling in the other room and lowered his voice again. "Am I right in thinking the treatment is working?"

Chloe hesitated before responding, her image on the screen

displaying one eyebrow raised. She chewed over the question, then fell into discussion with Demetri about how alive she felt (well, not technically at that moment after dying). About how real and beautiful the world was, and how for the first time ever, she felt truly *free*.

"Seriously, if you're not careful, I'm never coming back." She laughed, hearing the timer announce she had one hour to go until re-immersion.

"Oh, you'll be coming back. It's more than my job's worth for you to remain immersed in that...game." Demetri laughed.

Chloe rested her head on the back of the chair. Demetri followed suit. It was nice catching up with Chloe, talking like old friends. He had always had a soft spot for her over the other Lagarde kids, and now that they were spending time together outside his professional practice room, he found that he could relax around her. She was fun, lively, and honest.

They continued chatting right up until the timer announced Chloe's departure back into the game. Over the last few minutes, Chloe had asked once more: "Doc, are you sure everything's all right with you?"

Demetri's lips tightened. He half-turned his head as the first sign of dawn appearing through the slatted blinds of the apartment. He had served as a professional in psychology for nearly two decades, detecting when others had problems and ironing them out using common sense and an objective lens. Now...

Was he allowing himself to do the exact thing he'd silently judged others for doing so many times over the years?

"Everything's fine," he said dryly. "Just concentrate on yourself, Chloe. I'm rooting for you."

He watched a flicker of concern wash once more over Chloe's face before she nodded and said her goodbyes. The screen flashed bright white, announcing her departure back into Obsidian.

Demetri placed the receiver down, leaned his head back again, and closed his eyes.

He was unaware of Mia standing silently in the doorway behind him with a mournful expression on her face.

CHAPTER TWENTY-SIX

Chloe had prepared for the worst, wondering if she would find herself back at the top of the mountain by the shrine. Having no idea what the difference between a fast travel point and a re-spawn point was, she had taken a hell of a risk choosing death over survival, but when she opened her eyes and saw several dozen shocked faces staring at her, she breathed a sigh of relief.

Ignoring the flummoxed faces, she patted herself down, rolling her eyes as she noticed that… Yep, once again, the top half of her clothing had been confiscated as part of the punishment for dying.

"Seriously?" She sighed. At least she was proud of what she was sporting.

Realizing that the message had read that half her items would be claimed, she opened her inventory, discovering that her rusty sword, croc meat, and—

"No! Not my tiny stick!"

True enough, Chloe's first Obsidian weapon was missing. At first, she had thought she was joking as she yelled her disdain, but she realized there was a hint of real sadness there. Although the stick had been next to useless, it had reminded her of where she had started in the game—a mental checkpoint to show her how far she had come.

Still, at least you have your coin, KieraFreya said in her mind as Chloe saw with mild delight that half the coins she had stolen from the skellies were still in her possession.

Chloe rubbed a hand over her face, stared once more at her own deliciously firm and fake game breasts, then resolved to sort out adequate protection. She looked around at the unsettled faces, suddenly remembering that her welcome had been worn out at this village.

"Maybe you shouldn't stick a respawn point in the center of your town if you don't want blessed suddenly appearing out of nowhere," she told them.

Spinning on her heels, Chloe resolved to find a quiet place to collect her thoughts and plan how to get new clothes to cover herself.

But not before she pulled up her menu and checked her messages from Gideon.

Wow...did not expect to open a message like that right now!

Just logged back in. Mom's going haywire over how much time I'm spending in-game and having a fit over the fact that bro funded it all.

Found a butt-ton more bugs in this game. We really need to patch together some kind of report to send back to Praxis, but I can't find the option to send stuff anywhere. If they're reading this now, then:

CAN YOU MAKE IT SO ENEMIES DON'T ATTACK WHEN WE'RE LOGGED OFF?

I get needing to find safe spaces just like in the real world, but seriously, I've got so many bug bites that I look like I've got poison oak. It's itchy as...

Anyway. Found no cleaning products in the mountains, but you should definitely watch out for those spiders. They get real... excited when they see women!

Hope you cleared your dungeon.

Gid

PS Say hi to KF for me ;)

Chloe couldn't help but smile as she read his words. She stared a little too long at the postscript, wondering who KF was until she heard KieraFreya tell her to keep walking into cover. Then it made sense.

Chloe hit Reply, hoping her message would help her achieve what she was looking for somehow.

Chloe made her way around the village as stealthily as she could. It was a strange feeling, having felt so welcome in this village before and then watching as the town waved her and her friends back into the forest.

Now, as Chloe snuck around, dodging behind huts and blending into the darkness, she wondered what would happen if Mantari or Mukkah discovered she was back in the village. Surely word of her return would have spread. Would they welcome her back with open arms? Provide her with more equipment?

Or would they nudge her back into the wilds without another thought?

Chloe weighed the two options. In the real world, she imagined they would be kind, welcoming, and open. But given Chloe's experience of NPCs so far in this game, they were unpredictable, turning on a dime and changing their stances. If there was one thing she'd learned thus far, it was not to trust everything she saw and believed. The last thing she wanted to do was get booted out by the leaders before she had a chance to cover up properly.

Not only that, but with every exaggerated effort to duck out of the way of passing tribespeople, Chloe felt the experience boost hit her **Sneak** skill.

Skill increased: Sneak (Lv 4)

Whether hiding from friend or foe, you're becoming one with the shadows. Keep hopping across darkness puddles, and soon you're sure to be as invisible as...well, an invisible person.

Bonuses: +4 dexterity

(NOTE: Increases in skill override any previous bonuses gained

from the skill).

Chloe silently pumped her fist, quickly ducking behind a stack of boxes as a woman carrying a vase filled with water on her head turned her way.

She blinked a few times, then stole across the street, waiting for a moment when the foot traffic dissipated. It was growing dark now, the shadows stretching across the ground. Chloe used this to her advantage, slipping quietly around the last hut and starting when she found the entrance to the weaver's hut.

A stocky woman with a stern face Chloe recognized from her days spent learning to whittle and craft sat cross-legged, sewing fabric together as she quietly hummed to herself. There was a small fire, and the edges of the hut were surrounded by boxes and lengths of cloth.

Chloe contemplated sneaking around the boxes and just finding some clothing for herself, the idea of just taking what she wanted and disappearing a little bit tempting.

After studying the woman for a little bit longer, she realized that was something she could not do. They had been good to her not so long ago. She owed them that at least—to be fair and offer coin for their services.

Chloe's form appeared from the shadows. She stood, waiting a long moment before realizing that the woman was so focused on her work that she hadn't noticed.

Chloe coughed.

The woman looked up, her eyes widening as she saw who was standing in front of her.

"You? The blessed one has returned?"

Chloe nodded.

The woman took a deep breath, held her head up, and screamed. *"The blessed one has—"*

Her voice cut off as, guided by KieraFreya, Chloe's arms wrapped around the woman's head. Her bracers covered the woman's mouth as she struggled beneath her.

How come every time I try to be civil to these people you end up attacking them? she asked in her thoughts.

Because you're never willing to do the things that will help you survive in this world.

Chloe considered this, shushing the woman as she stopped struggling and stared up at her with scared eyes.

"Please," Chloe urged. "Despite...this, I'm not here to make trouble. Look, if I lower my arms, will you *promise* not to cry out again?"

The woman nodded.

Cautiously, Chloe removed her hands from the woman's face. The woman took a deep breath, and Chloe was certain that another scream would follow. Instead, she waited patiently, watching Chloe blankly.

"Thank you," Chloe said softly. "I realize how this may look, but I'm really not here to cause trouble. The truth is that I...well, I died and found my way back here. There's literally nothing I could have done about it, but now, as you can see, I have something of a problem."

Chloe waited for the woman to act in the way any sane person might in the real world. For the eyes to hook down to her exposed breasts, all thought gone as the blood traveled from the brain to the southern regions of sexy-time land.

Instead, the woman studied Chloe with a quick flicker of recognition.

Of course, idiot, Chloe chided herself, seeing the woman's own exposed body. *That's just the norm here.*

Chloe shook her head. "Anyway, if you could please just sell me something to wear on my top half that might also offer some kind of protection, I'd be most grateful."

The woman continued to stare.

"I have coin." Chloe pulled several gleaming gold coins out of her satchel.

And there it was. The woman's eyes grew so wide that Chloe was certain her eyeballs might pop out and start rolling on the floor. A second later, Chloe received a message.

Junita has offered you a trade!
Accept: Y/N

Chloe hit Y and a window popped up, not dissimilar to her own inventory window except the left half housed a list of Junita's items and the right half was her sad excuse for stock.

Chloe perused the items while Junita waited patiently. She had an interesting selection. Tunics, jackets, cuirasses, gloves, trousers, and more. Nothing of the quality or protection level that Chloe's Oakston leather cuirass had offered, but she knew the risk she had taken by forcing her death.

Chloe purchased a cotton tunic and a leather waistcoat that boasted additional pocket slots. She wasn't sure what she'd use these for but figured they might come in handy to stick her small dagger or other items she might need to reach for in an instant.

She also purchased a waterskin and a pouch of dried berries, the sight of which reminded Chloe that there was a chance she might not get a warm meal from the town tonight.

When she was finished, she blinked away the trade menu and handed over two of her eight gold coins.

Junita's breath caught, her hands unable to lift to accept the payment.

"What's the matter?" Chloe said, studying the coins in her hand. "Oh! Sorry, too much? Here."

She took Junita's hands in hers and pried them open, dropping one gold coin into her palm and closing them tight.

"Keep the change."

Junita nodded enthusiastically. Chloe was sure she didn't stop for a long while after she ducked out of the hut and melted back into the darkness.

Chloe edged along the borders of the village, passing few tribespeople along her way. At one point, she saw Mantari through a gap between buildings, standing by an open fire and having a desperate discussion with two of the chief's sentries. The beast of a man searching around, his eyes finding hers for a second.

Chloe dissolved back into shadow and headed toward her next destination. She had one more person she wanted to pay a visit to before she set off on the road once more.

CHAPTER TWENTY-SEVEN

The forest was deadly quiet as Chloe approached the shaman's hut. It was as if, just in stepping over the borders where the trees gave the house peace, her head had submerged underwater and now all that she was aware of was her own breathing.

Not a single light was on inside the house, though Chloe now knew that that didn't mean anything. The shaman's house was a maze of trickery and deceit, a bona fide house of mirrors. Sure, it might look abandoned and empty on to the casual observer, but Chloe's stomach tossed as she remembered the queasy feeling of falling through the portal she had experienced the last time she was here.

The door was unlocked.

Of course, it was.

Chloe took a deep breath, preparing for whatever test the shaman had concocted this time. Another poison flower attack? How about some quicksand? Perhaps even the possibility that she was walking into a sentient house that spurted stomach juices through the doors and digested her without chewing?

Chloe stepped inside. The minute the door closed, the walls melted away, the filth on the floor making way for that same familiar white she had experienced before. The light was so blinding that it was hard to believe it was the middle of the night.

In the center of the room, the shaman sat. He was cross-legged once more, puffing on that familiar hookah.

"It's not often that I get repeat custom," he crooned, voice as silky and soft as the purple smoke that ribboned from his mouth.

"I'm not surprised. My last visit left me almost staining this floor with my vomit."

The shaman grinned. Chloe realized that he was floating an inch or two off the floor.

"You're floating?"

"Everyone can float," the shaman replied.

"Not really."

"Floating is nothing more than an illusion of the mind, a state of perception that results from your own biases and experiences clouding your vision. What you perceive as floating, I know to be sitting comfortably on the ground, deep in my thoughts."

Chloe studied the shaman suspiciously, dropping to the ground so she could get a better look. Sure enough, she could see straight through to the other side of the room.

"You *are* floating."

The shaman chuckled. "Or is that *you?*"

Run, KieraFreya thought. *The dude's bat-shit crazy. Get out of here while you can!*

Chloe snorted derisively and looked down, her face falling as she realized that she too was now cross-legged and floating several feet off the floor.

"Argh! Put me down," she complained.

Chloe felt the ground meet her ass as she smacked into the floor. She bent her back and reached behind, rubbing her backside. "What did you do that for?"

But the shaman wasn't there anymore. Now when he spoke, Chloe heard his words inside her head.

You got what you asked for. Isn't that what you are hoping for here? For me to grant you the boons you seek?

"I mean, yes, but that hurt," Chloe complained.

Not all requests result in positive feelings. Some require the injection of punishment and pain to create the action one desires.

KieraFreya snorted. *Get a load of this guy. Smokes the special herb and suddenly thinks he's a prophet. Come on, Chloe. Get out of here before he poisons you again or sends you on a kamikaze mission.*

What do you mean? Chloe thought.

Who do you think made the shrine crumble after we were granted the map? Don't you think it's a little suspect that a hermit out in the middle of the woods, shunned by the townsfolk, sends you on a trip to a shrine through a croc-infested bogland and when we finally reach our goal, the rocks topple and get us lost and stuck in an ancient passageway?

Oh, come on, "hermit" is a bit too far. I like to think of myself as a social pariah.

Silence followed. Chloe's spine chilled. "You can hear her?"

The shaman reappeared, once more sitting upside-down on the ceiling. Chloe prepared herself for another fall to the floor, but this time, he floated down to meet her. "I hear a great many things. Many don't tune their ears to the calls and whispers of the ancient world, but when one sees a girl at your level with armor like *that*, it is obvious to those who are aware that there is great magic here."

Chloe wasn't sure how to take that. She had been so *careful* not to let anyone know about the goddess within her armor, but here a shaman had just *known*. If that was the case, what was the likelihood other people throughout her journey would discover the truth of what she was searching for?

"Don't overthink it, child," he reassured Chloe. "Your secret will be kept from the world around you...for now."

Chloe took the offered hookah and inhaled deeply.

The world spun beneath her. She was floating now. *Really* floating, the soft plushness of a purple cloud under her as she stared up at the backlit figure of a woman who stood at least twenty feet tall. There was a bright light behind her, and her ponytail blew triumphantly in the breeze.

Chloe gasped as the figure came into clarity. She was staring at herself as she was now. Emerald and gold bracers, tunic and waist-coat. Although, the longer she stared, the more the image changed. Pieces of armor appeared as if from the mist like jigsaw pieces clicking their way onto her body.

"As your journey continues, your strength will grow," the shaman's voice boomed from nowhere at all. "Each piece of armor will bring with it talents and skills straight from the gods. Two, then three, then four, and you will be well on your way to protection and strength unknown by anyone here in Obsidian. You will find a great many friends and citizens prepared to follow you. You will make a great many enemies."

Chloe watched in awe as more pieces clicked onto the giant. Gauntlets, greaves, the breastplate, all gleaming and decorated with ornate markings that sparkled and glowed with a powerful aura.

"With this great power will come great danger as you learn to wield and harness the powers of the goddess you have inherited."

Chloe glanced at her bracers, expecting some kind of quip or retort from KieraFreya. When nothing came, she saw something move out of the corner of her eye.

A small distance away, the clouds beneath her blacker than the deepest shadows, a woman sat in chains, mouth covered with a black bandana. Chloe wasn't sure how she knew, but she called her name almost involuntarily, panic rising in her: "KieraFreya?"

"She cannot hear you right now. She cannot speak. Heed this warning, child, for it will serve you well to learn caution along your journey."

The bandana multiplied, a segment of the cloth tearing off and flying through the air like an eel. It found its way beneath the giant Chloe's clothes and snaked its way around her mouth, neatly tying itself into a knot behind her head.

"You have greatness locked within you, Chloe. Great strength and power that could wield the truest strengths of Obsidian." The shaman's voice turned dark. "Do not let the voice of retribution cloud the good inside you."

Chloe turned once more to look for KieraFreya, but she was gone.

She studied the giant version of herself who was standing as triumphant as a champion on Olympus. Then she heard a click, and the vision dissolved.

When Chloe opened her eyes, she was sitting on the tangles and vines that populated the facade of the shaman's hut. Her head was covered in sweat. She stood up sharply, wobbled slightly from the head rush, and tapped her bracers. "Kiera? KieraFreya?"

"Hey! What the hell?" came KieraFreya's response.

Chloe smiled, her heart still beating double-time. "Nothing. It's nothing." She looked around the room. "Where did the shaman go?"

KieraFreya moved Chloe's hand, pointing to the corner of the room where a wisp floated lazily. Chloe approached the ball of light, reaching out to touch it.

The wisp flew behind her, erupting into light as the shape of the shaman appeared once more.

Chloe gasped. "It was *you*? The wisp was you?"

The shaman laughed, a strange sound like fingers dragging over gravel. "Indeed. Help can take many forms in this world. It honored me to be able to accompany a fine adventurer on her road to greater things." The shaman's smile faded as he turned to the window. "You came to me to ask me to perform a magic that is greater than you know. Is this not true?"

Chloe blinked stupidly, the remnants of the shaman's vision still very clear in her mind. His words sizzled in her thoughts as she wondered what he had meant by them.

"Come on, girl. We haven't got all night," KieraFreya said, losing all pretense of keeping quiet now that she knew of the shaman's awareness of her.

Chloe nodded. "I wanted to know if there was a fast way to reunite with my friends Gideon, Ben, and Tag. They may have journeyed far already. What their destination is, I do not know. I only know they are alive and navigating the dungeons somewhere in the surrounding hills."

"This will take strong magic," the shaman said. "And I see that you are a pupil of the etheric arts yourself now. Tell me, would you be willing to learn the ways of the shaman in exchange for a small request?"

Don't trust him—

"Shut up," Chloe interjected, holding her hand out to the shaman. "Not you. I mean Her. You're fine. What do you ask in return?"

"To accompany you once more on your travels. I have spent a good portion of my years on the outskirts of this village, waiting for a blessed one such as yourself to roam the world with. There are great magicks to be learned, far beyond my capabilities, and it is these I seek to embrace."

"Join us in our company? Is that really all I have to do?"

The shaman nodded. "I will accompany you as far as I wish. It may not be far at all, it may be to the ends of the universe. I will adopt wisp form, and you will speak of me to no one. Those are my only terms."

Chloe's heart sank. *Another* secret to carry? What with her enchanted armor and a wisp floating around her all the time, what would people think? *Could* she keep her silence on both of those fronts, juggling responsibility for two people?

Chloe let out a breath. "And in return, you will grant me my wish?"

"I will reunite you with your friends, yes."

The deal was a no-brainer. Without outside help, there was no telling how long it would take to find the others. What if they'd located a new respawn point out in the wilds already? Would they ever make their way back to Oakston to find her? Probably not. If it meant having a tag-along as Chloe went on her journey, surely there were far worse things that could happen.

And besides, what harm would it do to have an extra (competent) magic user around, someone who could teach her and advise along the way?

Shaman Decaru has asked to join your party.

Accept: Y/N

Chloe sighed, selected Y, and shook the shaman's hand.

KieraFreya grumbled, "I don't trust him."

Sure, Chloe thought. *Just don't ask what he thinks about you.*

CHAPTER TWENTY-EIGHT

Chloe poked her head around the hut. Torches cast ghostly glows, making the shadows of the tribespeople dance and sway.

There were a lot more of them now. Mantari's figure was a foot taller than the rest of them as small groups of two and three reported back and were sent on their way again. Chloe couldn't help but feel a small note of hurt at how hard they were looking for her. What did they plan to do if they found her again?

When *they find you again*, KieraFreya offered.

For they surely would. This plan was ludicrous.

Chloe felt the presence of the shaman around them but could no longer see any sign of the strange man or the wisp. The bright white orb would have brought way too much attention to them, so Chloe had somehow agreed that the shaman would be tucked away in her satchel.

Another bug to report, Chloe had mused, looking at the disruption and distortion of cells and blocks as the space that held the wisp displayed a series of lines of error code that ran into the blocks around it. She wondered at that point if she would be able to pull the wisp back out, or if it was now imprisoned in unhealthy lines of zeroes and ones until someone had the wherewithal to fix it.

Chloe crept forward, going as far as she dared toward the bundle of bodies in the center of town. Behind them, Chloe could see a strange collection of sacks and bags piled high. A little closer and she saw the respawn point, stars etched into the ground. Her target. Their mark.

The growl of some creature rang in the distance, and several of the tribespeople drew their weapons and disappeared. Mantari clucked instructions to others, who headed in the opposite direction.

Now was her chance.

Moving swiftly, Chloe hopped across the shadows and moved toward a closer building. Another round of maneuvers and she was within sprinting distance. Just there, behind Mantari's back.

Chloe took a series of steadying breaths, remembering the shaman's plan.

Okay, here we go...

Chloe tore open her satchel and the wisp launched out. Like a whirlwind, the orb whipped in a wide circle around the respawn point, snatching the light from the torches and plunging the towns-people into darkness.

Taking advantage of the cover, Chloe charged over to the respawn point, crouching. She heard cries of alarm as figures rushed into the clearing. Mantari's silhouetted figure whirled about, following the blazing trail of white light.

"Now!" Chloe shouted, and the wisp tore back toward her and embedded itself in the ground. The light was bright beneath her, and Mantari's face melted from anger to fear to disbelief.

"Chloe? You have returned?"

He sounded almost...happy. Relieved, even. Chloe hadn't been sure of what to expect when she made her presence known, but she should have believed that Mantari would be pleased. His smile lit up his face, if only for a second, before it clouded with worry.

"Chloe? What is happening to you?"

The star shone in bright whites and blues, pulsing in light that looked like flames. Chloe felt herself being pulled out of this reality, although now that she had seen Mantari and the others, she wanted a moment to explain herself. To clear up what was happening.

"I wasn't sure I was welcome anymore," Chloe shouted as the flames began to take her. "You sent us on our way. Told us we were taking your resources."

Mantari laughed, head shaking. "You are more than welcome whenever you like, Blessed Chloe. Just, your fat little friend can no longer eat us out of house and home."

Tears pricked Chloe's cheeks as the heat of the flames lifted. The wisp began to chant unspeakable words into the dirt. She could even hear KieraFreya grimacing from the power of it all.

Mantari reached forward.

"No!" Chloe shouted. "This is what I want. This is the way I have to go."

"To go where?"

Chloe thought about that, struggling to arrange her thoughts as the pressure built. "Nowhere. Home. It's one and the same. You can call off your men now. We'll be gone soon."

"Call off my... We were hunting, Chloe," Mantari said, the grin returning to his face. "There are beasts in the wood that are scarier than you."

"You haven't seen me when I'm angry." Chloe winked.

And then it happened. The chanting voice reached a crescendo, the voice seeming to be a thousand-person choir. The flames erupted into a series of mystic flames of red, blue, purple, black, and green. Chloe watched as the village of Oakston was ripped away from beneath her feet, Mantari's face melting into nothing. What Chloe had mistaken as a pile of sacks and bags blinked at her with shining eyes, and Chloe realized then that Mukkah had somehow known all along and had lent her power to the shaman for safe passage. The blubbery woman's face showed the faintest trace of a smile in the etheric glow of the flames.

Chloe felt the blaze wash over her. Felt her skin prickle but not burn. Her hair whipped around her as she gritted her teeth, holding onto what remained of the earth for dear life. Wishing and hoping that everything would come back to her, and she wouldn't have to feel the searing pain of death as she—

Chloe grunted as the floor became firm once more. The flames vanished. The roaring sound of magic died.

She panted as she pulled herself up from the floor. "Well, that was intense. You could've warned me."

"Would you have gone through with it if I had?" the wisp asked, adopting the form of the shaman once more.

KieraFreya scoffed. "I don't see what the problem was. A little fire never hurt anybody. You should have heard yourself: *Arrrgh! Ohhhh! Noooo! Help me! I'm a poor defenseless girl who can't stand the heat!*"

"I did *not* say that," Chloe growled, crossing her arms.

"You might as well have."

Chloe huffed, choosing to ignore KieraFreya, and for the first time trying to work out exactly where they were.

They were standing in what appeared to be a room carved out of gray rock. For a second, Chloe panicked, expecting to see the Seat of the World in the center and tumbled rocks on either side.

Instead, what she saw was walls lined along their length with decaying bookcases. Dusty, crumbling tomes sat at odd angles on the shelves, gently frosted in cobwebs. There were work benches with strange empty vials and flasks, and in the center of the room was the star-shaped symbol of a respawn point, which now glowed a faint white.

"You can choose to bind yourself to this space if you wish," the shaman explained. "Bind points are sigils loaded with magic that cause the blessed to automatically resurrect to whichever point they've chosen. As I understand it, your current bind point is set at Oakston since that was the first location you discovered which housed safety and citizens. Now that you have one set, you can select any number of others when you find them, though be warned, there is no way to re-select a deselected respawn point unless you're within physical distance of the mark."

"But the travel point at the shrine told me I could fast-travel to them at any time. You're saying I can't do that here?"

KieraFreya sighed, clearly tired of having to explain things to Chloe. "Respawn points and fast-travel points are completely different. One is a forced resurrection space, but the other you can use whenever you like."

"Aw, man," Chloe moaned. "It would be more useful if they both acted the same."

The shaman nodded, wiping a finger over the dusty bench and leaving a trail behind him. "Indeed, it would. Fast-travel is a gift granted only by the gods. One must make the sacrifice and be blessed in travel in order to use the functionality."

Chloe glared at KieraFreya, remembering that she had almost considered chopping her hand off, thanks to her.

Chloe shook her head. "So where are we now?"

It was a rhetorical question, really. Chloe pulled up her map, spotting her icon in her field of vision with a little legend that read Kingsholme Cave.

"Great. Another cave. Just what we needed," KieraFreya complained. "Give it a few minutes, and we'll be swimming in skellies again. Hey, Chloe! You remember that, right? When you chose to commit suicide instead of running to safety. I would take it personally, thinking that you're coming up with any excuse to get away from me. But, y'know, you keep coming back, so I guess I can't be all that bad."

"I don't think we'll have to worry about skellies this time," Chloe said, pointing toward an open door where the piles of skeleton bones were laid. She looked back at the shaman with questioning eyes.

The shaman nodded back, enough confirmation for Chloe to run off ahead.

"Hey! Slow down! You don't know what dangers are ahead," KieraFreya yowled. "Do you know how *boring* it is waiting for your ass to respawn while I'm just hovering somewhere in the etheric? *Ridiculously* boring! And then you just come back as if nothing ever happened..."

KieraFreya's words were drowned out as Chloe ran, fueled by excitement. Guided by the series of torches that were lit along the tunnel wall and mildly aware of the wisp now floating at speed behind her, adding his own light, she turned down tunnels, narrowly avoiding slipping on rocks, and followed the trail of the dead until she reached a large stone door that was standing slightly ajar.

"What's gotten into you?" KieraFreya asked, somehow sounding out of breath herself.

Chloe squeezed through the gap in the door and found herself in a large chamber. A set of stairs ran along the far wall leading to an over-watch that skirted around the entire room. There were crypts all around that had been smashed open, and skeletons littered the floor.

Chloe continued on ahead, smiling as she saw the scorch marks on the wall—blackened stars of ash from recent fireballs. They were in the right place.

At the top of the stairs, they turned back on themselves, and she found a door on the upper levels with black carvings on its front. Chloe entered through into a secondary chamber, this one with glowing green fungus lining the walls. Great mushrooms added a sickly glow. In the center of this larger room was a large treasure chest, its top already open and the contents looted. But that wasn't what Chloe was staring at.

"They really did it," she murmured, marveling at the rotting corpse of what she presumed was the skeleton overlord. The skeleton wore a dark, thin helmet, and sported a set of rudimentary armor that the others must have deemed not worth looting. Chloe moved closer, noticing a dent in the center of the skeleton's chest where someone had sat at some point.

Me and the guys found the sickest dungeon. We managed to take down a small army of skeletons between us and got massive gains from it. Right now we're taking a quick break in the main chamber. I'm sitting on the skeleton overlord! Lol.

The message returned unbidden to her memory. The words had come from Gideon a short while ago. She wondered if he had already received her message, or if it had reached him during one of his log-off times. If it *had* reached him, surely he would be here, waiting for her in this room.

Unless his friends didn't want to retrace their steps on account of some girl who thought she was better off doing her own thing.

Chloe shook her head, not quite sure if that had been her thoughts or KieraFreya's.

"Well, they're not here." She sighed, nudging the skeleton with her toes. "Looks like they did a heck of a job clearing out this dungeon, though."

There was a small flash of light as the wisp returned to shaman form. "And what makes you think this dungeon has been cleared?"

"Erm, maybe the surrounding piles of bones and the big boss man that's currently at our feet?"

The shaman laughed, although there was no humor in there. "This overlord is but one checkpoint on the journey to dungeon completion. Your conversations with your friend are where your knowledge draws its line. Expect the unexpected and prepare for battle. There is more to come."

Chloe sighed deeply, starting once again for the door ahead. She nudged the heavy door open a tad further, spotting more torches lighting the darkened corridor.

Man, why is it that everyone *can read my mind? Where the hell is the privacy anymore?*

You want privacy, you'll have to pay for the Pro Membership, Kiera-Freya teased.

Do you even know what that means?

Nope, but it sounded funny to me.

Chloe tried her best to empty her head and set off into the dark.

CHAPTER TWENTY-NINE

"Y'know, I thought it would be a *lot* more glamorous than this," Chloe whined, the slime from the rock walls coating her skin as she squeezed through a crevice.

They had been walking for what felt like hours in silence and now Chloe had thrown away all pretense, her mind going back to lazy afternoons cuddling with Blake on the sofa while the ignorant pig focused more on his in-game character than showing any kind of affection.

"What do you mean?" KieraFreya retorted. "What's not glamorous about this? You're practically glowing. Who knew the secret to beauty was sweat, rock slime, and not bathing in over a week?"

Chloe sniffed her pits and instantly recoiled. *Damn, she had a point. Where the hell do you bathe in a place like this?*

"When Blake played, he spent time in towns and cities around *normal* folk. Where's the civility here? Where's the domesticity? So far all I've managed to do is hop from forest to bog to mountain. I've fought enemies. I've died, and I've learned spells, but really all I want is a nice warm bath and to sit in a tavern for a few hours with a—" *beep* "—cosmo."

"What's a cosmo?" KieraFreya asked.

Chloe sighed, explaining the delectable sweetness of the cosmo and the effects the alcohol had on her body.

"Sounds like a good way to hide your problems," KieraFreya said when Chloe had finished. Behind them, the wisp floated along like a buoy over waves. "Numbing yourself and erasing all memories of the night before."

Chloe eyed her bracers suspiciously. "Did the doc put you up to this?"

"Seriously, who's the doc?" KieraFreya replied. "Why do you keep assuming I know things from your world? Moreover, why do you assume I care?"

They approached another steady downslope in the tunnel. This time the path wound into unknown territory. Chloe gripped the walls, learning from her previous mistake in which she had run a little too eagerly, letting gravity speed her journey, only to find that a steady drip of water filtering through the rock had made the floor slippery.

Chloe had smacked down on her backside, grimacing from the pain and taking a second to recover as she slid and whirled a few feet down the slope without effort. The rock was freezing on her backside.

KieraFreya had laughed.

The shaman had not.

"But seriously," Chloe continued, ignoring KieraFreya as she worked her way down, passing the body of another large rat lying limply on the floor. "There's got to be more to this game than dungeon-hopping and chasing our tail. Tell me, Wispy-boy. You must know of the cities?"

The shaman's voice appeared in her head. *I know* of *the cities, but I have never been to one. I've lived my life with the Oakston people, and the limit of my adventures was the woods and dark places that bordered our lands.*

"Damn. What about you, KF? Surely you must have some knowledge of the cities, having watched them for years from way up in your ivory tower in the clouds?"

"Okay, first of all, 'KF?'"

Chloe shrugged. "I'm just trying it out. KieraFreya...well, it's just a bit of a mouthful, y'know?"

"It's my name."

"So?"

"It's a *goddess'* name."

"And? People give nicknames to gods all the time in my world. Jesus, for example. I've heard all kinds of people switch his name up. 'The Son,' 'Christ,' 'JC,' 'J-bomb.' You always give nicknames to the people you love."

Chloe deliberately chose not to look at her bracers in case Kiera-Freya spotted the fib in her eyes. Who was she to know that Chloe was telling a little white lie?

"You're saying you *love* me?" KieraFreya repeated, disgust clear in her voice.

Chloe bit her lip. "I mean, I *guess* so. As much as anyone can love someone they're stuck with in a realm they've been thrown into. You *are* one of my closest friends both literally and figuratively, and we have already been through some shit. So, yeah, I guess on some level I *do* love you."

Chloe felt her bracers shudder on her wrists.

"Hey!"

"Secondly," KieraFreya retorted before Chloe could continue speaking, "what makes you think I had nothing better to do than watch the people in Obsidian go about their daily lives? Sure, I'd take a peek from time-to-time, but there's just as much drama with the gods as there is with lowly folk. You think you've seen drama down here? Wait until you see what the gods have to offer. They may keep themselves hidden and out of arm's reach, but it's like a whole 'nother level of theatrics up there."

They finally reached the bottom of the spiral. Chloe opened her mouth to reply to KieraFreya but stopped when she saw the blood splatters glistening on the golden doors that lay ahead.

In the center of the doors was a large lock in the shape of a flame. Chloe was impressed to see that a decorative object of the same shape was already embedded in the door, a key the others must have found on their travels to allow them safe passage.

Chloe placed her ear to the door. She could hear people talking on the other side, muted words through the rock. Her heart skipped a beat.

With a smile, Chloe winked at the wisp and shoved the door wide open.

"Don't worry, boys. The party is *here! Err...*"

Chloe cut her words short, her breath catching as she saw the monstrous creature lying in the center of the room.

The troll was enormous. Even lying on its back, it was double Chloe's height. In its boulder-sized head was a cavernous mouth, with two tusks set into its lower jaw. There was a club lying just out of its reach that was the size of a small tree.

Chloe's mind traveled back to her first encounter with these creatures. The two had blocked the way on the Deathwalk of the Gods and launched boulders at her as though they weighed little more than pebbles.

"Is it...alive?" Chloe mumbled to KieraFreya, noticing now the splatters of blood that stained the rock around the troll's form.

"Do you see it breathing?" KieraFreya replied.

The truth was, she couldn't. The troll was lifeless, as still as the rock around it. Chloe was sure that if she viewed the room from another angle and had no idea what a troll was, she might've stood a chance at missing the troll altogether. She moved closer, seeing small cuts and bruises on the troll's skin. Tiny areas that were charred and burned. Suddenly Chloe felt a sense of pride.

Her friends had taken this troll down, three novices attacking a creature the gods had deemed worthy to use as a guardian on the path to protect a mythical treasure. The smile returned to her face as she wondered where were they now.

As if in answer, Chloe heard a hissed whisper. "Pssst. Who goes there?"

"Shut up, Tag. It could be anyone. You really want to draw attention to ourselves *now?*"

"We need to do *something*," Tag's voice replied.

Her heart lifting, Chloe skirted the troll's bulk. Her eyes widened as she ran toward the back of the room and she found her three friends locked up in three individual cells set into the rock.

"Chloe?" Gideon said, disbelief clear in his voice as he rose from his darkened corner and held onto the bars. "What are you... How have you..." Gideon gathered his thoughts. "What are you doing here? Did you get my message?"

Chloe reached through the bars and hugged him. "I did. How's the rash doing? Did you get *my* message?"

Gideon squeezed Chloe tight. As she pulled away, he gave her a strange look. "No, my other message. I replied after I logged back in and saw your request. I figured it was ironic, you telling us to stay where we were, given that we were already trapped in here with nowhere to go."

Chloe searched her memory but could find no glimmer of recognition for what Gid was talking about. She brought up her messages, and sure enough, there it was, the text from Gid telling her they'd gotten themselves trapped in one of the dungeons and had no way of freeing themselves without any kind of key.

"I'm sorry, the last few hours have been a bit of a whirlwind. I haven't had a chance to check my notifications. Are you guys all right? What happened?"

Gideon, Ben, and Tag took turns explaining their adventure. How everything had been fun and glorious. How they had stumbled across the dungeon by luck and taken their chances.

"You don't level up unless you take chances and...revel...up?" Tag's voice stumbled to a halt.

Ben rolled his eyes. "I thought you were good with poetry?"

"When they're not *my* words..."

They had swept through the skeletons, working almost seamlessly like the three had in so many games before. Even Gideon had had fun taking down skellies with his fireballs, Ben picking them off from afar before they'd even had a chance to reach the pair fighting back-to-back.

Then had come the skeleton overlord. A skeleton with heightened defenses, increased HP, and regenerative magic.

"That one was tougher," Ben said. "He burst out of the crypt just as we were finishing off the other skellies.

"Yeah, if *someone* hadn't been so fast to loot the treasure." Gideon glared at Tag.

"*Hey!* I was curious, okay? There could've been something useful inside to help us take them all down." Tag folded his arms.

"You could have waited one extra minute!" Ben complained. "That would've been *more* than enough to pick off the final dregs. But *noooo*, you *had* to open the chest and trigger the overlord's rising."

"How was I supposed to know that would happen?"

Gideon pulled at his hair. "Because there was a chest *next to a giant stone coffin*! How many times have we done this before? If there's a treasure chest in the center of the room and a load of things around it that seem like they house baddies, *the treasure box is the trigger*."

Tag snorted and fell silent.

"Was there at least any good treasure in there?" Chloe asked.

Tag shuffled his feet. "A couple of coins and a battle axe."

"Well, that's something, right?" Chloe offered, keen to diffuse the situation as much as possible and help Tag.

"Meh," he replied. "Its attack value was lower than the one I managed to get in Oakston. It wasn't worth it, really, so I left it in the box, took the coins, and turned on the attack."

"That's the first *we're* hearing about the coins," Gideon said.

"Well, *I'm sorry*. Forgive me for focusing on the job at hand," Tag replied. "In case you haven't noticed, there's a giant troll keeping us prisoner."

Chloe spun. "It's alive?"

"Of course, it's alive. You think we're in here by choice?" Ben said.

Chloe studied the troll, finding literally zero sign of the monster moving. "Are you sure it ain't dead?"

The three guys craned their heads, trying to see through the bars as best they could.

"I don't know." Gideon shrugged. "It doesn't *look* very alive."

"Hold on," Chloe said, whirling back to face them. "How in the hell did a *troll* lock you up in these cells? His hands are huge. Those locks are tiny. I haven't had a whole lot of experience with trolls, but are they that dexterous that they can use keys as easily as we pick teeth with toothpicks?"

"There was a mage…" Ben began.

Chloe threw her hands in the air. "Oh, of *course*, there was a mage. Why is there *always* a mage?" Her mind filled with the glowing eyes and rage of the black mage who had killed her not half a day ago.

"Woah, what's got *her* riled up?" Tag asked.

Chloe briefly explained the situation, detailing what had happened at the shrine and acknowledging her new glowing companion after the guys finally spotted the white wisp.

Then they moved on to the jail situation, Chloe's stomach sinking as the guys explained that the mage, combined with the troll, had effortlessly outdone them all. Even with Gideon's magic, Ben's archery, and Tag's bulk, they had been defeated easily. The mage had drawn the attention of the troll and paralyzed the three of them while the troll bashed around with its club. Tag got the brunt of the damage, trying to run while covered in his own blood before being dragged back by the power of the mage and staining the door.

The three ended up surrendering to the mage in a desperate effort to avoid losing their friend. After getting locked up in the cell, Gideon had cast **Healing Hands** on Tag and brought him back to full health. The mage had disappeared with a dark smile, some other purpose driving him forward.

"So *I've* got to go ahead by myself to get the key to save you guys?" Chloe moaned.

"Not exactly," Gid said, nodding at the troll. "The mage didn't take the key. He left it in the one place he thought it would be well-guarded."

Chloe looked forlornly from the troll to her friends.

"For—" *beep* "—sake."

CHAPTER THIRTY

Chloe's nose wrinkled. Up close, the troll smelled worse than she'd feared. She stepped around the beast, the filthy linen of its loincloth pulsing off stink in physical waves.

"Do I really have to?" Chloe whispered across the room. Although the troll hadn't moved when they were talking at top volume, now that she was closer, she didn't want to know what would happen if she was right beside him and he woke up.

Gideon and Ben nodded. Chloe hated Tag for the smug smile on his face.

Chloe tiptoed up, craning her neck to see the key. She reached, digging her hand as far into the pocket of the loincloth as she dared. Her arm disappeared up to her elbow, but she was nowhere near deep enough.

Whipping out her arm, she attempted to wipe the stink off her flesh. It was no use. She grabbed a fistful of material and began to hoist herself up, grunting and groaning as she jumped and climbed on top.

"I've only been in this game for a week or so, and *still* I'm trying to climb the shoulders of giants," Chloe mumbled, getting unsteadily to her feet. She wobbled slightly as she felt the instability of the troll's lungs rising almost imperceptibly.

She gently dropped to her knees and lifted the material of the pocket. A thick wave of stink hit her and she had to stop herself from heaving. She faced away and took a couple of steadying breaths, then dove into the pocket. From afar, she must have looked a sight, like a cat playing beneath a duvet. Chloe crawled as fast as she could, emerging a second or so later looking waxen and pale.

"No luck?" Ben called.

Chloe shook her head, unable to form words.

"Oh, that's right," Tag said, slapping his forehead. "It was the *other* pocket."

Chloe glared at Ben and forced back a dry heave. With a heavy disposition, she crawled over the giant, repeating the same process and emerging a few seconds later with a large silver key.

She wasted no time in sliding back off the troll and unlocking the cells. She saved Tag for last, letting him sweat it out as she teased that she could just leave him there if she wanted to. It would be amazing revenge for not being clearer about the key's location.

"Come on, just let me go. I'm sorry, okay?"

"Turn three times on the spot and bark like a dog," Chloe teased.

Tag coughed. "You're not serious?"

"What do you think, fellas? Am I serious?"

Ben chuckled, a juvenile glint in his eye. "I've never known you to joke, Chloe." He stretched his arms and cracked his back. "Better do what she says, bud. Freedom feels *good.*"

Chloe laughed so hard that she doubled over. Even Gid laughed with them. She took a deep breath, trying to refill her aching lungs with oxygen and getting a slight hint of something stale and foul in her nostrils.

She looked at the far corner of Tag's cell where the wall was dark and a small trickle of something yellow trailed across the floor.

"Oh, my God," Chloe said. "Is that—"

Tag's eyes widened. In a flurry of movement, he spun three times so fast that he almost fell over.

"Woof woof. Woof woof!"

Chloe, Ben, and Gid burst into laughter once more. Chloe's eyes went blurry as she giggled, trying her hardest to find the lock through tears of laughter. She finally found it and turned the key.

"Woof woof. Woof...wurgh?"

"What is it, Lassie? What is it, boy?" Ben cooed, slapping his knees.

Tag wobbled, readying his hammer as he pointed behind them all to where the sound of something gigantic was moving.

"Aw, man!" Chloe sighed, turning slowly to find the troll rising to its feet, a hungry stare on its face. Great globules of saliva spooled down its chin, finding their way into the cracks and folds of its bulk.

Chloe glanced at Gideon and prepared a fireball. He prepared his own with shaking hands, eyes fixed high on the beast. She cast **Creature Identification** and absorbed the information.

Mountain troll (Level 15)

982HP

982HP? The black mage was the same level and had far *less than that,* Chloe thought, taking her stance and joining Gideon and Ben as the first long-range missiles fired toward the troll. The troll flinched, its health dropping by around 3%.

The shaman's voice appeared as Chloe summoned another fireball, strafing left as all four of the party split in several directions to confuse the beast. *Remember, every creature is different, Chloe. While a wolf may be fast, a turtle may be slow. An elephant may be bulky, but a horse may crumble under the sword.*

Wait, Chloe said, drawing her sword and chancing a cut at the troll's knees as she sprinted closer to him. The sword caught skin but barely made an impression, leaving behind a pathetic cut that dribbled blood before it coagulated. *You're telling me there are elephants in Obsidian?*

There are. I've heard tell of their existence in the eastern plains, out toward Narlath, where the lands are drier and the rains sparse.

Enough of the biology lessons, please, KieraFreya chided. *Maybe you've got some useful information on a troll that's currently trying to turn us into jelly?*

Chloe nodded and steeled herself for the attack, dashing between the troll's legs and going for another slice. This time the sword had even less impact, the silver seemingly bouncing off the troll's hide.

Chloe emerged on the other side, narrowly avoiding the troll as it swung its club in the direction of Tag, who was currently sprinting as fast as his little legs could carry him, holding up a makeshift shield that looked like it was made of wood.

"Come and get me, bro!" Tag shouted, passing a groove in the cave wall where Chloe could just make out the flashes of arrows appearing as if from nowhere. Clearly, Ben had been working on his **Sneak** skill and was now taking advantage of the small pocket of darkness to pick away at the troll's HP.

Gideon, meanwhile, had run back to the protection of the cell and was flicking through the shaman's tome that Chloe had given him as a parting gift. He flicked feverishly through the pages, shaking his head, glancing up as Tag passed his cell with a "What the *hell* are you doing, lad?" moments before the club bashed the metal bars, denting them on impact.

Chloe wondered what the hell Gideon *was* doing and how he expected to not get crushed when he remained a static target. Come to think of it, Chloe had been standing for a moment or two just watching the action as Tag tore around the room and the troll followed.

It suddenly clicked. The troll was trying to finish his work. Gid and Ben had said it themselves: Tag had almost been crushed to death. Surely an *almost* death must have really pissed off the troll when it saw its victim spring back to life as if nothing had happened.

To further cement this theory in her mind, Tag kept hurling abuse, occasionally ducking through the troll's legs as Chloe had. A couple of times, he smashed its toes with his hammer, making the troll yowl.

Chloe examined the troll's health. 793HP. They were making a dent, but surely Tag wouldn't be able to keep this up for long before his own stamina began to wane.

"Whenever one of you is ready to jump in, that'd be *real* nice!" Tag said, slipping as he skidded on some loose debris and crashed into the wall. He bashed his head, blinking as the pain set in. The troll loomed over him, a strangely triumphant grin on its face.

The club came around, it swung down. Chloe ran for Tag and threw her body over him, hoping against hope that her **Reckless** nature would yield some benefits, or maybe the gods would take pity on her again. Her eyes screwed shut as she waited for the blow.

A few seconds passed.

No pain came.

But the smell of fried meat did.

Chloe peeled herself away from Tag, eyes meeting the grumbling dwarf's. "Thanks, lass," he said awkwardly, rubbing his head as they rolled away from each other.

The troll was frozen solid. Still as a statue.

Well, not quite as still as a statue. It still moved, the club lowering at an infinitesimally slow speed as something sizzled. Chloe heard the sound of cooking bacon and peeked around the troll to see Gideon rubbing his hands together as if he were holding defibrillators. Every few seconds he would remove them from the troll and pump up the electricity, then throw lightning-charged palms against the backs of the troll's knees.

"You know you're making us hungry, right?" Chloe said, Gideon offering her a cursory glance as he continued his desperate attempt to chip away at the troll's health.

"Slow-time curse," he gasped between rapid breaths. "Didn't think it would work at first. Turns out it's pretty useful."

Chloe examined the troll's health, pleasantly surprised that it was now down to 547HP. A large chunk had gone after all of Tag's running around, Ben's arrows, and Chloe's cuts. But she could see that more damage was being done by Gideon each time he zapped the troll's legs.

Tag moved away from the club, finding refuge near Ben, who had stepped out of the shadows. "How long do we have?"

Gideon shrugged. "No idea. That's why I'm pouring MP into these attacks. It could be seconds. Could be minutes. Could be days."

"How much MP have you got left?" Chloe asked.

"Not enough," Gid said, rubbing his hands and producing nothing but a mild friction burn. "Sh—" *beep*.

"Then let me step in," Chloe said, drawing her sword and placing a palm on her blade. Muttering the words that were now ingrained in her memory, she set the sword alight with pulses of electricity, took her place next to Gid, and hacked and slashed. There were minor scorch marks where Gid's hands had affected the troll, but Chloe watched with dismay as no marks appeared from her sword.

She reared back, channeling her strength to hack and slash once, twice, three times. Still no effect, although she did notice the troll's health drop a significant chunk.

"What the hell? How is nothing happening?" Gideon asked.

"Something *is* happening," Chloe replied. "Look!"

Gideon craned his neck up to where Chloe was pointing to the troll's health bar. He blinked and squinted. "What am I looking at?"

Chloe tutted. "Right. You don't have **Creature Identification**, do you? The troll's health is dropping. It's got about 30% left. Regenerate your MP as best you can. Tag, rest and eat something quickly to restore your health. Ben, keep firing."

"I'm out of arrows," Ben replied, drawing a poor excuse for a blade and holding it out. "This might work."

"Go for it," Chloe replied. "Gid, how are we doing on that MP?"

"Slow to recover. I'm going to need a few more minutes."

Just then, Chloe saw something that made her eyes grow wide. "I don't think we've got that long."

"How can you tell?"

Chloe pointed at the back of the troll's leg. Where she had slashed at the skin with her lightning blade, thin lines began to slowly appear. The skin unzipped along the length, achingly slow, as thick red blood began to drop, then pour out. The troll began to noticeably move forward, time beginning to catch up as they heard the slowed-down timbre of the troll's growls.

"Clear the area," Chloe shouted, running to meet Ben and Tag at the recess in the wall. Gideon was the last to join, moving out of the way just in time as the troll returned to normal speed, the impact of the attacks from Gideon and Chloe now accumulating as time struggled to catch up with reality.

The backs of the troll's leg gushed open, blood fountaining out. The troll was pushed forward with an unholy force, its hand slipping on the club that smacked into the wall where Tag and Chloe had been a moment ago. Its head forced hard into the corner and they heard an almighty crack as bone broke.

Chloe watched with gruesome fascination as the troll's health deteriorated to zero in a second. The final impact with the wall had been enough to end the creature's life.

Monster defeated: Mountain Troll (Lv 15)

+590 exp

Light washed over Gideon and Ben as they leveled up, celebrating as they hovered in the air.

Tag grinned, standing as if waiting to level up. When nothing happened, he said, "Hey! What? I use myself as live bait, and the wizard and the archer get the points?"

Gideon and Ben laughed, shrugging.

"If it helps, I didn't get anything either," Chloe said, bringing up her character sheet to examine how far she might be from level 10.

<u>Bio</u>

Character name: Chloe (*click to select a new character name*)

Level: 9

Class: Null

Race: Human

<u>Stats</u>

HP: 250/250

MP: 180/180

Stamina: 330/330

Active effects: Null

<u>Attributes</u>

Strength: 22 (+19)

Intelligence: 6 (+13)

Dexterity: 20 (+16)

Endurance: 25 (+18)

Etheric Potential: 9 (+14)
<u>**Skills**</u>
Languages: Human
Acrobatics: Lv 3
Armed Combat: Lv 1
Cooking: Lv 1
Crafting: Lv 1
Creature Identification: Lv 4
Dark Vision: Lv 4
Dual Wielding: Lv 2
Experimental: Lv 1
Fishing: Lv 1
Herb Identification: Lv 1
Sneak: Lv 4
Swimming: Lv 1
Reckless: Lv 4
<u>**Available Points:**</u> **0**

"Hey! I did get *something,* though," Chloe said, noticing a minor increase in her strength and endurance. "Woah. **Reckless** level 4!"

She heard Tag groan behind her as she pulled up the notification and read about the increase.

Skill increased: Reckless (Lv 4)

Did you really just throw your body over a dwarf like he was a landmine? Can't say we've ever seen that before. Here, have a bonus.

Bonuses: +13 strength, +7 endurance

(NOTE: Increases in skill override any previous bonuses gained from the skill).

"Is anyone else's AI, like, super sassy with their descriptions? One minute it's straight-talking, the next minute I feel like my brother caught me stealing his Advent calendar chocolate again."

"Yeah, I've had that a few times," Ben said, strolling around the room and recovering his arrows. "I think it's just the AI trying to be funny. Y'know, trying to make sure the game is friendly to kids when they play it."

"The game's an 18, Ben," Gid chipped in. "Who are they trying to impress?"

"That's not going to stop underage kids from playing," Ben retorted. "You know that my brother was playing 18s when he'd just turned 11. Yeah, Mum didn't care what the game was, she just appreciated that it kept him quiet. Didn't even matter that I had to put up with him pretending to slash me open and jump around every corner when I was getting ready for bed for a week."

Chloe flicked away her notifications, taking a sip of water from her skin. "Still, maybe that's another thing to report to Praxis. A bit of consistency goes a long way." She offered some to Gideon, who accepted gladly.

Ben sat down by the wall, taking a deep breath and wiping the sweat from his brow. "Can you believe we *survived* that?" He let out a laugh. "What should we merry band of four do next?"

Gideon nodded toward the open door. "In case you've forgotten, we've still got a mage to catch."

"Okay," Chloe said, a determined expression on her face. "But first let's loot this mother..."

Her voice trailed away as ash flew into the air and the troll began to disintegrate. They all turned and saw Tag's tiny form appear as the troll's bulk vanished, leaving behind a neat pile of treasure.

"Er..." Tag said with a guilty smile on his face. "Splitsies?"

CHAPTER THIRTY-ONE

They tried for some time to walk the tunnels in relative quiet. Chloe was impressed more and more with her **Sneak** skill, noticing how lightly she trod now compared to the troubles she'd had when entering the goblin cave. With every skill point gained across her specific talents, she felt stronger in a way she didn't believe possible in the real world.

She wondered what it would be like to take the logic of the game and use it back home. What skills would her brothers and sisters have? Would there be a way to increase her skills in charisma, business, work ethic, and negotiation to catch up with the gods of her own life? Those who were held in much higher regard on their black-suited pedestals?

Her mother and father would be king and queen, of course, atop their thrones, looking down on them all. Her six brothers and sisters would be the lords and ladies of the land, and Chloe the outcast. The jester of the family, working her ass off to reach the stature of the others.

Was it even possible at this point?

"I'm really glad you found your way back to us," Gideon said, interrupting Chloe from her thoughts. "The others won't say it, but they missed you, too. We make a good team, don't you think?"

Chloe smiled. Tag and Ben were a short distance ahead, leading the way with a torch they had stolen off the walls.

"Yeah. Yeah, we do."

"If you don't mind my asking, what was it that brought you back to us? Last I understood, you were setting out on a quest solo. Haven't you got bigger fish to fry than dungeon-looting with us three?"

Chloe nodded. "The funny thing about frying bigger fish is that you need a bigger pan."

KieraFreya clicked her tongue.

Gideon raised an eyebrow. "What?"

Chloe laughed, turning back to where the shaman's wisp floated behind them. Inspired by the great magic user, she had tried to wax philosophical but had proven in that moment that intelligence definitely wasn't one of her strong points.

"Nothing. I guess I just managed to discover that this world is not kind to those who travel alone, especially those of lower levels than the monsters that are out there. I had a choice: should I push through and work my way up in the levels slowly, struggling out there by myself, or should I join three brave adventurers I've grown to like and trust, and we can help each other boost our experiences?"

"When you put it like that, it's a no-brainer."

"That's what I'm saying," Chloe agreed.

"You know you won't *just* be joining us, right?"

"What do you mean?" Chloe asked as they ducked beneath a piece of low-hanging rock and veered around a corner.

"I mean, every group needs a leader, Chloe. Every group needs someone to take charge in situations and command the group for the betterment of all. When the three of us played other games, it would usually be me taking charge. The warrior normally takes the brunt of responsibility, getting thick into the heart of battle and guiding the rest of his men—" Chloe shot Gideon a look "and women to victory."

"Then it can be you again," Chloe said, placing a hand on Gid's shoulder. "Just do what you normally do and lead us all to victory, pal."

Gid smiled, shaking his head. "Not in this body. In case you haven't noticed, my confidence is gone. I've spent years studying the art of the warrior, training in combat, learning strategy of battle and war from the angle of a man with a sword and shield. Now?" He raised his hands in front of his face "Now my power lies with these and, and while I'll admit this is all pretty cool, I have a long way to go before I can call myself a leader again. Didn't you see me at the house? With the bears? In the woods with the wolves? What troop is going to follow a clumsy, inexperienced mage into battle?"

"What troop is going to follow a confused girl with little experience in gaming mechanics?"

Gideon studied Chloe with a knowing look on his face.

"What?" she said.

"You don't even see it, do you?" He nodded at the other two, who were deep in their own conversation. "They already are. Didn't you hear yourself back there with the troll? You *owned* it. You gave the orders, and they listened."

Chloe scoffed. "Yeah, right. It takes a great leader to awaken a troll and shout at people to do stuff."

Gideon laughed. "No. It takes a great leader to be listened to in the thick of battle and for others to *willingly* follow. That's the mark of a great leader. That was what I saw today."

Chloe thought about it as they journeyed onward. Her, a leader? Ever since she had been dumped into this game, she had felt like nothing more than a clumsy excuse for a player who happened by chance to stumble across a great opportunity.

Now, though?

Now she was being told once again that there was something inside her. The shaman had spoken of greatness within her. Gideon believed in her ability to lead. The shaman had even followed her, trusting Chloe to keep him safe on his first true adventure far away from the village in which he had resided all his life.

Could this be true? Could there really be something inside me that is destined to lead others?

No, KieraFreya contributed.

"Oh, shut up," Chloe mumbled. When Gideon gave her a look, she added, "Not you, *Her.*"

Gideon's eyes found the bracers and he nodded.

When they at last came to a stop, it was at the head of a flight of stairs that led down into a dark, cavernous abyss in which the group could see nothing.

"Eyes up, folks," Tag muttered. "Boss battle ahead."

"How do you know?" asked Chloe.

"Ordinarily you'd get the typical battle music," Tag said. "Y'know, like *da-nuh-nuh-nuh-na-na-na...boom. Da-nuh-nuh-nuh-na-na-na...whoosh.*"

Gid and Chloe sniggered.

Ben's face remained stern. "But here you can just...feel it. Can't you?"

Chloe closed her eyes, and sure enough, she felt...*something*. Great tension in the air. Pressure. Finality.

"Everyone recovered and fully ready to battle this thing?" Chloe asked, scanning the group. "Gid, how's your MP?"

"As full as we're going to get in this timeframe. Ordinarily I'd love to have a few potions for backup for when we make the charge, but unfortunately, this game doesn't seem to be yielding many of those yet."

"Where do we find them?" Chloe asked.

"Cities, usually," Ben replied. "Or sometimes hidden deep in dungeons. My guess, though, is that the mage has looted anything that might be of use to us just on the off-chance that we might follow him."

Chloe nodded. "And no one here has any idea what the mage is doing traipsing ahead of a group of adventurers through the dungeon?"

The other three shook their heads.

"And no one has any clue of any potential danger that may be lying ahead?"

Another shake.

"And all three of you have lost your tongues and can no longer speak English long enough to answer me with actual words?" Chloe smirked.

Another headshake, this time accompanied by smiles.

"Screw you guys, let's just get this over with. Hey, Wisp, want to give us some light to see by?"

The wisp vibrated as if excitement had run through its body. It floated ahead, gliding down the stairs and illuminating the way with ghostly pallor.

Chloe and Tag took the front, Tag's torch adding extra light as the wisp made its way ahead. It paused at the bottom of the stairs. Gideon and Ben prepared themselves as they followed the first two, Ben's arrows already nocked and ready to fire. Gideon's hands were in place, ready to create magic should the need arise.

All was deadly silent. Chloe ducked her head, struggling to make out what lay on the floor beneath. The stairs went on and on, winding ever so slightly toward the wisp's glow. All else beyond the reach of the light was in utter darkness, but the pull and pressure Chloe had felt at the top of the stairs had intensified.

When they were halfway down the stairs, they heard their first sign of movement.

And it was a big one.

"*Igne iudicii!*" came words bellowed through the darkness, a bright ball of emerald-green fire appearing from nowhere and streaming across the room. The fireball smashed into the stairs, causing them to crack and crumble.

"Run!" Chloe shouted, shoving Tag forward and leaping over the falling rocks as fast as she could. Gideon and Ben leaped after her, managing to make their way over the debris and sprinting the rest of the length of the stairs.

A gentle croak of laughter echoed around the room as darkness resumed.

"Gideon, **Purple Blaze**, now! Fire into the darkness to find him!"

The pair of them summoned their own fireballs, casting the orbs into the shadows. The balls followed a straight trajectory past huge carved pillars with rustic runes along their height, the light fading as it moved farther away. They revealed nothing more than air and dust until they finally extinguished.

They cast several more balls as quickly as possible. Still nothing.

"Save your MP," Chloe said, feeling a little breathless.

"What do we do?" Ben whispered, his bow readied and sweeping arcs in the dark.

"Aw, let's just take the fight to him!" Tag shouted, rallying his war cry as power emanated through the four of them. "Come at me, you filthy—" *beep*.

To Chloe's disdain, Tag sprinted into the shadows. His body melted into the darkness, and they could hear his feet stomping around. His hammer made loud whooshing sounds as it sliced through the air. At one point, they saw a gentle glow of something that illuminated Tag and a figure cloaked in black before there was a yell of pain and Tag reappeared in their sphere of light, sliding on his back across the cavern floor.

"Well, that wasn't fun," he breathed. "Want to step in and help, people?"

"We really didn't want to hurt you," Chloe replied.

"*We didn't really want to make you cry,*" Tag sang in a high falsetto. "Man, I loved that song."

Words were muttered in the darkness.

"Focus!" Chloe said, dragging Tag back to his feet. "Here it comes!"

"*Meus mortuus est surge et vivorum DOMINETUR!*"

"Anybody here speak Latin?" Tag asked nonchalantly as an eerie glow appeared from the darkness.

Ben fired, the arrows soaring and one of them finding their mark. The mage groaned, turned away its glowing blue eyes, and vanished.

The ghostly glow remained as a steady stream of mist kicked up from the ground. Something crackled, hard things walking across hard things. Chloe recognized that sound instantly, her heart sinking.

"Get ready, guys. Looks like it's skelly time."

"I didn't think you were ready for this skelly." Ben grinned, already firing at where the skeletons were appearing.

Chloe lit her blade with purple fire, shedding a little more light on the situation. "Wisp, circle and dazzle the skellies. Show us where they are, and we'll follow."

Like a dutiful hound, the wisp trailed into the gloom, its weak glow casting a ghoulish glare over the skeletons. There were dozens of them, a whole sea of the dead for as far as Chloe could see.

She nodded at Tag. Tag nodded back.

They sprinted toward the skeletons, weapons raised. Chloe felt alive, reaching the first skeleton and taking it down with a simple hack. It must have been low-level, she mused, unable to concentrate and stand still long enough to utilize **Creature Identification**.

Another skelly down, then another. Chloe felt a bony hand claw her shoulder and spun, the fetid stench of the skeleton causing her to recoil. Before she could bring her sword back up, the skeleton crumbled into a thousand pieces. Tag winked at Chloe, his hammer back in his hand.

"I got your back, girl."

"Literally." Chloe smiled. "But who's got yours?"

Tag's face dropped as a pair of skellies put their arms around his throat. "Help!" he cried as he was dragged backward.

Arrows flew through the air, finding their target in one skeleton's chest, a little higher than Tag's shoulder. Another whistling arrow and the next skeleton was no more.

"Maybe shoot a little closer to me next time?" Tag yelled at Ben, who had now climbed a few stairs to gain the advantage of height. "You nearly got *me*, dumbface!"

Tag shut up as another arrow came straight at him, just nicking the leather on his shoulder before taking down a skeleton that Tag hadn't noticed coming.

"Concentrate!" Ben grunted, returning to the problems that were closer at hand. Even though he was taking down skellies left, right, and center, they were making headway, surrounding him on all sides.

Only Gideon remained with him, pulsing lightning from his hands and sending waves toward the skeletons, toasting them as they fell.

"Way to harness your powers, Gid!" Chloe shouted.

"I gained a level! I can now choose their trajectory," Gid said between breaths.

"Nice!"

Chloe turned her attention back to the problem at hand and resumed sweeping through the darkness with her purple sword ablaze. She felt energized and wore a huge smile on her face as she took down skeleton after skeleton. The bones piled up around her feet, and she wondered what kind of goodies she would find in these skeletons when it came to looting the bodies.

"Chloe, this way," Tag said, smashing the skull of a skeleton and nodding into the gloom ahead to where the mage floated in the darkness, the wisp now circling him like a candlelit target.

"Good job, Decaru!" she called. "Stay on him!"

"Decaru?" Tag asked.

Chloe gave Tag a look as if to say, 'You expect me to explain this to you now?'

They made their way closer to the mage, the location now lit by the wisp. Chloe and Tag whirled around each other, Ben and Gideon thinning out the crowd around them as their defense turned to offense and purple fireballs found their way into the crowd of skeletons.

Purple flames lit up the great cavern, and Chloe was shocked to see just how many skeletons there were. She peered over their heads to see where they were coming from and saw the mage staring at them darkly, its hands aglow as the bones of their defeated enemies were brought back together. The dead rose once again to become the...living dead?

"We have to take him out. He's the source of it all. They're going to keep coming back unless we can take him down!" Chloe shouted, her voice hard to hear over the ruckus.

"Nice plan, girly," Tag growled between attacks. He took the shaft of his hammer in both hands and swung in a circle. After several revolutions, he summoned his rally cry again, that familiar mystical blue haze returning to the battlefield. Tag laughed as he was suddenly shrouded in bright light, his body floating off the floor as he leveled up in front of them all.

"Ha! At last!" Tag shouted out. "Level 7! Woo!"

Chloe felt the power of the **Call of the Valiant**, her body swelling with the temporary buffs Tag had bestowed upon them. Allowing Tag to charge ahead, Chloe followed in his wake, taking out any skellies that had somehow survived the wrath of his hammer.

"A little farther." Tag was panting, determination on his face.

They made quick progress across the floor, now only a short distance from the mage. When they were within striking distance, Chloe shouted for Tag to crouch. She sprinted toward him, used his back as a springboard, and leaped into the air, her sword leaving a blazing trail of indigo behind.

"Take this, you mother—" *beep*!

As the beep rang around the cavern, Chloe smiled triumphantly, preparing for her sword to meet the flesh of the mage. She laughed, then her face fell as the mage disappeared in a flash of blinding light. Chloe fell straight through where the body should have been and stumbled clumsily as she found herself on the floor.

Skeletons swarmed her and her mouth opened in panic. Somewhere far off, past the stink of decay and death, she could hear Tag's shouts as he smashed his way toward her. Gideon and Ben roared somewhere beyond the noise.

Chloe couldn't believe it. She had been so *close*. She had almost had him. One inch closer and he'd be dead on the floor, Chloe using his body as a landing pad rather than flailing helplessly as her sword extinguished and she felt the skellies clutching and clawing at her body.

Not now, Chloe thought, panic rising within her. *Please, not now*.

KieraFreya sighed. *I've got you, bitch*. Chloe's arms began to move of their own accord, blocking many of the attacks—but not all.

Chloe watched as her health began to decrease, feeling the pain like daggers in her side. She closed her eyes, thinking back to her previous death. How she had been all alone in a cave. The lengths she had gone to to reunite with her group. She couldn't go through that all again. She couldn't lose, not now. Not this time.

Block after block, scratch after scratch. Chloe's anger rose. There was a fury deep inside her, a determination she had never felt before. She had a purpose here. These men needed her. Without Chloe, they would surely all fall to the mage's wrath.

A sound began to gurgle from the back of Chloe's mouth—a roar from the belly of a beast, growing louder as she cried out. The anger bubbled from within and found its way out of her body as a triumphant roar that gave the skeletons pause in their attacks. At that moment, she was no longer Chloe but someone different. Someone greater. Chloe flexed her arms, closed her eyes, and screamed until her lungs burned.

That was when everything changed.

CHAPTER THIRTY-TWO

For a moment, all Chloe knew was white. Every inch of her vision was as blank as a fresh canvas, and her body moved without her thought.

She became aware of an almighty scream, worried now that her throat might grow hoarse from the effort. She finally realized that it wasn't her scream at all. The sound was coming from in front of her.

Chloe strained to see, her vision a drunken blur. The dazzling light was emanating from her hands as KieraFreya's pushed the magic out in a column of white in front of her, wiping out skeletons as she cleared the path ahead.

What...what are you doing? Chloe asked.

KieraFreya struggled to talk. *Getting...us...out of...here.*

Chloe straightened, her strength returning to her as control of the magic began to slowly transition from KieraFreya to her. Where before Chloe had fought *against* KieraFreya for power, this time it felt as though KieraFreya was handing over something with precious potential and any wrong move would hurt them both. There was compassion and care in the transition and Chloe took the power in her stride, rising to her feet and aiming the swath of light in a sweeping arc.

"Duck!" she shouted to Tag, who wasted no time in obeying.

The skeletons fell the instant they were touched, the light strong enough to reach the whole room. The mage floated somewhere in the distance, the faintest trace of fear on his face.

Chloe started running toward him, clearing a path for herself and the others.

"Gid, *now!*" she shouted, not waiting as Gideon started with surprise and began to sprint across the room.

"Don't leave me!" Ben called, giving chase until all four were once more united in the center of the room.

Chloe stumbled as she stopped, feeling the MP drain as the light extinguished and the mage leered at them, lit now only by the wisp once more.

"Tag, keep the skellies at bay," Chloe commanded. "Ben, help Tag. Gid…" she gave him a wink, "you know what to do."

They all obeyed, Ben, Tag, and Chloe keeping their enemies away as Gideon sank to his knees and began to chant, his concentration entirely on the job at hand. Chloe whirled her sword around her, keeping her eyes on the mage as much as possible, watching as he studied them with great interest, marveling at the woman and the powers she had produced.

As Chloe fought, she watched her MP regenerate. *Not fast enough,* she complained. *Not fast enough.* She got assistance from KieraFreya and found that battling was easier than it had ever been before.

The mage resurrected the crowd once more, Chloe's shoulders slumping as she felt the weight of what was about to happen in the pit of her stomach. The skeletons outnumbered them almost 100 to 1. If they didn't pull this off, they'd be screwed. All this fighting would have been for nothing. They'd all find their way back to Oakston with nothing more than the memory of a battle lost.

Unless the others have set their respawn points to the entrance to the dungeon, Chloe thought sadly. She hadn't confirmed her set point, not knowing if she was going to find the others there or not. The last thing she had wanted to do was keep respawning miles from familiarity and hope.

Chloe's MP hit a modest 25% regen. She glanced at Gideon, power now seeping through his hands.

"Whenever you're ready, Gids," she called.

Gideon nodded, then stood and manipulated the magic flowing through his hands. "I'm not sure I've got enough, Chloe."

"Just try!" Chloe said desperately. "Just *try!*"

Gideon attempted to fire his spell, but the magic dissipated the instant it left his hands.

"Come on, Gid!" Chloe shouted, her magic vibrating in her hands, KieraFreya once more grunting with exertion.

The thin mage tried once more, his eyes screwed shut in concentration. The spell was taking every last ounce of magic within him to summon. He shaped his hands while Ben and Tag fought off the tide, focusing on giving the two magic-users enough space to finish the job.

"Gid, *NOW!*"

With a sudden movement, Gideon threw his magic at the mage, now caught unawares as Chloe cast her own spell and threw a column of light directly at his chest.

The mage's mouth opened wide, then froze. The light hit the mage at exactly the same moment the mage's time clock slowed down. The mage hovered in mid-air, his robe flowing with the minutest of movements as he were in a vat of treacle.

And now came Chloe's moment. As Ben and Tag beat the rhythm toward her final victory, Chloe once more grasped her sword, launched herself, and slashed at the mage. Her sword glistened in the wisp's light, and there was a glint of fear in the mage's eyes. Chloe came at him again, and again, wondering how long the time freeze would hold the mage still.

She landed gracefully on both feet, feeling her stamina and MP drain. Behind her, Gideon folded over on the floor, his breath coming in short bursts as the skeletons closed in.

Yet still, the mage remained frozen. Skeletons launched at her as she made her way back to the others, her sword singing as it cracked skulls and cleared a path for her return.

"How long is that magic going to hold?" Chloe asked Gideon.

Gideon did not reply, his hood cloaking his face as he panted to try to recover.

"If it holds much longer, we'll be overrun," Ben shouted. "We can't keep fighting. Our stats won't allow it."

Chloe's eyes flicked back to the mage, where thin slices were beginning to appear across his robes, slowly threading deeper toward his skin as time tried to catch up with what Chloe had done.

Another skeleton down. Another. Chloe remained by Gideon's side, protecting and keeping him sheltered as the skellies came to grab him. "Gid? Now would be a great time to get up and help us."

Gideon's eyes were unfocused, his face dark. "Need...mana..." he struggled to say.

Chloe turned once more to the mage, the cuts now beginning to bleed in slow globules running down his body, his eyes widening so slowly it looked like a trick of the light.

A skeletal hand caught Chloe's ankle and pulled, dragging her off-balance and bringing her to the floor. She kicked at the skeleton, her sword doing its best to take down the others crowding her.

Beep "—off!" Chloe shouted, kicking and thrashing, her mind thrown back to her last death as skeletons piled on top of her, ripping her to shreds before she had found her way back to the white room with the doc.

Chloe felt a hot, searing pain in her leg as a skeleton's fingers gripped her skin...

And then it was all over.

Chloe watched with gruesome fascination as the skeletons suddenly crumbled around her, dropping to the ground as if they'd just given up any semblance of life they once might have had.

Above them, the mage was spared the briefest of cries of anguish before time caught up, the impact from the column of light making his body into a blinding display of white fireworks. The cuts and slashes from Chloe's sword divided him into a thousand tiny pieces.

A great pulse of power erupted from the mage in concentric shockwaves. Chloe and the others were thrown to the floor to join the skeletons. Tag's laughter filled the air as he fell.

Quiet washed over the room, the only sound coming from the purple fires that crackled in various locations across the room.

"We did it." Chloe smiled, staring up at the ceiling and letting herself rest. "We goddamn well did it."

A blast of golden light showered over them all as they were suddenly lifted into the air. Chloe, slowly getting used to this feeling of gloriousness, beamed as her hair whirled about her and she felt the power increase that came from leveling up. Behind her, she heard Tag and Ben laughing. Beside her, Gideon came alive again as his stats restored to their full capacity, his laughter joining the ringing sound of their leveling.

After they had returned to the ground and the light disappeared, Tag pumped his fist, letting out a weak "Woo!" that set them all laughing again. The wisp hovered above them, a strange warmth that gave them strength being emitted from its light.

"Woah," Tag exclaimed. "Guess who's gone up one more level?"

They all checked their updates, Ben exclaiming that he had gone up two more levels, while Gideon had achieved another as well.

By Chloe's memory, that would make Tag, Ben, and Gideon even on level 9.

Chloe brought up her own character sheet, beaming as she saw the number 10 next to her level.

<u>Bio</u>

Character name: Chloe (*click to select a new character name*)

Level: 10

Class: *Click for more information on selecting a character class.*

Race: Human

<u>Stats</u>

HP: 275/275

MP: 200/200

Stamina: 345/345

Active effects: Null

<u>Attributes</u>

Strength: 22 (+19)

Intelligence: 6 (+13)

Dexterity: 20 (+16)
Endurance: 25 (+18)
Etheric Potential: 9 (+21)
<u>**Skills**</u>
Languages: Human
Acrobatics: Lv 3
Armed Combat: Lv 1
Cooking: Lv 1
Crafting: Lv 1
Creature Identification: Lv 4
Dark Vision: Lv 4
Dual Wielding: Lv 2
Experimental: Lv 1
Fishing: Lv 1
Hand of the Gods: Lv 1
Herb Identification: Lv 1
Sneak: Lv 4
Swimming: Lv 1
Reckless: Lv 4
<u>**Available Points:**</u> **4**

"Aw, yeah! Level 10!" Chloe celebrated. "Woah, I've unlocked classes?"

Gideon, Tag, and Ben looked up at Chloe with envy.

"You're kidding?" Tag asked.

"Told you!" Ben elbowed Tag, a smile on his face. "It's level-based, like with *Arcane Hunter IV*. I knew it had to be something like that."

Chloe cast a quizzical look their way.

Ben answered for her. "In every MMORPG, a person gets to select a class for their character, like warrior, mage, cleric, or thief, for example."

"Some games unlock these from the start," Tag interrupted, "meaning that you shape your gameplay around what you want your character to be before you've even dived into the world."

"Whereas most modern MMORPGs," Ben said, taking back control, "let you discover what you like doing most in the game before presenting you with options. I thought I had what it took to be a tank in *Relic Hunter*, but once I picked up my bow and arrow, I fell in love with long-range combat."

"I was going to be a bard," Tag said, "until I learned to love steamrolling into battle and smashing things. I don't get to do a lot of that at home."

"None of us do," Ben added, bopping Tag affectionately on the head.

Chloe's attention turned to Gideon. "So that means you *could* just pick up a sword and go warrior, right? Screw what your brother thinks. Just change your style of play and pick up the warrior class."

Gideon looked forlornly at his toes. "Afraid not. My brother watches what I'm doing whenever I'm home. He's still threatening to pull the plug on my account if I don't do as I'm told."

Ben and Tag sniggered. "Sucks to be you!"

"Hey!" Chloe snapped. "That's no way to talk to your teammate. We're all in this together now. If one of us suffers, we all suffer, got it?"

The pair nodded.

"Now," Chloe continued, her attention returning to her activity log. "How the crap did we gain so many levels?"

Chloe opened up her Activity Log.

Monster defeated: Skeleton (Lv 2)

+20 exp

Monster defeated: Skeleton (Lv 2)

+20 exp

Monster defeated: Skeleton (Lv 2)

+20 exp

Monster defeated: Skeleton (Lv 2)

+20 exp

Monster defeated: Skeleton (Lv 2)

+20 exp

Okay, let's skip ahead a little bit here, Chloe thought as dozens more notifications of skeletal defeats sailed past her. *Ah! Here we go.*

You've unlocked a new (unique) skill: Hand of the Gods (Lv 1)

Well, dear mortal, you have earned the favor of the gods.

Guiding your hands, the gods can do terrible and wonderful things. Summon the use of this skill when you are in a dire situation and the gods will lend you aid. The results of this skill may vary.

Bonuses: +7 etheric potential

New spell acquired: Deic Light (Lv 1)

Thanks to the gods, you have been bestowed with Deic Light. Cast this spell to summon a powerful column of light to dispel enemies who associate themselves with the darkness.

Requirements: n x 100MP (where n is equal to the number of seconds taken to cast the spell)

More and more notifications of skeletal defeats, and then:

Monster defeated: Mage (Lv 16)

+1,300 exp

Monster defeated: Skeleton (Lv 2)

+20 exp

Monster defeated: Skeleton (Lv 2)

+20 exp

Monster defeated: Skeleton (Lv 2)

+20 exp

Oh, for goodness sake, Chloe said, zipping through more notifications. She stopped when she found what she was looking for.

Level increased! You are now level 10

Congratulations! You have proven yourself a true adventurer of Obsidian. By making your way to level 10, you've unlocked a selection of new classes for your character. Click the info icon to find out more.

+4 attribute points

(Attribute points must be assigned within 24 hours of gameplay. If unassigned after 24 hours, any remaining points will be randomly assigned.)

Chloe clicked the icon, her eyes turning greedy as she scanned the information.

CHAPTER THIRTY-THREE

New classes available!

Now that you have reached the standard level for any adventurer who is ready to go from crawling to walking and test their mettle in the land of Obsidian, you have unlocked a number of classes to further improve your character and help you specialize and find your true path.

NOTE: A class cannot be changed once selected.

<u>Class unlocked: Warrior</u>

You've proven yourself a deft hand with a blade, now take on new heights as you harness your strength, train yourself in combat, and fight at the front of every battle. Warriors will have the opportunity to join the royal guard or can sell themselves as hired protection, and are often highly revered in populated communities.

Boons: The warrior class will gain you favor in cities, granting negotiation and charismatic benefits to your character. Warriors are among the first to receive new quests and benefit from discounts in local taverns.

+10 strength, +10 endurance

Class unlocked: Mage

So, you've dabbled in the arts of the etheric. You've played with the mystical and the unexplained, now unlock the opportunity to shape the very fabric of reality. Mages have the ability to further specialize their magic across three subcategories: mystic, destructive, and restoration. However, mages are often seen as dark threats by those who do not understand the ways of the etheric. A word of caution: mages make enemies faster than most.

Boons: The mage will be able to access further training from the Mystic Academy, and will find that a place will open among the magical guilds once inducted. Mages benefit from discounts in local apothecaries and stores that sell potions and ingredients.

+10 intelligence, +10 etheric potential

Class unlocked (unique): Berzerker

Thanks to your determination to excel at being reckless, you have unlocked this unique class. Berzerkers gain many of the benefits of warriors but have a tendency to fly off the handle and charge into battle without conscious thought. Your visible class will be set to Warrior for public viewing since your Berzerker status is private.

Because of this, you gain all the benefits of the warrior class. However, when the red mist descends, you will be unable to control your character for a limited amount of time. Anyone who witnesses your Berzerker status during this Red Rage will be made aware of your true class.

Boons: Berzerkers gain the skill Final Stand when health is critical, granting a sudden surge of strength and empowering players through a Red Rage. They are also viewed as more desirable to the opposite sex, holding influence over potential lovers due to their reputations as bad boys and bad girls.

+15 strength, +10 endurance

Class unlocked (unique): Battle Mage

You've learned the basics of combat. You've gained the use of spells. You can't decide which path to travel down. Well then, Battle Mage is for you.

Battle Mages are dual wielders with the ability to manipulate destructive magic and combine this with the art of combat. Battle Mages are able to follow both the paths of the mage and the warrior, although they will be at a disadvantage across both disciplines, seen as less than their pure counterparts. They also suffer from a lack of discounts at both taverns and apothecary stores.

Boons: Battle Mages are an experimental class who aren't afraid to try new combinations of magic and weaponry. They also benefit from increased intelligence and are able to unlock unique and hidden spells.

+15% luck in experimental magicks.

+15 intelligence, +10 etheric potential

Class unlocked: Cleric

You have been touched by the hands of the gods, now devote your life to their purpose and increase their favor among the mortals.

Clerics are highly revered among all spheres, able to take up residence in cities and towns for free as well as benefitting from increased boosts to the study of restorative magic. As a Cleric, you will be trusted among folks of Obsidian without question, and be able to learn the secrets of the world around you.

Boons: Increased trust among all folk, boosts to restorative magic, able to talk to gods through prayer.

+15 etheric potential, +5 intelligence

Chloe chewed her cheek as she read through the class options again. And again. Her attention finally distracted when Tag asked her, "Would you like to do the honors?"

Chloe shook her head, sending away the class information. Her mind was full of the possibilities of what was now available to her. She wanted to select a class that would most benefit her, but now wasn't the time. From the sound of it, a person's class choice was a big decision, and the last thing that Chloe wanted to do was rush into something so permanent.

Chloe chuckled, reminding herself of how she had sounded the day she had turned 18 and agreed to legally be hired by her mother's and father's company.

"I couldn't," she said, seeing Tag pointing to the mage's corpse. "The victory is *ours*. We should all do it."

They nodded, Gideon still a little woozy on his feet. As one, they crouched and touched the mage's body, activating the looting process. His skin melted into ash that flew into the air, leaving behind the mage's clothes, a selection of coins, and two small scrolls tied in the center with red ribbon.

"6 copper and 5 silver," Tag tallied, scooping up the coins and attempting some mental arithmetic. "Divided by four, that's...um, okay, so carry the one. One each, and that's...two left over. Don't know how many coppers are in silver in this game yet, so let's call that...um..."

Ben snatched the coins out of the dwarf's hand and, with a chuckle, distributed one silver to everyone, and one copper. The remaining two copper and one silver he handed back to Tag. "Here. For your hard work."

Tag grinned. "Showoff. Just because my intelligence is shit in this game..."

"Right," Ben replied. "Only in *this* game."

Chloe inspected the scrolls, untying the ribbons and gasping as she perused the text.

Scroll item: Spell of Resurrection

New spell acquired: Resurrection (Lv 1)

There are a great many forces at work in this realm. Though many choose to pursue the path of the light, magic can also be found in the path of the darkness. While life is sought and clung to with iron claws, death is the inevitability that comes to all.

Or so it would seem.

Summon the powers of this spell to bring the dead back to life. Higher tiers of this spell will allow control of the dark forces of the dead, while lower tiers will allow the resurrection of fallen comrades.

A note of warning: there are those within the realm of Obsidian who frown upon the dark arts. Be wary of your

surroundings before toying with the gods of darkness and snatching away their prizes.

Requirements: 100% of player's MP

(NOTE: The Spell of Resurrection can only be cast once within a 48-hour period. Players must be a minimum of level 10 with a specialization as a magic user in order to cast this spell.)

"What is it?" Gideon asked, looking over Chloe's shoulder and reading the scroll.

"Woah," he exclaimed. "That's pretty sweet."

"You've acquired it too?" Chloe asked.

Gideon nodded.

"What? What is it?" Tag said, shoving Ben aside and hopping up and down to try to read the scroll in Chloe's hands.

Chloe lowered the paper and presented it to Tag. Ben read it too, and both their mouths dropped open.

"Sounds like some dark magic there," Ben said. "How does it work, though? Are there any words or incantations you need to know to summon the power?"

Gideon and Chloe looked at each other.

"No? Didn't you just get the notification saying that you'd just acquired a new spell?"

Tag's eyes went hazy for a second as he perused his notifications. "Nope. Nothing." Then, under his breath, "Friggin' magic users."

Chloe smiled, wrapping up the scroll and replacing it where the mage's body had been. She unfolded the second scroll and read the text.

Grinyada,

It is with urgency that I burden you with this quest of mine. A disruption has occurred in the wilds of Obsidian, a disturber of the peace on a mission to claim what is by rights my treasure.

Seek out the girl who has obtained the mythical bracers and bring her to ruin. Return with the bracers to my manor in Nauriel to receive your not insubstantial reward. My spies claim she was last sighted among the Oakston people, accompanied by three of the blessed. Remove them from the equation to ease your journey.

But remember, don't waste your time on their deaths. The blessed only return.

Tohken.

P.S. Tell no one of this request.

"Holy…" Chloe said, not quite able to believe what she was reading. She showed the paper to Gideon and the others, who raised their eyebrows in unison as they made their way to the bottom of the message.

"Oh," Tag said.

Gideon nodded. "I know."

"That is…*awesome!*" Tag bellowed, his voice reverberating around the cave.

"What do you mean, 'awesome?'" Chloe said in disbelief. "What's awesome about this? Didn't you read the paper? Someone is trying to *kill* me!"

Ben nudged Tag. "Get this, the woman who has died more times than we can count on one hand is worried about death."

Chloe couldn't believe what she was hearing. The note was there in her hand, the words written in ink to tell someone to hunt her down and kill her, and these guys were…*laughing?*

"Look," Ben said, placing an arm around Chloe's shoulder. "This kind of thing happens all the time in these kinds of games. You piss someone off, they come after you. You show exceptional talent, someone gets jealous. All we've got to do is track down the guy who sent this note, and we'll get a nice bit of a boost to our experience. If I were to guess, I bet there's already a notification—"

"Yep!" Tag exclaimed. "Right here: '**A most bloody request.**'"

Chloe opened her notifications. Sure enough, there it was.

Quest unlocked: A most bloody request

Someone has it out for you. Find the sender of the death note in the land of Nauriel and discover what truly lies behind this request.

Difficulty: 3/10

Rewards: 2,000 exp

Accept quest: Y/N

Without hesitation, they each accepted the quest. Ben asked to re-read the note to look for clues.

"Seems strange that someone would be out to get you just for a set of bracers," he said. "They're just regular armor, right?"

Chloe felt her blood run cold. She hadn't even thought of the implications of showing the others the scroll. She had only hoped they would throw some kind of light or clarity on the situation. If someone was out to get her, she needed help.

Now, though, the spotlight was on her and her magical armor. She cast a glance at Gideon, who was staring at his feet.

"I don't know," Chloe said with as genuine a sense of confusion as she could manage. "All I did was find these in a cave. They give me a nice bonus to my stats, but otherwise, I can't work out what the problem would be."

Tag's face lit up with excitement. "Oh, God! I love a good puzzle." He rubbed his hands together. "Maybe there's a hidden story behind them that we don't know about?"

"Maybe they belonged to a high-status family and got lost in an accident years ago, and now the long-lost heir is on a mission to reclaim them," Ben chipped in.

Chloe turned once more to Gideon, their eyes catching this time, unbeknownst to Tag and Ben as they continued imagining scenarios and trying to guess what this Tohken guy wanted with something that was otherwise quite unremarkable.

They're on to you, KieraFreya whispered in Chloe's head as they retraced their steps, looting as many skeletons as they could while they passed back through the cave.

No. They're on to us, *remember? We're a team.*

KieraFreya sighed. *Don't remind me.*

Chloe let the others go ahead, trailing slightly as she tried to process everything she had just discovered—the classes, the spells, the letter—in her mind.

EPILOGUE

Rain pattered lightly against the window. Outside, the wind picked up, heralding the coming of a storm. In the buildings all around, people stayed in the comfort of their warm rooms, happy in their sheltered bubbles as the world whirled by outside.

Mia stood against the window, arm leaning on the glass as condensation gathered and crept down her arm. They had warned of power cuts. Of surges and blackouts as the wind built and tore through the city. She glanced at Chloe, wondering how the emergency backup would fare. Chloe's pod was the first of its kind; the others had been replicated and produced based on this model. Should something happen, would everything be all right?

The door opened. Demetri grumbled as he entered, lowering his umbrella, his hair soaking wet.

"Wouldn't think you'd be so soggy with an umbrella," Mia said blankly.

Demetri shook his head, fine droplets of mist spraying around him. "Damn thing got stuck on the way out of the subway. Had to wrestle like mad to get it open. Kinda wish I hadn't bothered. It made no difference."

Mia gave an empty laugh.

Demetri removed his wet jacket, placed his umbrella in the sink to drain, and sat in his place in front of the TV screen. That was his normal routine, now. Ever since that night, he had watched Chloe like a hawk, drawn in by her adventures and making a permanent ass-print in Mia's armchair.

"How's she doing?" Demetri asked.

"Fine."

The display showed Chloe trailing down a mountain, her sword drawn as a pack of wolves came at the adventurers. Something large and feathered flew overhead, joining the fray. Demetri smiled when Chloe said something wildly inappropriate as the soaring beast dived at her, a censoring *beep* ringing out from the speakers.

Mia watched Demetri with a morbid kind of fascination. Ever since *that* morning, he had changed around her. Had become different. Not cold, exactly, but more closed off. Clinical. The psychologist she was sure his patients would see.

There had been no more kissing.

There had been no more lovemaking.

There had been only Chloe and her adventures as they sat side-by-side in silence, waiting until night came to sleep and waking up early to watch some more. Demetri disappeared to his sessions and returned when the city fell dark.

Mia wondered, if he had the chance, would he send an assistant in his place to check on Chloe? That was surely all that he was here for now, right?

She shook the thought away. The doc cared about Chloe more than he probably should. She was his charge and he was her keeper, protecting her from anything that might go wrong while she was locked in her VR world.

Mia left the window, finding her seat beside Demetri as she unscrewed the lid of a bottle of Coke long since gone flat. She took a swig and tried to catch Demetri's eye. When he ignored her, she said, "Demetri, we need to talk."

Demetri's lips tightened and his brow went stern. He raised his own flat drink and took a sip. "*Now* you want to talk?"

It seemed strange to Mia that Demetri would be so cold at this moment. So calculating. Particularly when things had been great not long before. Then again, Demetri was only human. Could he be faulted for not following his own advice in circumstances such as these?

"I…" Mia began, offended by the weakness of her voice and mad at *him* for making her feel this way.

"You what?"

"I'm sorry," Mia managed at last.

The words hung like a vapor cloud around them. The glare from the TV was bright in the darkened room, the only thing that flickered or showed any kind of movement.

"Fine," Demetri said, giving Mia the curtest of nods and returning to the TV.

Mia's nostrils flared as she felt those stupid feelings rise. That strange concoction of everything she had avoided since moving to the heart of the big city and pursuing this career. The feelings she had bottled inside her after reuniting with Demetri after all these years, but which came springing out into the open anyway. Those feelings…

Those *damn* feelings.

"I'm sorry," she said, turning sharply now. *Commanding* his attention. "I'm sorry, okay? I never meant to not tell you that Chloe died and we spoke. I never meant to keep it a secret from you. I know how much you've got invested in this operation, so I understand why you'd be pissed, okay? If you want to hate me, then hate me. It wasn't *me*. It wasn't who I am."

She grabbed his hand with both of hers, and her heart sank as he withdrew it and placed it on his lap.

"Then why did you do it?" Demetri said. "Why did you do it, and why did you *lie* about it?"

Mia bit her lip, the question hitting her with a physical force. She had no idea why; that was the truth. When Demetri had questioned her in the morning, rolling over with a stony grimace, why had she lied? Moreover, why had she held onto the lie until they were shouting at each other? Until they were red in the face and unable to breathe?

The answer was simple. It was just an answer she didn't want to admit. Couldn't admit.

Had to admit.

Mia closed her eyes as she said the words, fighting off the hot tears that collected in the corners.

"Because...because I like you, okay?"

Demetri froze, his stern expression melting like icicles on a hot day.

"That's your excuse? You 'like' me?"

Mia rolled her eyes. He had her on the fence. She had to give him more, and when she started, it just flooded out of her. "No. I mean, I like-like you. Like, a lot. And it's just… This whole thing is new to me. I don't *do* this. I don't fall for guys or think about them all the time or let their presence cloud my work. I don't play hooky or get distracted from the things I love. I work in a male-dominated profession, and I've never once let a guy distract me from what I was focused on."

Mia stared straight into Demetri's eyes. "And then I met you."

Demetri's face softened completely and his eyes dropped to the floor.

"Are you serious?" he asked at last. He took her hand.

Mia nodded. "I'm sorry I lied. I guess part of me wanted you all to myself, and although she's stuck in the video game, it was hard for me that she was taking your attention all the time. I wanted to help *you*, too. You looked so tired and stressed, and...we know what a good stress reliever is right?"

Demetri flushed, and they both laughed.

"I like you too," Demetri said. "After spending years analyzing couples and individuals and working out their kinks, and getting the inside scoop on how couples work, you'd think I'd get it a bit more, wouldn't you? I know how hard it is to admit you like someone. It's not what I came here to do, but seeing you in that cafe, and all the time spent together? This whole thing has felt like a dream."

"A good dream, I hope?" Mia winked.

They smiled at each other then, Mia finding her way onto Demetri's lap as they said more sorrys and kissed until it all felt better. After a while, Demetri offered to make them both some tea. As the kettle boiled, he rested his hands on the work surface and watched Mia as she sat up and wiped her eyes.

She turned coyly, leaning on the arm of the chair as he pottered around and fixed the tea. He came back and she stood, allowing him to sit once more before resuming her place on his lap, her arms around his neck.

Demetri stared for a long time into her eyes before acknowledging the prickling feeling that Mia still had more to tell.

"What?" she said, pulling back to look at his whole face.

"There's something you're not telling me, isn't there?"

Mia exhaled. "It's scary how you can see through me, Doc."

"I've told you, don't call me 'Doc.'" Demetri grinned. "The last thing I want to be doing when I'm doing...you...is thinking about the daughter of one of the wealthiest families in the country as she traverses a VR game."

"I thought you were into that." Mia winked.

Demetri's face straightened.

"Okay, but you might not like it."

"I'm a big boy, I can handle it."

Mia sat back and took a deep breath. "I've got some good news and some bad news. The good news is that the bug reports have been seen by the dev team and they're making progress in fixing all of the problems Chloe and the others have raised. Pretty soon they'll run a patch, and they'll be able to change their appearance throughout the game. Level ones won't be able to discover or harness mythical weapons and enchantments thanks to intervention from the gods, and when a player is logged off, as long as they're in a safe place, their avatar won't suffer any damage."

"That's great news. That means that the beta test is working, right?" Demetri said. "So no more pain for the players either?"

"See, that's one of the things. Since Chloe is our first tester and is the only player currently in total-immersion VR, it means we can't run the patch for her until her time is up. The guys will receive the advantages but Chloe won't."

"So Chloe will still feel pain, but everyone around her won't?"

"Oh, no. The others will," Mia explained. "But a vastly reduced variant of it. Nothing more than a scratch or tickle."

Demetri blew out a mouthful of air. "I don't know how I'm going to be able to tell her that the next time she suffers immeasurable pain and dies."

Mia nodded sympathetically. "You might want to double up and add that, due to the success of the initial weeks of testing, Praxis Games is moving ahead on the national primary rollout of the game. Pretty soon the game is going to be alive with new players."

"That's good news, right?"

Mia sighed. "And with that, they'll be opening the public live-streaming channels. Every player is going to be searchable and watchable. Pretty soon, Chloe Lagarde's adventure is going to become a whole lot more public."

Character Sheet

<u>Bio</u>

Character name: Chloe (*click to select a new character name*)
Level: 10
Class: *Click for more information on selecting a character class.*
Race: Human
Stats
HP: 275/275
MP: 200/200
Stamina: 345/345
Active effects: Null
Attributes
Strength: 22 (+19)
Intelligence: 6 (+13)
Dexterity: 20 (+16)

Endurance: 25 (+18)
Etheric Potential: 9 (+21)
Skills
Languages: Human
Acrobatics: Lv 3
Armed Combat: Lv 1
Cooking: Lv 1
Crafting: Lv 1
Creature Identification: Lv 4
Dark Vision: Lv 4
Dual Wielding: Lv 2
Experimental: Lv 1
Fishing: Lv 1
Hand of the Gods: Lv 1
Herb Identification: Lv 1
Sneak: Lv 4
Swimming: Lv 1
Reckless: Lv 4
Available Points: 4

Skills-dex

Skill increased: Acrobatics (Lv 3)

Congratulations on performing a full triple rotating front flip while falling. Front flips can be quite the crowd pleaser. There are some who make an honest buck performing tricks, like jesters and acrobatic hobos. Welcome to their ranks.

Bonuses: +5 dexterity

(NOTE: Increases in skill override any previous bonuses gained from the skill).

You've unlocked a new skill: Armed combat (Lv 1)

Good job. You can now fight stuff. Y'know, s'long as they're low level, like bunnies and stuff. Let the battles begin!

Requirements: Acquisition of first weapon

Bonuses: +1 strength

You've unlocked a new skill: Cooking (Lv 1)

Rip out some herbs, shove in some meat, add some fire and there you go! Now you can cook basic recipes with a decreased chance of setting the damn thing on fire. Go you!

Requirements: Cook your first meal

Bonuses: +1 dexterity

You've unlocked a new skill: Crafting (Lv 1)

Those who can craft gain a fair advantage in Obsidian. Create your own armor from leather. Make your own weapons. Or continue paying others to do it because at this level, your chances are still relatively slim.

Requirements: Create your first item

Bonuses: +1 dexterity

Skill increased: Creature Identification (Lv 4)

You can now view the HP of your opponents with a simple cast of this skill. Watch their health decrease in the form of a progress bar as you hack and slash your way to victory.

Bonuses: +6 intelligence

(NOTE: Increases in skill override any previous bonuses gained from the skill).

Skill increased: Dark Vision (Lv 4)

The night is fast becoming your mistress. Dark shapes become more refined, night terrors lose their fuzz, and oh the pranks you can play as you dissolve into the darkness and lead your friends astray.

Bonuses: +5 intelligence, +8 etheric potential

(NOTE: Increases in skill override any previous bonuses gained from the skill).

You've unlocked a new skill: Dual wielding (Lv 2)

Many don't understand the diversity of battle style that dual-wielding has to offer. Some stumble across this by chance. Like you. You're a chancer, right? Now you can combine both magic and the physical in battle. *Boop!*

Bonuses: +2 dexterity

You've unlocked a new (unique) skill: Experimental (Lv 1)

Your mind works in mysterious ways. In the heat of the moment, you choose to take the path less...well, never traveled. Continue working on this skill, and your experiments will become more successful and less likely to backfire with each level gained.

Bonuses: +1 intelligence, +1 dexterity, +1 endurance, +1 etheric potential

You've unlocked a new skill: Fishing (Lv 1)

See those things in the water? They're fish. You can catch them. Well done.

Requirements: Catch your first fish

Bonuses: +1 dexterity

You've unlocked a new (unique) skill: Hand of the Gods (Lv 1)

Well, dear mortal, you have earned the favor of the gods. Guiding your hands, the gods can do terrible and wonderful things. Summon the use of this skill when you're in a dire situation and the gods will lend you aid. The results of this skill may vary.

Bonuses: +7 etheric potential

You've unlocked a new skill: Herb Identification (Lv 1)

No more walking around and throwing the first thing you find into your mouth. The world is full of dangerous plants and shrubs. Identify them with a simple look.

Requirements: Study herb-lore from a practitioner

Bonuses: +1 intelligence

Skill increased: Sneak (Lv 4)

Whether ducking from friend or foe, you're becoming one with the shadows. Keep hopping across darkness puddles, and soon you're sure to be as invisible as...well, an invisible person.

Bonuses: +4 dexterity

(NOTE: Increases in skill override any previous bonuses gained from the skill).

You've unlocked a new skill: Swimming (Lv 1)

The water is fine, come on in! Swimming is a great skill to have in Obsidian and can grant you passage to many of the realm's hidden pathways. Not a level 1, mind you. You've got a ways to go. Get practicing.

Requirements: Take a dip in the water

Bonuses: +1 dexterity

Skill increased: Reckless (Lv 4)

Did you really just throw your body over a dwarf like he was a landmine? Can't say we've ever seen that before. Here, have a bonus.

Bonuses: +13 strength, +7 endurance

(NOTE: Increases in skill override any previous bonuses gained from the skill).

Quest-dex

Open Quests

Quest unlocked: A Fallen Goddess

The Goddess of Retribution, KieraFreya, has fallen from grace. Her form has been divided and scattered across the land of Obsidian. For eons she has lain in wait, hoping for an adventurer who is brave enough and strong enough to unite the pieces of her armor once more and restore KieraFreya to her former glory.

Find all [x] pieces of KieraFreya and return her to the gods.

Difficulty: 10/10

Rewards: 100,000 exp, + rare items (locked).

Accept quest: Y/N

Quest unlocked: A most bloody request

Someone has it out for you. Find the sender of the death note in Nauriel and discover what truly lies behind this request.

Difficulty: 3/10

Rewards: 2,000 exp

Accept quest: Y/N

———————

Complete Quests

Quest complete: Walk the Deathwalk of the Gods

You've done it! You've outwitted the trolls, trodden through the realm of fire, swum the unforgiving lake, and emerged victorious through the fractal labyrinth of death. You've truly proven yourself—

#ERROR404

—a champion among champions—

MISSING_SEQ

REBOOT_POPUP

—Carry on, adventurer Untitled, and soar to ever greater heights!

Bonuses: 10,000 experience + Bracers of KieraFreya

Quest unlocked: We didn't start the fire.

Some idiot has lost control of his flames. Help him to put out the fire before the whole house is burnt to cinders.

Difficulty: 1/10

Rewards: 50 exp

Accept quest: Y/N

Quest unlocked: Crossing the language barrier

There are many in the Oakston village who can speak your language. There are, however, also many who can't, and this might become tiresome for you.

Unlock new quests and interactions in Oakston by either learning a new language or finding an interpreter. The rewards that you gain will be based on the choices you make.

Difficulty: 2/10

Reward (Interpreter): 100 exp

Reward (Learn a language): FAILED

Accept quest: Y/N

Quest unlocked: Where's the shaman?

You've quite the inquisitive mind. You've found the shaman's house, but the shaman is nowhere to be found.

Use your powers of curiosity to track down the shaman before the poisonous gas that has been filling your lungs from the Death-bell flowers sends you into your final slumber.

Difficulty: 4/10

Rewards: 500 exp, Final slumber potion recipe

——————————

Failed Quests

Quest unlocked: One of us

The chief has summoned you to her chambers to accept a permanent position as part of the tribe. The tribespeople of Oakston may be basic, but there is opportunity for growth and development here. Learn from local experts, hone your skill under the tutelage of others, and make Oakston your home.

Difficulty: 1/10

Rewards: 5,000 exp, Title unlock (Oakston Villager), New language (Tribal: Primitive).

Spells-dex

New spell acquired: Deic Light (Lv 1)

Thanks to the gods, you have been given Deic Light. Cast this spell to summon a powerful column of light to dispel enemies who associate themselves with the darkness.

Requirements: n x 100MP (where n is equal to the number of seconds taken to cast the spell)

New spell acquired: Purple Blaze (Lv 1)

Congratulations on learning your first spell! Now that you've taken your first foray into the realm of the etheric, you'll be able to call upon the mystical and the unexplained to aid you in the heat of battle.

Requirements: n x 20MP (where n is equal to the number of seconds taken to cast the spell)

New spell acquired: Resurrection (Lv 1)

There are a great many forces at work in this realm. Though many choose to pursue the path of the light, magic can be found in the path of the darkness. While life is sought and clung to with iron claws, death is the inevitability that comes to all.

Or so it would seem.

Summon the powers within this spell to bring the dead back to the living. Higher tiers of this spell will allow control of the dark forces of the dead, while lower tiers will allow the resurrection of fallen comrades.

A note of warning: there are those within the realm of Obsidian who frown upon the dark arts. Be wary of your surroundings before toying with the gods of darkness and snatching away their prizes.

Requirements: 100% player's MP

(NOTE: The Spell of Resurrection can only be cast once within a 48-hour period)

New spell acquired: Volt Shock (Lv 1)

Thunderbolts and lightning, very, very frightening! You can now summon the power of electricity to inflict damage upon your enemies. Find creative, unique ways of using this skill as you develop and grow.

Requirements: n x 30MP (where n is equal to the number of seconds taken to cast the spell)

AUTHOR NOTES MICHAEL ANDERLE

JUNE 19, 2020

Hello!

My name is Michael Anderle and I'm beyond honored you have read this story and are joining me in the back for the author's notes.

If this is your first time to connect with me, THANK YOU! If this is your 40th, or 400th, thank you (that many books) over again.

A little background for those who don't know it.

In November of 2015, I release the first three stories in what has become The Kurtherian® Universe. In 2016, I released (about) another 10 books of my own, and started collaborating with four other authors to provide collaboration stories in that universe based on fan's demand.

Since then, we started branching out with different models and stories and collaborators.

We like to produce books in the urban fantasy, science fiction, and paranormal genres. Occasionally, we have a couple of romance / pnr (closed door) and action / adventure genres as well.

I stayed out of the LitRPG / GameLit (closer to what I consider this series) for a while. Not because I wasn't a fan of the genre, but rather there were certain rules in the genre I didn't think I understood very well.

So, better to stay out than get in and do it badly.

I happened to get a chance to speak with a well-known author in the genre (Aleron Kong), and ask him specifically what the rules are for LitRPG, and other authors for what GameLit was. With that knowledge in hand, I set off to create a series.

The only problem? I like telling stories, and I couldn't personally deal with all of the stats in "crunchy" LitRPG.

So, I ditched the parts of stats keeping and updating in the story I didn't personally enjoy (many readers do, I'm just not one of them.) I talked with another best-selling author in the GameLit arena and asked him how he worked his stats.

While a bit confusing, I sorta understood it. But, I kinda failed there, too.

Now, I realize I'm a GameLit…Light…*really* light like 1% milk type light GameLit author/creator. I like putting in the stats that are relevant to the story, but not really mess around with the complete list or with just the stats that affect what's going on RIGHT NOW.

Especially the funny stats.

Case in point, Dakota Krout has a system he has explained to me, and he is the first author who put in snarky negative type talents that I happened to read. I have no idea who was first, he was just the first I read.

I come from a D&D background. This was about 30 years ago and I haven't played in decades.

(If you don't count World of Warcraft or a little Skyrim. It would never have occurred to me to do snarky AI negative talent tree work but I love it both in stories and creating AI's with that personality.)

So, it's with a bit of a 'tip of the hat' to Dakota Krout for first introducing me to a snarky Game AI character and that is how you get a character who keeps losing her clothes in this book.

Please join me in the next book, where we have a lot of fun, and just a bit more shenanigans.

Each book, I try to do an update (at least a weekly update) diary entry. I live in Vegas with my wife Judith and no cats or dogs. We have three kids (all guys) living out of the house in Texas at this time.

Diary June 14 – 20, 2020

So, Las Vegas is a little weird right now. You have pockets of people who are very Covid-19-aware around the valley area, and then you have the casinos. Some of the casinos are very Covid aware and more stringent, and others aren't.

No casino (that I've been to) mandates wearing a mask.

The Station Casinos shoot that temperature gauge at you when you enter their establishment but are pretty open after that.

Caesar's Hotel and Casino (for this latest weekend) was packed with people, and they try to encourage social distancing, but occasionally people get a little close together—and by occasionally, I mean all of Friday night.

I can't speak to Saturday or Saturday night since I didn't get to continue playing. My budget was used up, so I worked and slept most of Saturday, catching up from some mixed up sleep during the week.

I'm at the Green Valley Hotel and Casino. Sitting in the food court, I can see at least twelve people playing on the casino floor. The mask to no-mask ratio seems to be about even, except for the person who has a mask, but is smoking, so the mask is pulled down.

I'm going to count that as a no-mask.

Here in the food court, the mask ratio is about one person with a mask to twenty without one.

We are fifteen feet from the slot machines.

I get why those of us in the food court have no masks (and there is no difference when I go to regular restaurants. Once a person sits down at a table, the masks come off almost immediately.)

I think I will be about done with these updates starting next week. Enough of my diary entries have dealt with Covid-19 and Las Vegas, it's time to just…talk about other stuff.

Like books, maybe?

Sometimes, it's hard to remember what readers want to hear about in our (author and publisher) lives. I eat, sleep, and breathe publishing and stories at this point in my career, and what's normal to me (and seems like would be boring to you) is probably not.

As always, THANK YOU for reading our stories. We would not be able to create the wonderful stories without readers like you supporting us!

Ad Aeternitatem,

Michael Anderle

BOOKS BY MICHAEL ANDERLE

For a complete list of books by Michael Anderle, please visit

www.lmbpn.com/ma-books/

CONNECT WITH THE AUTHOR

Michael Anderle Social

Website: http://lmbpn.com

Email List: http://lmbpn.com/email/

Facebook:
https://www.facebook.com/LMBPNPublishing

www.ingramcontent.com/pod-product-compliance
Lightning Source LLC
Chambersburg PA
CBHW050031120726
47903CB00006B/1995